9½ Couples

9½ Couples

LIFE

LOVE

INTIMACY

A Novel by

Dr. Wendell Scales

Capulet House

West Bloomfield, Michigan

Capulet House Publishing,
P.O. Box 250662,
West Bloomfield, MI 48325-0662.

Visit our Web site at *www.CapuletHousePublishing.com.*

This is a work of fiction. Other than historical events, the situations and scenes described are inventions of the author's imagination. The author created all of the characters, and none of the character portrayals is based on real people. Any similarity, therefore, to anyone living or dead is purely coincidental.

Note: This work contains the opinions and ideas of its author. It is sold with the understanding that the author and publisher are not engaged in rendering professional services in this book. If the reader requires personal assistance or advice, a competent professional should be consulted.

First printing 2003

ISBN 0-9728728-0-9

LCCN 2003103125

1. Fiction   2 Relationships

Cover and book design by Sans Serif, Inc.

Printed and bound in the United States of America.

Printed on acid-free paper

To those who are juggling,
have ever juggled, or will juggle,
the relationship trilogy:
Conflict, hope, and love.

Acknowledgements

Writing a book is no small task, and it would not have been possible without the help of my family, special friends, teachers, editors, agent, muse, and He who guided my fingers across the keyboard whenever I came to a crossroad. I couldn't ask for a better writing team or support group. Much love and many thanks.

The Couples

Dexter and Epiphany

Joel and Harriet

Darren and Claudia

Dominique and Christian

Blair and Marcy

Charlie and Kathy

Tyrone and Tyra

Mark and Adrian

Julia and Victor

The diary is an art form just as much as the novel or the play. The diary simply requires a greater canvas.

—HENRY MILLER, *The Cosmological Eye*

A Note from the Author

Have you ever loved someone so much that everything seems to remind you of them? A song flows from the radio and instantly you're transported back to a party, slow-dancing in the arms of that special someone. A familiar fragrance trapped within the folded edge of a magazine page escapes and whips your senses into a sensual frenzy, releasing yet another memory of that special person.

He saw a couple cuddling by the fireplace and, without warning, the rich flavor of hot chocolate, marshmallows, and Simone's honey kisses excited Jean-Paul's taste buds.

Over the years, my friend and colleague Dr. Jean-Paul Lefervre counseled hundreds of patients who have lost their loved ones. He guided them through the grieving process, explaining the emotions that would manifest immediately and those that would materialize down the road. However, not until he lost his wife Simone, did Jean-Paul really understand grieving.

When Simone made her transition, the pain within Jean-Paul's heart was so intense it took every ounce of his mental energy to block the excruciating heartache throughout the day. Jean-Paul endured his sleepless nights with the help of wine, long walks, and prayer. He was so crushed and distraught that his patients counseled *him* during their therapy sessions. Denial, pain, loneliness, fear, shock, anger, anxiety, and that most-devastating of human emotions—guilt—hit him like a two-ton wrecking ball, turning Jean-Paul's peaceful life into a living hell.

The road to recovery wasn't short or easy, but Jean-Paul eventually accepted the reality that his Simone was gone—and that ab-

3

solutely nothing was going to bring her back. After a short leave from his practice, after hours of intensive counseling and analysis of the case histories of patients who had lost someone dear to them, Jean-Paul was able to rebuild peace in his life.

Yes, by studying the case histories of his patients who had lost a loved one, Jean-Paul discovered a way to let go of Simone. He was able to cheat the cliché, "experience is the best teacher" by using the collective experiences of his patients as a map to shorten his road to recovery. Jean-Paul refined this road-map therapy and incorporated it into his bag of treatment "tricks." He found that sharing the misfortunes of former patients with new couples coming in for counseling dramatically decreased the number of appointments needed for therapy and increased the patients' success rate. Judging from the attitudinal changes in my friends who were being treated by Jean-Paul with his new "journal therapy," the results were phenomenal.

Then the idea hit me—why not compile a series of stories, in journal form, dealing with relationship problems? Couldn't Jean-Paul use such a book as a therapeutic aid in his practice? He thought it could.

Before long, we compiled several entries and put them into book form. Jean-Paul told his patients that this book was like a crystal ball—that they could see the past, present, and future outcome of a couple in a conflict like theirs. The patients loved it. Soon they started requesting chapters unrelated to their problems. Weeks later, Jean-Paul was bombarded with phone calls from friends of his patients, requesting "that crystal ball book."

There must be much truth in the cliché "misery loves company," because the response to his initial book was overwhelming. I'd like to believe it's not that misery loves company, but that those of us who are miserable want to know that we are not unique—that other people have the same problems we do. In fact, we gain comfort when we discover that other people have successfully dealt with similar issues. I believe that this awareness gives us the strength to forge ahead.

For those of you wondering about patient confidentiality, Jean-Paul has changed the names of each couple presented in this book.

Permission was given by those patients still living, and by those family members surviving the deceased. The original content of the patients' thoughts expressed in their journals has not been changed; however, the thoughts have been enhanced to clearly reveal the essence of each conflict.

Do you remember Aesop's fables? His stories contained subtle suggestions and hidden meanings, wrapped in metaphors. Aesop designed his fables to entertain his readers, while subtly conveying a moral truth or some cautionary advice. You might think of Jean-Paul's collections of case studies as interesting fables about life and love inside of intimate relationships.

9½ Couples is about relationship ecology, the study of the consequential problems that occur in relationships because of human nature and lack of communication.

Jean-Paul reconstructed the stories of nine couples from the personal journals his patients kept while they were in counseling. Each "fable" was designed to make you the proverbial "fly on the (heart) wall" of the couples during their conflict. Complete with twists and turns, multiple layers of meaning, and unexpected endings, each fable is, in itself, a complete story. Also here, is the underlying story of our ½ couple, Jean-Paul, and his now-passed wife, Simone.

Each couple's conflict, their journal entries, and Jean-Paul's commentaries set the stage for the dramatic events that have shaped Jean-Paul's life—as a man, lover, husband, and father.

If your challenge is that of infidelity, you may connect with Darren and Claudia's heart-wrenching thoughts. If you have the formidable task of dealing with an unromantic partner or trying to extend the one-minute horizontal waltz to several hours, the extremes of Julia and Victor will make for interesting and stimulating reading. If your challenge deals with an inability to "stand up," you may appreciate the carpetbagger approach taken in Tyrone and Tyra. Forbidden fruit may look different to you after reading the poetic prose in Dexter and Epiphany. Joel and Harriet's story offers several not-so-obvious insights into May-December relationships. And if you're reading just out of curiosity, I'm sure you'll find Jean-Paul's book informative and entertaining.

Whether you read these stories to shed some light on a situation that exists in your life or just because you're curious, I believe you'll walk away with a broader perspective on the saying, "there are two sides to every situation."

When I asked Jean-Paul how a person could use these stories, his reply was simple, yet profound: "Whenever you come to a crossroads in your life—and there will be many—use these journal entries and the information in this book as a crossing guard—to foresee and hopefully prevent, emotional accidents."

If you're able to use the essence of these journal thoughts to avert potentially damaging arguments or conflicts, or to prevent your heart from being broken again, the time you spend reading Jean-Paul's book will be the best emotional investment you've ever made.

Prologue

My name is Jean-Paul V. Lefervre and I'm an incurable romantic. I'm also a psychiatrist with a practice limited to my specialty of couple's counseling. Over the years, I have worked with couples in various countries and from different walks of life. I have listened as they poured out their deepest darkest secrets, their failures, highs and lows, infidelities, and a multitude of other conflicts within their relationships.

In my early years of practice, I felt as if my therapy sessions did little, if any, good for most of my patients. My patients would separate, divorce, or continue to live out the same miserable dramas within their dismal relationships. I realized that my patients were ultimately responsible for their own emotional well-being. Even so, I felt like a failure as their doctor.

I was so frustrated with my low success rate that I became hellbent on finding a technique that would yield better results. My long search for that magic bullet left me even more frustrated and feeling helpless. I desperately needed a method that would give me more insight into the couples I counseled—that would allow me to read their real thoughts about the truth—something that *all* of us have difficulty talking about.

I found the answer to my problem quite by accident. I was paging through my old university textbook on nineteenth-century romantic art, when a well-known painting caught my eye. As I savored this work of art, it revived a fond memory from my childhood. My grade school frequently took field trips to the *Musée du Louvre*, where we would study the great masters of art. During one visit, I strayed away from my class and entered the romantic art gallery. It

was in this gallery that I first saw the painting which I now redis-
covered in my art book.

Liberty Leading the People depicted a woman bearing a French
flag, beckoning the commoners to forge into battle against the aris-
tocratic rulers. I'm sure the artist intended to use the French flag
waving valiantly above Liberty's head to inspire the commoners to
fight. As for me, at that age, I would have followed Liberty just because she was beautiful.

The book also included the artist's written works. You see, in
France, everyone is a philosopher, but *Liberty's* creator, Eugène
Delacroix, was a Frenchman of extraordinary perception. The following entry from his journal started the wheels turning within my
frustrated mind:

> I am carrying out my plan, so long formulated, of keeping
> a journal. What I most keenly wish is not to forget that I
> am writing for myself alone. Thus I shall always tell the
> truth, I hope, and thus I shall improve myself. These
> pages will reproach me for my changes of mind.

As I finished that passage in Delacroix's journal, the answer to my
problem was illuminated in beams of brilliant white light.
Delacroix's *written* works of art, not his painting, excited me this
time.

I had to act on my discovery. I would require my patients to write
each day in a diary, a journal, just as Delacroix had suggested. They
were to write whenever a situation created an emotional imbalance
within them. Next, I would have individual sessions with each partner to discuss his or her most disturbing issue. The joint counseling
session could not occur until I had met with both partners individually. Having armed myself with each partner's view of the conflict—
via their journal and our discussions—I could guide the couple in a
direction that would position each of them to see the conflict
through the eyes of their partner. Hopefully, they would see the underlying causes of the problem and move towards resolving it. Addi-

tionally, as they periodically reviewed their journal entries, they would gain valuable insight into their lives.

It was strange, but I found that most of them would write only about the experiences that left them in an emotionally low state of being—they wrote only about the crap in their lives. Were their negative experiences so powerful that the positive moments of their lives were overshadowed, even drowned, by the downpour of life's woes? At the very least they could've written, "Every day above ground is a great day. Today I woke up. Today is a great day!" But they didn't.

The journal entries from hundreds of couples made me realize a factual *cliché*, "the truth has many wings." The truth can be interpreted in many ways because of the dirty laundry, childhood wounds, and old baggage stored within our heart's memories. These things are the exposed nerves that have been left unprotected in each of our backgrounds, laid bare by the unresolved conflicts in our past.

When a new conflict activates these painful nerve endings, they induce a sort of tunnel vision, which prevents us from seeing any point of view other than our own. We see, hear, and feel only the pain they have created within *our* lives. This old baggage eventually breaks the lines of communication with our partner, wreaking havoc with our relationship.

Once opened, the musty contents of the old baggage can suffocate and extinguish the love within a relationship. It's important to rid yourself not only of the stifling contents, but also of the old luggage as well.

I have introduced each couple's story in this book with a quotation. It's meant to give you a clue about the conflict within this couple's relationship. As you read each journal entry, keep an open mind. If you must judge, at least first consider both of the partners' journal entries and my commentary.

Each journal entry has multiple layers of meaning. Seek the core of each partner's thoughts; if you do, your understanding of the conflict will increase a hundredfold.

Refrain from making assumptions. Most situations in life are not as they appear. Take note of how each partner viewed the situation that generated the conflict. Imagine how they felt during the conflict and how they arrived at their decisions—resolutions that were often fatal. More importantly, as you read, remember this twist on a cliché . . . *There are two sides to every situation, and each side has sides (conflicts) of its own.*

My reasons for revealing these patients' thoughts to you are simple. I believe that we *want* and *need* to be in control of our lives. If within this book you should read a thought that resonates with your soul, quiets your heart, inspires you to reshape your destiny, reminds you of your life's purpose, renews your love of self, averts an argument with a loved one, helps you to better understand your loved one, gives you hope for a better tomorrow—or if one thought relieves a burden in your heart, my purpose in revealing these patients' thoughts will have been accomplished.

There is one more agreement I would like you to make with me, promise that you will read the couples in the order in which I present them. Each chapter builds upon the preceding one; reading them out of sequence would put the material out of context, leaving you confused. Confusion is exactly what I hope this book will eliminate from your relationship.

After each couple's story I discuss each partner, their point of view regarding the conflict, and then comment on the *real* conflict. There are also questions for you to ponder about the couple's conflict, and a few for you to answer regarding yourself. Finally, I tell you how their conflicts related to my life and the major life-changes they produced that have made me who and what I am today—despite myself.

1

Dexter and Epiphany

Faith is not a thing which one "loses,"
we merely cease to shape our lives by it.
  —GEORGES BERNANOS,
    The Diary of a Country Priest

Dexter—October 18

The forbidden passion imprisoned so long ago within the deep chambers of my soul erupted, spewing pleasures beyond belief throughout my body.

Over the years I found comfort, even satisfaction, from a book of poetry. I read the love poems so many times they became second nature to me. Little did I know these heavenly words would guide me through this, our maiden voyage. As I whispered those love songs in Epiphany's delicate ear, she slowly relaxed. Having lost the battle with her curiosity, she opened Pandora's box. With her most intimate thoughts . . . desires . . . and . . . fantasies exposed, my goddess Epiphany finally surrendered, and gave in to her mortal nature.

When she opened that box, Epiphany transcended the puritanical concerns she had harbored in her past, and opened a portal leading into an unknown and unexplored territory; where a woman's carnal nature rivals the rapture of heaven and the sweltering heat of hell.

I tied a lover's knot in a blade of hay, and laced it through Epiphany's hair. Just lying next to her made the passion buried within me boil. It was a feeling that had to be satisfied. Unable to contain the desire that for so long has been smoldering deep within my core, the words of my love mantra floated gingerly off my lips . . . *"Your lips are like a scarlet ribbon; your mouth is lovely . . . "*

With that my tongue began its virginal journey. Traveling away from her ear, my tongue crept downward and across her cheekbone, into a delightfully deep dimple. Climbing out of this beautiful quirk of nature and continuing its journey, my organ of taste explored more of Epiphany's velvety skin.

My tongue wandered about until it found the sharp angle of her mouth, the angle where her orifice of oral pleasure begins. Slowly, diligently, and nervously my tongue traced the outer edge of her full bottom lip . . . *"Your lips drop sweetness as the honeycomb . . . "* So soft, and so sweet was the taste of her lips, it made me wonder if the petals of her virginal water lily were just as delicious.

Suddenly, the hot tip of her twining tongue shattered my thoughts about her heavenly lips below. Curiously, it rubbed against my top lip in such a way that I was driven to meet it head on with mine. *"Milk and honey are under your tongue . . . "*

Our tongues began a dance: A love ritual powered by the mutual feelings in both our hungry hearts. Our tongues connected—talking to one another in ways our conscious minds could never comprehend, in a language that has never been recorded on paper. How could you possibly use words to describe this feeling? Our tongues spoke to one another in God's divine language—love.

Driven by the heat of passion within my body, heart, and soul, I drove my tongue into Epiphany's mouth . . . oh my God . . . the wetness, the warmth, the sweetness. Is this not more than one man can stand? Is this not heaven?

Each dart of my tongue into Epiphany's mouth was countered with a sensuous thrust of her broad hips against my throbbing scepter. *"Your waist is a mound of wheat encircled by lilies . . . "* It wasn't just a thrust! No, it was a strong push with a slow sway, first to the left . . . then to the right, in a circular motion circumscribed by the tuft of hair upon her exalted Mound of Venus. Epiphany's movements were free of the guilt ingrained within her by the ones who had prepared her for marriage.

"How delightful is your love . . . much more pleasing is your love than wine . . . " Inching southward, my tongue happened upon her bare melons . . . *"and your breasts like clusters of fruit . . . I will climb the palm tree . . . I will take hold of its fruit . . . "* Holding the stem of her melon between my teeth, a stiffening occurred within my loins as my tongue licked her hardened breast bud.

The moonlight glistened off the small pool of perspiration within her navel . . . *"Your navel is a rounded goblet that never lacks blended wine . . . "* I anointed the tip of my tongue with this sacred salty water and became intoxicated with ecstasy.

"You are a garden fountain, a well of flowing water streaming down . . . " Epiphany's water lily was dripping with the perfumed nectar of love . . . *"I have eaten my honeycomb . . . "*

No longer able to restrain the molten liquid within my scepter, I cautiously slid inside my love's wet lily. Moments later . . . hours later . . . or . . . perhaps an eternity later, the buried passion within me spewed out . . . *"I have come into my garden . . . "*

It happened three months ago, and I haven't been able to think of anything else since. I know it was wrong to make Epiphany surrender to me. Wrong to make her commit adultery so shortly after marrying; it has been less than a year since her wedding day. I pray God will forgive her for this transgression. As for me, without celestial intervention, I will burn in the fires of hell.

I was able to ignore her subtle advances at first. The casual eye contact that lasted a little longer than normal, and the way she bowed her head and smiled innocently at me. However, after a while my defenses crumbled. I found myself seeking her smiles and long glances. Soon I found my heart would flutter when I was in her company and hurt when she was away.

Later, during one of our weekly talks, she disclosed her true feelings for me. Instantly, confusion wreaked havoc with my mind. I'd already exchanged vows twelve years ago, yet when she whispered the words "I love you Dexter," my heart leaped into hers and abandoned the covenant it had taken, along with my promises of an exclusive love. There was no choice; Epiphany would have all of my love, until my last breath.

Although she is ten years my junior, this twenty-six-year-old has resurrected emotions within me that were supposedly slain twelve years ago.

It has been written that a man is only half a man without a woman—Epiphany made me whole.

In school, I was taught about the epiphany of Jesus. It was the manifestation of the divine nature of Mary's son, Jesus, to the Gentiles. But its new definition is the manifestation of the woman I love and adore—Epiphany.

How can I persuade her to join me? How can I convince Epiphany to leave her safe haven and venture with me into the unknown? I know I cannot compete with her heavenly love, but I must find a way to have her as my wife. Blessed Mary, I pray Jesus' father will be merciful and forgive our trespasses.

"Place me like a seal over your heart . . . " God, please allow our union to occur, or I will surely die, *" . . . for love is as strong as death . . . "*

Epiphany—January 6

"Forgive me, Father, for I have sinned, it has been three months since my last confession . . . I have broken my marriage vows, and worse I . . . "

No! Those words are not right for this—the most important confession of my life. I have been searching for the right words for the last three months, to beg forgiveness for my beloved Dex. Why should he be punished for bringing joy into my life?

What made me bait, lure, entice, seduce, and corrupt Father Dexter?

I was wrong to allow my desires of the flesh to overrule the covenant I made on my wedding day. Worse than that, I made love to a man who has given his life to serve You. With my one sinful act, I have taken half of his heart, when all of it rightfully belongs to You. Father. God. What have I done?

I allowed my curiosity to overcome my vows, because I wanted . . . no . . . I had to release the passion I have been denied for so long. Dex was not at fault. Yes, he fell onto my web of seduction, but once he touched it, there was no turning back. My earthly desires were so intense, so ripe for the picking that any mortal man would have succumbed. Father, he never had a chance, and so I take full responsibility for his sins. He has worked so hard to serve You faithfully for the last twelve years. Please do not let this one transgression wipe out all those years of hard work and devotion. Deny me entry into Your house, not him.

When Dex recited the verses from the Songs of Solomon, a wave of calm flowed over my soul. Oh Father, how could I not surrender to the weakness of the flesh, when those words speak of Your greatest gift to mankind—your gift of love? Did You not intend for the words of love spoken in the Song of Songs to be a guidebook for the conjugal rights of a couple?

Solomon himself, a powerful and wise man could not resist being drawn by the cleverness and bewilderment of a woman's love charms. Certainly, my beloved Dex could do no better or worse than King Solomon. No Lord. I'm not making a mockery of Your blessed Solomon; I am desperately pleading for my selfless Dex, because he believes he has brought shame on his vows, Dex has already judged and condemned himself to hell.

You have countless people who love You. I know, because I am one of them. But Father, is it too much to ask of You to share Dex's love with me? I'm not asking him to turn away from You; only the

Monarch of Hell would be foolish enough to demand such a thing. I'm only begging You to share his love with me—please.

It's ironic, today is January 6, the day we celebrate the feast after which I'm named, and here I am pleading for Dex's soul. Jesus was manifested to the Gentiles as the Savior—an epiphany. Love was manifested to me by Dex—Epiphany's epiphany. Blessed Mary, even my sense of humor has taken a sour turn. Please forgive me, again.

Once more the time has come for me to confess. I missed the last two cycles, and it is imminent that I confess before it is brought to light. The archangel Gabriel, the spirit who resides over the ripening of fruit, would gladly herald this revelation. But maybe he won't. What if he doesn't bring Mary's lily to signify her blessing? Instead, what if he brings his horn and sounds the undoing of Dex's seed, our child that I now carry?

No, my God is not cruel; He would never do such a thing.

It's time for class and, as the school's only catechist, I mustn't be late. This Q & A session covers the Lord's Prayer, a liturgy that I have recited many times in the last three months. This also happens to be my last session. I must leave. I will not bring disgrace to the name of my precious Dex.

There is time to light one more candle for my darling Dexter . . .

"Hail, Mary, full of grace, the Lord is with thee; blessed art thou among women . . . Father. God. This is Your unfaithful bride Sister Mary Epiphany, please forgive our Dexter, it was not his fault . . . Hail, Mary, full of grace, the Lord . . . give Your blessing to his child growing within my womb . . . Hail, Mary, full of grace . . . do not let this child come into the world without knowing its father . . . Oh, hell . . . "

Every time I read the words of Dexter and Epiphany, a multitude of questions floods my mind. The answers have changed over the years, but the questions always remain the same. What is it about a forbidden fruit that brings out our most intense feelings of love? Would I, or you, for that matter, have the courage to enter Eden's garden, pick and then ravish that golden apple? Would we have the courage to risk everything, including our souls to love someone even though loving him or her was taboo?

I wonder which advocate of Beelzebub's came up with the concept of forbidden love. They also termed this kind of love guilty love. How could the heavenly love that Dexter and Epiphany felt for each other be of a guilty nature? What horrible crime did they commit that would make a jury of their peers render a verdict—guilty of love?

Could God himself have consecrated their relationship? After all, isn't love the foundation of the Good Book? Is it God's law or man's interpretation of His word that prohibits the union of a man and woman of the cloth? Is this the same law that didn't allow or recognize interracial, interdenominational, or same-gender marriages in the past? As the great Fats Waller said, "One never knows, do one?"

One thing of which I am certain; Dex would have made a great Frenchman. During our few counseling sessions, I came to know a great deal about the kind and gentle man who pollinated the convent's forbidden apple blossom. I learned that Dexter's father had abandoned him and his mother when he was eight, a critical time in the development of his personality. Because his only model of fatherhood was what a father didn't do, he vowed to be the best father a child could ever hope for, and to be a loving husband to his wife.

In probing his background, I discovered it was not Dexter's wish, but his grandmother's that forced him into seminary. He tried to please his grandmother and family by committing his life to God. But in his heart, he had always known his destiny wasn't saving souls—it was to express God's love as a mortal man. His ability to transform Solomon's *Song of Songs* from the written realm into the physical world was a confirmation that his heavenly purpose on Earth wasn't delivering God's words of love to the masses, but expressing God's words of love to the woman he loved.

Father Dexter's guilt wasn't a result of breaking his vow to God; it was *not* being able to express God's greatest gift to Epiphany—the gift of love.

Put yourself in Father Dexter's place. Imagine the pain he must've felt having his heart torn apart with God as his witness. Feel the delicate

fibers of his heart being ripped apart as the conflict within him escalated. Should he break his vow to the Holy Father and shatter his
grandmother's dream in the process? Should he remain lukewarm, stay
in the fold with the other sheep, and endure his purgatorial suffering
for loving Epiphany? How would you react if you were forced to
choose between two loves that were equal, yet unequal?

It wasn't his fault that he broke his vows and promises, nor was it
the taste of Epiphany's forbidden flower that made Father Dexter go
against the rules of his church—it was in his human nature. Love made
Dexter break from the path forced upon him by his well-meaning
grandmother. How can you condemn or cast out the children of God
just because the passionate fire of His lightning bolt of love has consumed them?

Wouldn't his sin have been greater if he had gone through life riding the fence of loving God, yet desiring the earthly love of Epiphany?
What do you think of Dexter? Better yet, what if you had to make that
same decision? What would you think of yourself?

I met Epiphany during an unwed mother's workshop that I presented
at her convent. She was a beautiful young lady, with a "quiet power"
about her. In fact, if you saw her walking down the street, you'd never
suspect she was capable of seducing any man, much less turning out a
man of the cloth. Although the more I think about it, there was a
uniqueness about Epiphany that many men find alluring. Her physical
features were like those of women painted during the Baroque period—sensual, attractive, and very desirable. The women portrayed in
these paintings are often referred to as being *Rubenesque*, because
they are similar to the models painted by the Flemish baroque artist
Peter Paul Rubens.

Epiphany reminded me of a painting by Rubens, *The Judgment of
Paris*. Yes, it's time for another art lesson, but I'm an incurably romantic
Frenchman—I relate most things in *my* life to love, sex, food and the
arts. The women in this painting by Rubens are rather healthy or, as Tyrone–another one of my patients–would say, "Gurlfriend is nice and
thick!" This painting is based on the Greek myth in which a shepherd
named Paris is asked by three goddesses to choose the one with the

most beauty. According to legend, Paris did choose one, which made the other two go crazy. This is supposedly how the Trojan War began.

Choosing one woman over another, or comparing one woman to another when they are both present, guarantees you'll get the death penalty—losing one or both of your heads in the guillotine. Unlike Dexter, Paris would *not* have made a good Frenchman.

God did not call upon Epiphany to become a nun; the sisters in the convent showed her the way. Raised in a nunnery, Epiphany could not help following in their footsteps. Unlike Dexter, she didn't consciously know what her purpose was supposed to be here on earth.

During a break in the workshop, Epiphany told me how delighted she was about the program, and how she was praying that these unwed mothers would use the information I had given them so far. I listened to some of Epiphany's remarkable conversations with the unwed mothers during the break. Curious, I later asked how she was able to connect so well with these young women. I learned that she was an abandoned daughter of an unwed mother. Epiphany's mother left her at a convent and ran off with Epiphany's father. She was told that her mother left in search of a better life for her little girl. Unfortunately, her mother seemed to have forgotten where she left Epiphany.

During the workshop, I prescribed my usual journal therapy for the attendees. The participants loved the idea of self-counseling by revealing their innermost thoughts on paper, but it was Epiphany who took full advantage of the journal therapy. Once she started writing, she couldn't stop. For the next three weekends, Epiphany ripped the confessional doors off, and waded through the troubled waters surrounding the thoughts of her lascivious actions as she feverishly wrote in her journal.

Epiphany's journal told me how guilty she felt because of the carnal thoughts she had about Father Dexter—how she fantasized about Father Dexter while indulging in self-pleasure. Epiphany made a good point in her diary when she said, "Did you not intend for the love spoken in the *Song of Songs* to be a traditional part of life?" If you read the words to each song, they read like a marriage manual written in simile form.

What about that secular woman trapped within Epiphany's breast, the one caged like a wild animal—the jailed woman serving a sentence for a crime she did not commit—the *femme fatale* forced into wearing a habit, a religious chastity belt? What about her? Could you be within a breath's distance from the man you love more than life itself and not inhale his love within you? Did Epiphany or Dexter stand a snowball's chance in hell when those words of love rolled off his tongue and into her heart? Was she wrong for allowing her desires of the flesh to over-rule her vow of chastity?

During the third and final weekend of the workshop, Epiphany re-vealed her most agonizing thought in her diary. Removing the habit's wimple from her head, she began reading aloud "I had to be with Dex-ter in the earthly sense ... the first time he penetrated my heart it felt so heavenly ... oh God, how I longed for ... no ... how I needed that ... *special* caress ... I wondered how it would feel ... if only for one time ... I needed to keep him inside of me for as long as it would take ... but ... I'm not being fair to him ... but I must have him around forever ... even if it is only ... half of him ... I ... "

All of a sudden, quick as a thief, Epiphany snatched the silver cross and chain from her neck as she muttered these words, "I knew ... I was at my most ... fertile period when I ... begged Dexter to chant our love mantras from the *Song of Songs* ... I don't know how ... but I knew he wouldn't deny me ... not *this* time ... not like he has in the past ... I just knew he wouldn't. Oh God, what have I done ... I knew better ... I didn't give him a say in the matter ... I ... *Damnit!* What have I done ... to my Dexter ... I ... "

Two hours later Epiphany stopped crying—at least she stopped cry-ing hysterically. Between her voice dissolving into sobs and drying the tears flowing down her cheeks, Epiphany was able to finish her diary readings. She mustered a half-smile. She placed the wimple on her head, straightened her habit, and left. I never saw her again.

Epiphany thought her greatest sin wasn't her infidelity to God, but the way she had selfishly used Dexter as a sperm bank—making a withdrawal without his permission, and with no intention of sharing the profit of his "begotten" product.

In her mind, she believed Dexter could never be with her, but that she could have a part of him with her, by having his child.

How many young women become pregnant just to carry the love of a man within them? Perhaps you know of a woman who clings desperately to her love child, and the man within this child. Better yet, what about the woman who tries to save or strengthen the love between herself and her man by having a child? I suspect this practice has been going on since the dawn of time, and it'll probably continue well into the future. Who's to say if it is wrong or right, good or bad? *Maybe it's just what* **is**—no more and no less.

What she didn't write about, which I believe is significant, was her need to be the kind of mother she never enjoyed as a child. Was it a co-incidence that she and Dexter both harbored a similar need to become the parent they never had? Were they soul mates destined to be together? Was it divine order that made their paths cross? Could it have been the work of the serpent from the Garden of Eden? These are the same questions I ask myself each time I read their journals.

What questions do you have concerning Dexter and Epiphany? You do have questions about them, do you not?

Epiphany did leave the convent for the reasons she wrote in her diary. She had mentioned during our last session something about moving to a small city in Switzerland. Epiphany believed she could raise her love child there without the stigma of being excommunicated, and without the town haunting her and her love child.

My last visit with Dex was six months after Epiphany left the convent. When Dex learned that Epiphany had left the convent, he was heart-broken. He blamed himself for not having the strength to take her away with him. For months, he tormented himself with the sweet memories of the night they enacted the scriptures from Solomon's *Song of Songs*. Not only had he lost face with the church—for he had confessed his sins to his superiors—he had also lost the love of his life. Had he known she was pregnant with his child, he would have been completely forlorn.

Unable to outright tell him Epiphany's whereabouts, because of patient confidentiality and the promise I made to the love of his life, I had to devise a way for Dexter to find his family. After all, I knew they both wanted the same thing and, like most couples, they had *not* communicated their inner thoughts to each other.

I quickly thought of a simple plan. I excused myself from the room to use the restroom. I left my progress notes from Epiphany's last session on the side table nearest to Dexter, with a bookmark on the page indicating her desire to move. When I returned forty-five minutes later, Dexter was gone. Lying on top of my notes was a three-word note written in black ink: "God bless you." It was written on his white clerical collar.

I told you from the very beginning that I am an incurable romantic. If he moved quickly, Dexter could arrive just in time for the birth of their child.

I was faced with a love triangle like the one that challenged Dexter and Epiphany: a conflict that caused serious problems early in my marriage, cause us to come close to legal separation.

After my father made his heavenly transition, my mother's health steadily went downhill. I knew she was lonely and having a hard time adjusting, so I started visiting with her almost daily to make sure she had taken her medication, take her to the market, and do any other thing that she requested of her *good* son Jean-Paul.

After a time of caring for my mother, I realized I had become a surrogate husband to her. I maintained the same routine with her for several months, probably several months too many. Mother, as you have probably guessed, had become extremely dependent on her son the doctor. I felt a real sense of obligation to take care of her, because she had been there for me as a child—not to mention how good she was at fabricating guilt trips.

Eventually, Mother moved in with us because she was unable to function anymore on her own. Simone was okay with the move and, as usual, she was there to lend her wonderful helping hand. God I miss my Simone.

Mother's physical condition steadily worsened over the years, but her mind remained sharp. The only problems we had during her later years were geriatric depression and the unhealthy dependency she had developed on me. I can't say exactly when it happened, but if I left mother's presence for more than my normal workday, she'd start calling, faking illnesses, and using her other tricks to get me to come home. As a practicing psychiatrist, you'd think I wouldn't fall for the guilty child routine, but my degree doesn't make me immune to years of childhood conditioning. Eventually, I realized what was going on—as with most doctors, family members are the last patients to receive treatment.

Simone, with her unique way of not interfering, brought up an interesting and important point to me one day. She mentioned that we hadn't taken a single vacation in the past year because of "your mother's delicate condition." As usual, Simone was right. Because of the new teaching position I accepted at the university and my private practice, I was working seven days a week. The combination of work and mother consumed all of my time. Not until I found several packages of C batteries and two marital aids from *Le Sex Shoppe* did I realize how negligent I had been of taking care of Simone. Within three weeks we took a week of holiday in Cannes for some sun, fun, and, privacy.

During our holiday, I received what seemed like a hundred phone calls from Mother, and she let me know in no uncertain terms how I had abandoned her. She told me it was obvious that I no longer loved her, and then she threw the ultimate guilt trip—she reminded me of the sacrifices she made for me while I was growing up—and this is how I repay her.

Even though I knew this "poor me" routine too well, the "childhood conditioning" crept in and I felt as if I had let her down. Isn't it funny how some of the buttons your parents pushed when you were a child still work in your adult life? I tell myself not to push my daughter's buttons now that she has become an adult, but just as I promised never to say "because I said so!" to her as a child, my finger can't resist hitting a button every now and then.

I guess life wasn't complicated enough for me, so Simone added a little fuel to my brush fire. She was offered a temporary position as an educational *attaché* in Washington, D.C. It would be a great stepping-stone for the advancement of her career, that she couldn't afford to pass up. It was also an opportunity for me to do some advanced study at John Hopkins's Hospital on a foreign-exchange program. Only a few wrinkles needed to be ironed out before we could leave home. Simone would leave immediately, and I would follow as soon as I could arrange a leave from my practice and secure a caregiver for mother. This transition should not have taken more than three months to complete.

That little brush fire I mentioned earlier turned into a raging forest fire when my mother realized I would be leaving her within two weeks.

Mother tried everything in the book to keep me from leaving. Four months later, I still hadn't joined Simone. The two most important women in my world were pulling me in opposite directions. I was torn between the woman who gave me a life and the woman who had become my life. As usual, when I found myself on the horns of a dilemma I would review the case histories of patients with problems like mine. During this conflict, I happened upon Dexter and Epiphany's entries in my progress notes.

Was my conflict any different from theirs? Wasn't Dexter torn between his love of God and his love for Epiphany? My mother, who was like a goddess to me, was demanding more than I could deliver. I could no longer be the remembrance of my father—her departed love. Like Dexter, I had to live my life with the love of my life, Simone. I hoped Mother would understand and release me, much in the same way Dexter and Epiphany knew God would understand and release them to live together as one. I joined Simone shortly after hiring Brigitte as Mother's caregiver.

During the years we were away, I made it a point to call Mother often and I would try to visit her at least every three months. During my one-week visits with her, I felt closer to Mother than I had since my father died. The first question out of her mouth was always "Have you been eating?" followed by, "You look thin. Have you lost weight?" Her health had declined, but her spirits were stronger than ever.

The last time I was with her, there was such a wonderful look of peace on her face. She told me things about my father that I had never known. Occasionally, she would tell me that my father said

hello, and how proud he was to have had a son like me. She was eld-
erly, so it didn't bother me that she thought she had spoken with my
father. It was all right with me if she talked to him, as long as it
brought her comfort. I joked with Simone over the phone before
leaving for the States about my mother wanting to get a ticket for
the "White Light Airlines" jet to visit my father.

Over the years, Simone has always picked me up curbside at
Dulles airport on my return flights from Paris. The last time, however, she came inside and greeted me. Simone hugged me much
tighter than usual and wouldn't let go. It was as if she hadn't seen
me in a lifetime. Finally, in a soft voice she whispered, "Brigitte
phoned . . . your mother's flight departed . . . she's gone to live with
your father."

I miss my mother almost as much as I miss Simone. There was
only one difference between the two losses. I don't have any guilt associated with the loss of my mother. Even though I was away when
she died, I knew she was in good hands with Brigitte. I knew I had
done all that I could for my mother. She was okay with me being
away, and we had become very close. Last, Brigitte told me she died
painlessly in her sleep.

I had a lot of guilt associated with the loss of Simone. I was right
there with her when she died. I should've done more . . . but I did-
n't. While we were very close, I felt as if we had only scratched the
surface in exploring the depth of our love. The way she died was
much too painful for her, and for me. In my mind, I still hear her
agonizing screams and the way she begged for death to take her
away. I remember at the end how she looked into my eyes, barely
able to move her lips, as she whispered, "Please forgive me . . . I
have . . . and . . . always will . . . love you . . . Jean-Paul . . . "
Damnit, it wasn't fair! I should've let her finish.

2

Joel and Harriet

Uncertainty is the refuge of hope.
—HENRI-FRÉDÉRIC AMIEL,
Journal Intime

Joel—December 23

It's killing me that she'll be alone for the holidays.

I can only imagine how difficult it's going to be for Harriet. After all, except for a few close friends, she'll be alone this holiday. I won't be there to snuggle with her in front of her marble fireplace. I won't be there to pour her vintage cognac or to keep it warm. I won't be there to catch the tears flowing over her cheeks as she watches "*An Affair To Remember*" for the thousandth time. Harriet won't have anyone there to beat at backgammon or jenga. All she'll have will be my brief phone calls to comfort the most wonderful person I've ever known.

I feel so responsible for creating this mess, but there isn't a single thing I can do right now to make Harriet's situation better. She constantly tells me it will be all right and that I shouldn't worry about her. "I'm a big girl. I can take care of myself," is her usual reply, but how can I forget she's going to be all alone? How can I pretend everything is all right, when I'm not going to be there with her to celebrate Christmas or New Year's Eve? After all, this *is* the season to express love. Harriet shouldn't be alone, but I can't be in two places at the same time.

Damnit! What made me think I was capable of handling this kind of situation? I feel like I'm back in high school, when I was trying to date Becky and Penny at the same time. I didn't pull it off then, so what in the hell makes me think I can do it now?

I still can't see what Harriet is getting out of this relationship. Why is she so understanding? How can she tell me everything will be just fine when everything I see indicates just the opposite?

Harriet continually tells me it's her decision, her choice to live this way. I know she is older and more mature than I am, but it has to bother her when I go home to Colette. She has to be thinking to herself, "I get the romance, sex, and his love, but in the end he still goes home to her." Harriet can't be so mature that she totally accepts my being with someone other than her. Doesn't she long for me to hold her tenderly as she sleeps?

I know she means what she says, but there is a small part of my ego that wants her to be a little less independent, less tolerant. I know she wouldn't lie to me about her feelings. She never has, and with her integrity she never will.

I'm constantly inventing ways to let Harriet know how much I love her—to let her know that even though I'm not there in person, I'm always with her in spirit. I've probably written over a hundred letters and poems to her in the short eight months we've been together. I wish I could give her more than my pitiful letters of love or my poems that never seem to rhyme. Unfortunately, these meager offerings will have to do for the moment.

I don't make enough money to buy the kinds of things she likes or to take her to the exotic places she wants to visit again. Hell, Harriet's net pay each month is three times my gross income. I just wish I could do more for her. The strangest thing of all, my financial position doesn't seem to bother Harriet in the least bit. That's just one of the many reasons I love her. So what made her fall in love with me?

I would love to take Harriet to Tiffany's for a breakfast of emeralds, cultured pearls, and diamonds, but I can only afford to give her my heart and all the love within its four chambers. It's sad, but if it wasn't for the hopeless romantic who resides within me, I wouldn't be able to give her anything. Harriet tells me my companionship is more than enough, and that I shouldn't concern myself with giving her "things." But what is it about my company that makes up for my inability to give Harriet the nice "things" she loves? The nice "things" I want to give her. The nice "things" she deserves for being such an exquisite jewel.

I can imagine how Christmas will be for her. Harriet's friends and their families will gather at her house for dinner on Christmas evening. After dessert, they will retire to the library and exchange gifts. They will sing Christmas carols by the fireplace, then laugh, and sip her expensive cognac. They will leave and she will be alone.

On several occasions she has mentioned to me how some of her green-eyed friends take great pleasure in prying into her personal life. Harriet is a very private person and doesn't like to talk about her personal life. There are things about her past that she hasn't revealed to me—and she considers me her best friend. I can imagine how upsetting it will be for Harriet during the Christmas party when they ask, "Where is this so-called special friend of yours?"

"Harriet, my dear, you *do* have a friend, don't you?"

How can she answer those questions? She can't stand up, and announce to the world that she's seeing someone seventeen years her junior. Harriet can't tell her stuffed-shirt friends that she's involved with a man whose gross income wouldn't cover her utility bills—that her "special friend" lives with a model twenty years her junior—or the *coup de gras,* that he's an hourly worker.

Harriet has told me several times that she can handle her friends. I know she is *very* capable of handling herself; I've witnessed her in action when we've been out together. She can call forth a cold empty stare and a frigid sound to her voice that signal, CAUTION: YOU ARE APPROACHING DANGEROUS GROUNDS.

I don't know why she tolerates her friends with their malicious behaviors, but Harriet is amazing when it comes to dealing with people. Hell, she's amazing when it comes to most things. But my question still has not been answered. Why does she place herself in so many awkward situations just to be with me?

Surely, there are eligible men who are equal to her in every way. Men who can provide all the things she deserves to have or who can dazzle her with their brilliance. Men who've traveled around the world. Men who could easily relate to Harriet as an equal. Men, unlike me, who have had life experiences like hers. Men more experienced in the art of love. Men who don't require explanations about certain aspects of life, death, or the pursuit of happiness. How can she want someone like me, whose travel experiences are limited to a few Midwestern states? Who can't afford the $368 bottles of 1923 Cognac she imports twice a year from France? Hell, I can't afford the crystal *tulipe* glass she uses to sip this very old and rare cognac. Harriet deserves a man who is her equal in every way.

If she chose a man who has realized his purpose in life, her life wouldn't be so limited. I know there's a purpose I must fulfill before I die, but it hasn't been revealed to me; at least I don't think it has been revealed to me. A man who knows his purpose wouldn't be looking for his missing piece. I didn't know a piece of me was missing until Harriet asked me, "What is the one *thing* you need, baby, to make your dreams come true?" Why me, Harriet? I don't have the experiences of Don Juan or the suave sophistication of James Bond. Why has she bypassed the men of her caliber and chosen me to be her companion?

I know it's selfish, but I don't want her to leave me for another man. She'll see, one day, that I'll be able to give the "things" she deserves.

Harriet is a wonderful, kind, and honest woman. Because of those qualities, and a bunch of others, I love her, and yet I know she's way out of my league. It's as if I've just started high school and she has already finished her PhD.

I must admit, Harriet makes me feel as if I'm her equal. When we go out, she doesn't mind eating at places that are within reach of my pocket change. It's amazing how she can attend a dinner meeting at the Ritz's Terrace Room one evening, and then eat with me the next night at Dan's Diner. That's just another reason I love her and one more reason she shouldn't be alone during the holidays.

"Why me, sweetheart?"

Could I satisfy Harriet for a lifetime? Will she eventually long for a more experienced man? Will I long for a younger woman? What about Colette? Will she ever realize how much more there is to her besides a great body and a pretty face? Will Colette leave one day with a designer, photographer, or a corporate exec who can give her the trinkets she so desires?

There's too much floating through my head to be sure of anything. But I do know one thing for sure—Harriet shouldn't be alone for the holidays.

Harriet—December 23

He's so sweet!

Ordinarily, I'd get pissed if a man called me every couple of hours, but Joel's calls are as refreshing as a Highlands' mist upon my face.

It's so nice of him to be concerned with my happiness. His thoughtfulness is concerned not only with the upcoming holidays, but also with my welfare in general. Joel's so thoughtful in that way, unlike the men of my past. I wish Joel could understand the reasons I'm okay with our part-time relationship; but, for him to accept the real answer, he would have to be a woman, or at least have been treated like one. As I think about it, Joel does have a high level of sensitivity for a man. Could he have been a woman in a previous life? That would explain his empathetic nature toward me.

To make Joel understand, I would have to unearth my past relationships. Where would I begin the sad saga of my dealings with the baby-boomer boys? Dare I mention the evil actions the older ones of his gender are capable of carrying out—the betrayal and deceit? I dare not mention the false promises. Should I reveal all, and chance corrupting my sweet Joel? Perhaps it's foolish on my part, but I don't believe my baby could be corrupted. No, not Joel. He'd never follow in the footsteps of those cesspool dogs! He views women as equals, and for that reason alone he couldn't possibly become infected with that most dreaded of male diseases—*machoism*.

Telling him about my past relationships isn't a good idea at all. It would only open old wounds and uncover those disgusting memories I would rather not revisit. Painful wounds that have taken too many years to heal. Goodness, just the thought of telling Joel about those relationships makes my heart cringe in sheer terror from the horrid memories. I won't taint our present with my disheartening past.

Oh shit! My floodgates can't hold back the bloody memories. Like a flash flood, disappointment, pain, lies, abuse, tears, exploitation, cheating, victimization, humiliation, desecration, torment, defilement, domination, phoniness, abandonment, STDs, despair, confusion, violation, frustration, disbelief, unfulfilled promises, anguish, misery, and heartaches are trying hard to drown the peacefulness that Joel has brought into my life.

No! I won't have it! I've suffered far too long, and spent too many hours in therapy to allow those demons to rear their ugly heads. No, the past must remain buried! My precious present is too valuable and mustn't be tainted with my terrible past. I will not jeopardize Joel's innocence with my *exposés* of the baby-boomer boys. Never!

How can I get my Joel to understand? I have passed that stage in a woman's life when she is concerned with whether her man has other pillow pals or not. Hell, the men I have dealt with in the past played musical beds every time a woman pulled her covers back and whistled, "Here boy! Good doggy!" I know it's difficult for Joel to accept, but his adoration, respect, and admiration mean much more to me than having a warm body lying in my bed every night. Most of my girlfriends wouldn't agree with my sharing concept, but I would rather have 10 percent of a sincere, compassionate and loving man, than 100 percent of a treacherous Machiavellian.

Joel wants to know why I'm so understanding of his situation—why I'm not more demanding of him. To most women it would be obvious: my relationship with Joel is refreshing. He has been very open and honest with me from day one. Joel doesn't play the infantile games of his *macho* big brothers. Maybe he doesn't play those painful games of deceit and betrayal because he's young and still innocent. Whatever the reason may be, it's easy for me to relax and be myself with Joel, and that is *extremely* important to me.

There are no pretenses, no need on his part to control me or act superior to me. I don't believe he cares that I make more money than he does, and by now he should know money can't buy my love. Joel doesn't love me because of my physical attributes, my accomplishments, or the things I've accumulated in my life, he loves me—the real me.

The baby-boomer boys I've known have always had the misconception that giving "things" *is* love. Joel gives me the only thing he can afford—the only thing of true value—his heart. That's the reason I'm so understanding of my wonderful man.

There isn't a need to demand anything from Joel; he gives his all to me every moment that we're together. With him in my life, I feel complete. I know it's foolish to hold such a belief, because it implies that I need a man to supply my missing part—but I'm only human and I need *someone* to appreciate the love I have to give. For those who understand this, it isn't necessary to explain; for those who don't already understand, no explanation will suffice. Joel is the only man I have loved who has taken the time to understand my point of view, my moods, and my thin skin. Joel is the closest thing I've ever had to a soul mate.

There is a good chance this relationship with Joel won't last. Love, like life, holds no guarantees. At some point my "sage" wisdom will falter, and my life experiences will wear thin. One day he won't be able to over look this maturing body with its less-than-perky nipples, its thickening waistline, and its ever-spreading hips. One day his live-in Barbie doll could regain top billing in his heart. But until that happens, if I allow it to happen, I'll love every moment that Joel is in my life.

It doesn't bother me to be alone on Christmas, New Year's Eve, Valentine's Day, or any other damned Hallmark cards day, because every moment I spend with my sweet Joel *is* a holiday.

May-December relationship. . . . Just who in the hell came up with this phrase to describe the love relationship between a younger individual and an older one? I spent several hours at the library, searched the local bookstores and the Internet to get its true meaning, and find out who coined this expression. Before I tell you what my research revealed, I'd like to define this figure of speech according to Daniel Webster.

May of course is the fifth month of the year, and according to Mr. Webster's definition, it is the springtime of life; represented by the young. The word *May* was derived from *Maia*, a mythological Greek goddess. Besides being a goddess, *Maia* was also a nymph—a beautiful *young* maiden—capable of inducing *nympholepsy*: a state of emotional frenzy. This ecstatic frenzy occurred whenever a nymph became manic, which would, in turn, cause her to become a nymphomaniac. This excessive sexual desire within the nymph was so powerful that she could seduce any man or woman with her intoxicating smile. In the vernacular of a generation-Xer, "She would sex you up!"

When I looked up December in Webster's, the definition was not quite as endearing as May's. It was defined as the twelfth month of the Gregorian calendar and it is also a period characterized by coldness, misery, barrenness, or death; the coldest season of the year (life). In my mind, this definition conjures up the image of an old person desperately trying to hold onto life.

What did my research reveal regarding this figure of speech? Absolutely nothing. I didn't find a definition in any of the dictionaries of idioms I read, and there wasn't a shred of information on the web concerning this spring-winter relationship. However, two things that I unearthed were quite interesting. There are more books written about younger women with older men than about younger men with older women—and women wrote most of these books. Why aren't there an equal number of books about the relationship between the younger man and older woman? If there were more books on the younger man with older woman union, by whom would they be written?

Because I couldn't find the architect of this idiom, please accept my rendition of the impregnation, gestation, and birth of the May-December relationship term.

I believe that December was a sixty-something male professor teaching English literature at an Ivy League school. Ms. May, a freshman student attending his class, was captivated by his interpretation of the romantic's literary works, his sage wisdom, his seemingly harmless wit, and his deeply chiseled Adonis-like face.

One day during class, Professor December elaborated, "familiar acts are beautiful through love" from Act 4 of Shelley's *Prometheus Unbound*. Ms. May was particularly aroused by the innuendo the good professor laced throughout his explanation of Shelley's quotation. After class and without a moment's hesitation, Ms. May surrendered her body and soul to this man who was in the winter of his life.

A sixty-something female college professor observed this merging of seasons, unknowingly, just as they embraced. This female professor was familiar, in the Biblical sense, with Professor December. She was shocked, hurt, and outraged. When she saw her beloved embrace Ms. May, the image of them caused a reaction deep within her heart and soul. Seeing her Professor December with Ms. May made her think of all the young women she has ever seen embracing older men. Because she was a professor of Greek mythology, it was only natural for Ms. December to think of the most promiscuous young maiden in ancient Greece, Maia, the goddess nymph.

As she detailed this painful incident in her journal, she looked out the window of her ivory tower, and saw a small cardinal perched on a barren and snow-covered tree limb. The bird's grip on the weathered branch represented the young woman's embrace, while the tree limb symbolized the old man—her *now-former* lover.

From the indecipherable scribbles, on the tear-stained pages of her diary, chronicling the painful thoughts of this shocking incident, the May-December idiom was sired.

Far-fetched, melodramatic, and bordering on the sublime, you say?

Yes, you're absolutely right, but it works. Now let's take a look at Joel and Harriet.

During our first session, I became aware of Joel's most-endearing quality. This quality allowed him to become an intricate part of Colette's life and be, as Harriet wrote, "as refreshing as a Highlands mist upon my face." It was his sensitivity. Joel was gifted with an other-than-conscious ability to step inside their topsy-turvy worlds and create a sea of calmness for both of them.

Harriet initiated Joel's counseling sessions with me. She felt that Joel would excel beyond his wildest dreams if he could put his insecurities behind him. She paid for the sessions and carefully followed the suggestions I gave her to prevent Joel's pride from being hurt because he couldn't afford my fees.

Joel was quite mature for his age, but was still inexperienced in the ways of life. This lack of experience accounted for his not understanding why Harriet was okay with the arrangements of their relationship. Joel would have benefited from studying the movie *An Affair To Remember* instead of drying Harriet's tears as she pined over the tragic car accident in the movie. Perhaps he would have recognized that he was something of value to Harriet, that he gave her something that money could not buy—a safe and secure haven.

Joel's limited life experiences weren't enough to prepare him for the delicate intricacies of dealing with a mature relationship. On several occasions, I had to spend the entire session explaining why Harriet was okay with being alone for the holidays, sleeping alone, and finally, why she didn't need him to buy her "things." If he had listened carefully to what she said *between the lines*, he would have recognized the answer to his favorite question, "Why me, sweetheart?"

When I gave him what I thought was her reason, he refused to believe it was that simple "You mean that it's just because I pay attention and don't hassle her, Doc? Come on, even Colette demands more than that!"

How could I expect him to understand how painful her past relationships had been when he's never experienced heartbreak? Unfortunately, some of his issues could only be rectified with time.

I must admit that my concern for Joel was a little deeper than in the usual doctor-patient relationship. He was the kind of young man that any good father would have wanted as a son. We had a daughter who I dearly loved, but there was still that paternal need within me to raise a son. Although we never verbally acknowledged it, he accepted me as his surrogate father.

Perhaps the biggest hurdle for Joel to overcome was the issue of making much less money than Harriet. The first thing we talked about, which should have been obvious to him, was the number of years she had been honing her earning skills. He understood that she had finished college, that she was born with a silver spoon in her mouth, that she was much older, but it still bothered him. This is when my fathering genes kicked in, and I felt compelled to teach him a few things, much as my father "took me to school" when I was about to make the biggest mistake of my married life.

My father saved my marriage, and kept me from throwing away my best friend. That was one of the reasons I wept so hard when Simone whispered, "Please forgive me ... I have ... and ... always will ... love you ... and only you ... Jean-Paul!" before she died in my arms. I guess I had blocked her saying, " ... and only you ... "

God, I felt so guilty when she apologized to me again with her last breath. I still feel guilty. If only I had told her, I'm sure she would have forgiven me as I had forgiven her ... but there wasn't enough time. I waited too long. For the remainder of my life, I will be plagued with the "shoulda woulda coulda syndrome." But, let me get back to Joel and the fatherly lecture I gave him regarding the income issue.

I told Joel that, in today's world, women frequently make more money than their male counterparts, especially in certain ethnic groups. The reasons are many: more women seek higher education than men, which converts into making more money. They're also more disciplined in money management as a rule than men, especially in my case; and unfortunately they still have to prove that they're equal to men. Those explanations got me nowhere.

He didn't realize that Harriet made more money than most of the baby-boomer boys she had dated, and that they also shared his concerns about her income. When she was dating the baby-boomer boys,

Harriet reluctantly tolerated their *macho* bullshit, as each jockeyed to prove they were superior to her.

One day I asked Joel, "Why do you think Harriet buys four-hundred dollar bottles of cognac?"

Before he could reply, I whispered, "Because it slyly delivers this powerful message, 'Top this, asshole'."

Harriet's subtle cognac message to the baby-boomer boys reminded me of Sabine, a friend we had back in France. She was a rather old aristocrat who deplored being a part of the upper class. But Sabine was without a doubt the queen of "one up on you" lines. Late one evening we were sitting around and Harvell, the Napoleonic asshole in our social circle, uttered, "There's nothing that can compare to the taste of Harvey's Bristol Crème after a good humping!"

In the most nonchalant voice Sabine could muster she countered, "Ahhh yes, but it will never compare to the silky taste of *old* bottled Harvey's Bristol Crème as one basks in the afterglow kindled by an evening of *coital bliss.*" Then Sabine slowly turned to Simone, and with a roguish look on her face said, "Let him hump on that."

Joel needed to understand that Harriet doesn't want breakfast at Tiffany's; she wants to sup on love's rare jewelry. Harriet, like many women, hungered for a carat of conversation, a solitaire of sensitivity, earrings of ecstasy, a tiara of tenderness, an amulet of appreciation, and a ring of respect. Only when Joel realizes that Harriet needs the things that money can't buy, will he have the answer to his question, "Why me, sweetheart?"

Joel will eventually understand that finding one's purpose in life is not dependent on age, wealth, or one's position in life. A person's purpose is revealed on their journey through life. Your journey is one in which experiences are gathered, arranged, refined, and stored until your purpose permeates your entire being. It is the culmination of all the things you have learned in this lifetime that leads to the enlightenment of purpose. There is a universal belief, one that Dexter and Epiphany strongly embraced, that the expression of love is the ultimate purpose for our existence. Joel didn't have a clue at the time, but he had already actualized his life's purpose by loving Harriet.

Finally, Joel must understand that none of us—no matter how old, young, experienced or naïve, wise or ignorant—can foretell the future. Whether he will be able to satisfy Harriet for a lifetime will be depend on: how he treats her; whether he can correctly interpret the signals that her needs are changing; whether he's willing to adapt to these changes; whether he properly maintains the lines of communication with her heart; and whether he's willing to do whatever it takes to be around forever.

Have you figured out why Harriet is in this May-December relationship? Was she living out some adolescent fantasy she harbored during high school? Could it be his buff, youthful body? Was he convenient? Was he her maintenance man? Was she trying to be his mother? What would make a younger person attractive to you?

As for Harriet, she was very clear as to why she was in this relationship—*she was in control.* Control had become Harriet's highest relationship value. Because she was in control, Harriet eliminated any possibility of getting her heart broken again. She accomplished this by regulating the amount of love coming into and out of her heart. There's nothing wrong with wanting to be in control of your life, but it does present a problem when you try to control your partner's life to gain more control over you own.

I believe that, right behind love, the next-most-important pursuit in a person's life is to be in control of their life. Think of the unlimited possibilities that would be available to you if you were in total control of your life. Would there be anything you couldn't do? Would there be any restrictions on where you could go? Would you have to worry about being home before the streetlights come on? Of course, being in total control of your life is not realistic, but the amount of control you have over your life will produce an equally proportional amount of happiness.

When Harriet finally allowed the truth about her control issue to creep out of her heart's mouth, she talked about how badly she had been hurt by the men of her past. Harriet related incidents to me in which she purposely screwed up so she wouldn't look better than her "boomer" boyfriends. She also told me how she tried to be subservient to them and, finally, how she desperately tried to be the traditional type of woman her baby-boomer men wanted.

Harriet wasn't a traditional woman by any stretch of the word. Harriet was independent, strong willed, capable—a woman of the new millennium—superior in many ways to her male counterparts. It's a frightening prospect for many baby-boomer males to deal with this type of woman.

There is a "natural" law that states that the person who has the most options available, and uses those options, will most likely be superior to those with fewer options. Option was Harriet's middle name. She had all the business skills her CEO father could possibly pass on to his child. Unfortunately, her father wasn't capable of filling the gaps that only a mother could bridge for her girl-child. Harriet's was thirteen when her mother died, so Harriet didn't have the benefit of her mother's experiences in handling, managing, or dealing with men.

Although he had father-daughter talks with Harriet about men, she wasn't able to transform his spoken words into usable defense mechanisms. Phrases such as: "be careful," "the seven greatest lies ever told to get into your pants," "you're the only one for me," or "it'll clear your skin," were translated for her by her father in an attempt to protect her. But, to Harriet, they were just words. They lacked the experiential pain of having been lied to, bitten, and maimed, by the marauding packs of two-legged dogs.

After being used, abused, and mistreated, Harriet raised a fortress around her heart that was totally impenetrable. She vowed to never lower her drawbridge again. Work became her lover and constant companion. Not until she met a young, entry-level administrative assistant by the name of Joel did her defense mechanisms begin to weaken.

With him, she felt safe and refreshed because she was—in control. She fell in love with Joel because of his respect for women and his need to please. In many ways he reminded Harriet of her father. Because of Joel's wonderful qualities, she overlooked his youth, his lack of experience in the world, and his schoolboy presentations of love. Those idiosyncratic things were of no consequence to Harriet, for she had found someone safe to love—someone she could control.

In talking with Harriet, it didn't seem to bother her that Joel was with Colette—at least not on the surface. I suspect she had the concerns that most mature women and men harbor when compared to their youthful counterparts. But it was Harriet's high level of self-confidence and self-esteem that allowed her to get past Colette's youthful body—at least for the time being.

Joel told Harriet he was with Colette because he thought they had potential. Harriet was able to ascertain something different from the conversations she had with Joel when he and Colette were at odds with each other. Harriet knew Colette wasn't interested in developing anything other than her body. Harriet also knew Colette would never be able to satisfy Joel's unquenchable thirst for knowledge, or his cat-like curiosity.

Harriet recognized Joel's great potential for learning, his ambitious nature, and his stick-to-it-iveness. She knew that, with the right direction, help, and mentoring, he would become a great success—the type of man any woman would want. Because of Harriet's insight and her ability to take Joel to levels that would satisfy him, Harriet dismissed Colette as a threat.

At the time of this journal entry, Harriet hadn't lured Joel from his peaceful existence with Colette for a number of reasons. She didn't have time for a full-time relationship; he wasn't ready; and she still feared that one day he would break her heart.

Is Harriet taking the path of least pain by being with Joel? I don't think so. She only wants what the rest of us want—to love and be loved in return. But that is just my incurably romantic professional opinion: What do you think?

Colette met the CEO of a large and well-respected modeling agency. The CEO wasn't trying to improve the company's roster by stealing Colette from the Ford agency; it was done purely for fun. With the help of her new employer, Colette became a super-model. Since then, Colette and Octavia have been living together and, in my understanding, they are happy and very much in love.

It has been my experience that, in love relationships—especially in the May-December unions—things work best when the lovers emotionally balance each other. As of this writing, Joel and Harriet have been together in a full-time, live-in relationship for the past seven years.

When I saw Harriet last month, she expressed an interest in marrying Joel. I believe Joel will stay with Harriet forever if she doesn't sabotage the relationship. Remember, her initial reason for being with Joel was because *she* was in control. It won't be too long before Joel exceeds her level of confidence and competence. Harriet may begin to feel as if she's losing control in the relationship, and this could cause her heart's protective fortress to raise its drawbridge once again.

In time, Harriet will see herself as getting older—while her sweet Joel will never seem to age. By the way, isn't it funny how men do not age? They simply become distinguished. I wonder if, in this new millennium, women will stop getting old and simply become—elegant.

Eventually, Harriet will have to acknowledge the physical differences between her and the women Joel's age. That will be when the Colette's in his world will become a threat to Harriet. The deadly combination of not being able to compete physically with the younger women and losing her control over Joel could well strangle the love right out of their relationship. Time will tell.

Are you presently on one side of a May-December relationship? If not, have you ever considered one or been approached with the possibility of being with someone much older or younger than you? What was the first thought that ran through your mind as you considered these questions? Did you immediately ask yourself, "What will people say?" Did you instantaneously reject the idea as disgusting? Did your first thought provoke the questions: "How will I fit in with his peer group?" or "Will I always be the odd one in her group of friends?" "Are we destined to be loners because we don't fit in?" Did your first thought catapult you into the far future to ask the question: "Because I'll probably outlive him, who will be there for me when I get old?"

Have I ever asked myself those questions? Actually, those *exact* questions went through my mind before I married Simone.

It was very easy to answer the question: "What will people say?" I made a decision not to concern myself with the frivolous comments of people who thought ill of our eleven-year age difference.

Somehow, I knew Simone would be patient with me as I stumbled through the maze of maturation. I didn't care what others had to say. It just didn't matter. I was in love.

"How will I fit into her peer group?" Instead of wondering how we were going to fit into each other's circle of friends, I wondered how *they* were going to make their adjustments to us. Early in our marriage when we socialized, we would feed off each other's people skills. Simone's intuition would alert her when an uncomfortable situation was about to smack me in the face. She would come to my side, and her presence alone would extinguish my anxieties. I was so attentive to my wonderful wife that I could recognize subtle changes in her voice that indicated that she was uncomfortable with a certain situation. Unlike me, she didn't need my backbone for support; however, she was pleased that I sensed her uneasiness. We were—a match made in heaven.

"Because I'll probably outlive her, who will be there for me when I get old?" That was the hardest of all the questions that ran through my head, after I decided Simone was the only woman for me. It's impossible for anyone to be there for me when I get old. It's impossible, because I haven't met a woman yet who could compare to my Simone. I get *really* lonely, but somehow the tape recorder inside my head always knows when to playback her soft voice saying, "I love you Jean-Paul, and only you!" Yes, I outlived her and I get lonely for her, but the sweet memories of our time together somehow keep my heart out of checkmate—most of the time.

I'd like to end Joel and Harriet with a question. The question is: Does Love judge?

3

Darren and Claudia

Those who are faithful know only the trivial side of love: it is the faithless who know love's tragedies.

—OSCAR WILDE,
The Picture of Dorian Gray

Darren—October 19

Sleep has become my only source of comfort.

I only wanted her to tell me everything was okay. Claudia knew what today meant to me. Maybe I should say she *should've* known what this day meant to all three of us. How could she be so insensitive to my pain when she runs so quickly to the aid of her friends?

It is not often the pain comes. In fact, it hasn't reared its ugly head in a month. Today it returned. It returned with such incredible intensity that it ripped my heart once again beyond human repair. I hope the angel of mercy still makes house calls.

How could she not see it in my eyes? Whenever she hurts, her eyes change. I remember her tear-filled eyes a year ago today, as I walked away. How frightened her eyes looked at the thought of my never returning. They looked lost—like those of a young toddler who can't find her mommy at the mall. Most everyone's eyes change in some way when things go haywire. Why in the hell couldn't she read the pain in my eyes? I read the icy stare she gave me today, when she finally *did* realize what this day represents.

It's exactly one year since I found out about "him." "Him," this man who dared enter the heart of the only woman I have ever trusted and loved in my life. "Him," that son-of-a-bitch who isn't worthy to flush the toilet for her. Yes, "him," that low-life, alcoholic, jealous, and violent excuse of a man! Why did she allow him to enter her body, her heart, and our lives?

I know the reasons she gave me, but . . . never mind, I've spent far too many painful nights with tear-filled eyes pondering that same question over and over. Right now, I must deal with this dreadful pain. Oh God, it hurts so damned much. It's as if "he" has slipped back into my heart, using a dull scalpel to slice every millimeter of its delicate lining. And like the sacrificial rooster at a voodoo ceremony, I can't do anything besides bleed, and die.

How will I ever get over the betrayal, the deceit, and the horrible pain inside my crippled heart? *Will* I get over it? Someone tell me . . . how do I let it all go? Why is it that I can forgive but I can't forget? Why does it hurt so much?

Shit! I did nothing to warrant this treatment. Yeah, I know there have been times when I've been an asshole. I know my workdays are too long, but I'm giving her the kind of life she wished her father could've given her and her mother—the kind of life her mother eventually got—the kind of life my Claudia dreamed of having as a child.

There have also been times when I didn't stop long enough to listen, when she was having a bad day—bad days she brought upon herself, as she martyred herself to her friends. It was rare that I received the kind of blessings she bestowed upon her friends.

I'm not perfect, but I'm far from being like most of the husbands she talks about. I made mistakes but I never missed a day in telling her how much I loved and adored her, or how she's still the most desirable woman, I know.

I'm not making any sense. I'm rambling, babbling as if I were one of the confused at the Tower of Babylon. This is not like me. I've got to muster up some strength, some courage to get through this night. Just this night, then morning will come and it'll be all right—at least until the sun goes down again tomorrow.

I have never felt pain like this before. Oh God, I hurt so badly, please don't forsake me now.

I *told* her I was having a rough time today. I only needed a simple hug to reassure me—a little assurance that we are okay. That's all I wanted, all I needed. Well, superficially that's all I desired. Hell, deep inside I don't know what I need anymore.

But instead of comfort, she kept asking, "What? What's wrong with you?" Doesn't she know what this day represents to me? To us? To them? I overheard her telling a friend how she misses "him" from time to time. How she wonders if "he" is doing okay. If "he" has cut back on "his" drinking. If "he" is sleeping better. Why in the hell doesn't she wonder if I'm okay—okay on the anniversary of that horrible night? Why don't I get the same consideration as this no-class, backdoor son-of-a-bitch that entered her heart, her body, and our life?

It isn't that they were physically together that haunts me most . . . that's not true. The thoughts of them together hurt like hell!

I often wonder if he is better-looking than me—if he dresses better, smells better, hell if he tastes better than me. Yes, I even wonder if he is better endowed than me. But none of that matters. It's that she told me I was her "all and everything"—that she looked into my eyes every morning and said, "I love you, honey." Every morning she would say those words, all the while scheming to get with him before lunch. I trusted her completely.

What a damn *fool* I've been!

Doesn't she know that each time she tells me, "that is in the past," she's talking about "their" past, not *mine*? She doesn't seem to realize how I pray throughout each day for just one night without "their" past visiting me on my pillow—how hard I fight every night to escape the images of them together in my—no, *our* bed—the bed where we conceived our children, and where we held each other while planning a better future.

Claudia doesn't realize that my past isn't behind me; the damned thing camps out right up front in living color with digital surround sound. Behind me, hell no! It's etched forever in the frontal lobes of my brain. No, she doesn't know. She couldn't possibly know, or she wouldn't tell me it's all in the past. That's why she could only ask, "What's wrong with you?" then got pissed off and accused me of being childish. To escape discussing it further, she would scream, throw things, and then storm out of the house. Maybe she's still see-ing him . . . no, I can't go there.

The pain! It's still here, reminding me of how frail my heart and soul have become. Will this pain go on forever? Will the delicate lin-ing of my heart ever heal? If it does, I suppose the permanent scar will always remind me of my foolish trust in her. It's the same fool-ish trust that makes me love her even now. God! It hurts so damned much. It hurts so deep inside of me.

Please rip this pain from my heart. Teach me how to forget to re-member. Take their pictures out of my head. Somebody please help me!

Just let me make it through this night. I'm not asking for much—just one night of peace. One night alone with her, without "him" in our bed. That's all. That and nothing more . . . please.

The clock says it's 4:37 A.M., but time doesn't have meaning to me anymore. I've got to get a few hours of sleep. I have a triple-by-pass surgery to do this morning and I wouldn't want to make an-other mistake of the heart. I don't want Mr. Payne's children to suf-fer his loss and feel the pain of a broken heart. I must get some rest for them. I would never want anyone to feel the pain I have in my heart right now. God, make it go away! Make everything all right, the way it used to be. Maybe it never was all right. No, I can't go down that road either. I would die if I knew she had done this . . . No. Stop!

Perhaps I can symbolically remove my hurt as I repair Mr. Payne's frail heart. I wish someone would replace *my* shredded heart. God, I wish it were "him" on the table today. Just a simple twist of the aorta, a single suture, and "his" past would be behind me.

Claudia—October 19

That damned look of his!

Why is Darren doing this to me? I keep trying to forget, but he constantly reminds me with those damned eyes of his. They look like Dad's.

Why can't he just leave it alone? His heart isn't the only one that cries from the pain. Damn him! Why does he always give me that look? It brings back the painful memories of the past when I was growing up.

Doesn't he know how much I want to forget the past and the pain it has brought me? He keeps throwing it in my face with his damned teary eyes. Then he follows with "Why Claudia, why?"

My father's line was "I bust my butt for you and the kids to have a good life and you repay me this way! Why?"

It wasn't my fault. I tried to make it better for Dad, but nothing worked. Every day after she left us, Dad would look at me the same way he looked at Mom before she left—with those teary brown eyes. Shit!

I know it wasn't right, but what about me? What about my needs? My desires? Darren is always working. We have enough money to last us a lifetime. He's been so damned worried about securing our future that he never took the time to secure "us" in the here and now. Yes, I did it, just as I have many times before. He only found out about Dante. He's gonna pay for the way he treated me after Mom left . . . shit, why did Dad take it out on me? I wasn't the one who screwed around on him.

Darren thinks *he* has pain. He doesn't know the meaning of real pain. Hell, from the time Mom left Dad to be with "him," I was in pain. I lost my Mom because she wanted more. I didn't deserve to be treated that way. She abandoned me for the good life.

After she left, Dad rarely smiled, laughed, or played with us. I remember him crying a lot at first. Then after a while the tears stopped. That's when his eyes changed. He had an empty, glassy-eyed, lost look. Damn you, Darren! I lived with that goddamned look for ten years, and now you throw me back into that same pain again with your fuckin' eyes! It's not fair.

I know Darren is trying to give me the kind of life I never had, the kind my mother left us to live herself. He doesn't deserve to be treated like this, but what about me? He leaves me everyday for fourteen-hour workdays, six days a week. What am I supposed to do?

He doesn't want me to work and I don't do the mother carpool thing very well. I can't stand being around his colleagues' phony-ass wives. They all come from blue-blooded families, where they've been trained from birth to be somebody's wife. It bothers the hell out of me when they say, "I'm Dr. Handel's wife." It's as if they're an appendage on their husband's body, with no brain or life of their own. They couldn't make it on their own if they wanted—not like I could.

I had to earn my way into this good life. No one gave me anything. I worked my way through City College while raising both of my younger brothers, after Dad committed . . . when he was no longer with us. Hell, most of these doctor's wives are so damned hung up on who is doing what that if a delicious man were hand-delivered to them, they wouldn't notice him. Well, Buffy probably would notice, but only if he was served on a Steuben crystal platter. That bitch is just as transparent as the ten-carat diamond wedding ring she wears.

Why can't Darren be like my father *before* Mom left him? Mom wouldn't have left if Dad had been home sometimes to "do her" instead of working so hard to keep up with the Joneses. Just who in the fuck are the Joneses any damn way?

Before Mom left, Dad played with me. He would sing songs to me, and tuck me into bed each night after we said our prayers. But then he changed. He left me completely, just because . . . damn, why doesn't Darren stop looking at me like that? He's not my . . . Daddy. Oh my God, he *isn't* Dad. What have I done?

The affairs and one-night stands I've had have nothing to do with the way Darren treats me. It wasn't Daddy's fault either. It's me!

What have I done? Have I become my mother? If only she would've stayed, I could've lived a normal . . . damn her!

Why me?

Will Darren forgive me? Will he forget the past? Better yet, will he allow the past to be buried? What will happen if he refuses to stay? I don't want our children feeling the pain I felt as a child—the pain of losing a parent and their love.

If only he would stay. If only I could change. If only . . .

What would make your loved one scurry to the arms of another? What physical or emotional satisfaction does your loved one seek, in the bosom of another woman that he couldn't get from you? What Casanova quality could another man have that would pull your loved one into his bed? What drives one person to take the life of his unfaithful spouse, while another commits suicide? What would drive you into the embrace of another, when you have loving arms waiting to embrace you at home?

I met Darren when he was a senior at Wayne State's medical school in Detroit, Michigan. He attended a workshop I conducted at the Midwestern Psychiatric Symposium, held in Chicago that year. At the time, he was undecided about the area of surgery he wanted to specialize in after graduating. He attended my workshop *Crossroads: Follow Your Heart*, in the hope that it would help him make the best choice between orthopedic and cardiac surgery.

After the workshop, Darren introduced himself and presented his dilemma. As always, I replied with some "if" questions: "If you knew which one to choose, which would it be?" "If you could choose *only* one, which would it be?"

He hesitated, as most people do. I felt compelled to ask Darren the life-or-death if question, "Think of someone you love very much. Now, if you had to save that person's life as a surgeon, which of the two specialties would you . . . ?"

It turned out that Darren chose cardiac surgery. In fact, he was the most-gifted cardiac surgery resident they had seen at John Hopkins in ten years. During his residency, we became such good friends that it wasn't unusual to find Darren comatose in our guest room after a marathon shift at the hospital. He finished his residency and opened a practice in Bloomfield Hills, Michigan, where he met and later married Claudia.

They moved back to Baltimore when Darren accepted a prestigious and very lucrative position at the Hopkins' Institute. After they moved, we stayed in touch with each other by phone and whenever we could arrange our schedules to meet at the same conferences. However, it wasn't too long after they moved back to Michigan that Darren noticed a change in his relationship with Claudia. A change that had become obvious to those of us closest to Darren: a deadly one at that.

Several days after that dreadful afternoon, Darren called me at home. The first words out of his mouth were, "Jean-Paul, sleep has become my only source of comfort."

For the next several hours, I pondered Darren's statement. What did it mean? Was he talking about blocking out the pain of her betrayal by sleeping? Was he referring to sleep as a "little death" that would temporarily take him away from the pain? During our final counseling session, Darren revealed the meaning of his *sleep* statement. It was a revelation, a truth I had never considered.

What about Darren's journal entry? Who or what was he wrestling with, as he scrawled in his journal the crimson-stained and painful words gushing from his butchered heart? An important issue that consistently appeared in Darren's journal entries was his obsession with Claudia's eyes. As we opened his old baggage, the answer to this question became clear.

When I asked Darren about the significance of a person's eyes to their emotional state, he recalled a trip his family took to Hawaii when he was young. While they were on the island of Oahu, his family attended a real Hawaiian luau. After they served *poi*, a rich creamy dessert, some islanders went on stage and performed a variety of dances. The dances ranged from the fierce war dances of Samoa to the poetic and seductively enchanting Hawaiian *hula*. Darren told me about a silver-haired woman who came on stage before each performance to explain the next dance. Her words describing the courtship dance were forever engraved in Darren's memory.

Darren's eyes slowly defocused as if he were going into a trance. Slowly, he began reciting the silver-haired woman's words: "Don't believe the words coming from their hands ... or arms ... don't believe the words coming from the undulating movements of their legs ... or hips ... believe only the words that come from their eyes ... the words from their eyes come directly from the soul's inner light ... and the soul ... never lies." After what seemed like an eternity, Darren's eyes refocused. His head dropped. He stared at his interlaced fingers. He blinked. Then a wave of tears crashed against his gifted and trembling hands.

Darren overlooked a painful truth, as most of us do, hoping that he was mistaken about Claudia. The images of "them" together, his painful heart, his endless tears, and sleepless nights were just a few of Darren's self-inflicted punishments for disobeying the silver-haired woman's words of wisdom.

What caused the pain to be so intense within Darren's heart? As we plowed deeper into his old baggage, one drama consistently, in Darren's words, "reared its ugly head." The pain centered around the less-than-ideal relationship he had with his mother. Darren was forced to become a surrogate husband to his very controlling and manipulative mother. You know the type, the conditional lovers—give me all your love first and *if* it satisfies me, I'll give you *some* of mine. She should have been jailed for willfully obstructing Darren's childhood development.

To receive a token of love from his mother, Darren had to work like a child in a "sweat shop" and, even then, he wasn't always able to collect his love wages. No sooner, than he finished one chore, there was another waiting for his gifted little hands to start, delaying his payment of love once again.

Darren soon learned not to trust his mother's word; as you might expect. This lack of trust generalized onto the other females who populated his world—aunts, cousins, and girlfriends, were all perceived by this immature and impressionable young Darren to be—untrustworthy.

Darren's mother was also great at devising and executing guilt trips. Her most-effective guilt-inducing line was, "This is how you repay me after all I've done for you?" This line, although in statement form, was always delivered as a question. This excellent question was designed to elicit the only response possible from a childhood of guilt conditioning—"No, Mama."

However, one great benefit generated from his mother's conditional love was his phenomenal ability to please. Darren found that when he guessed what his mother wanted from him before she opened her mouth, and gave her what she desired before she could finish her sentence, he wouldn't get punished as much. What he perceived as not being punished was his mother expressing her love—in a minimal way. With practice, Darren was soon forecasting his mother's demands accurately ninety percent of the time.

Consequently, he became a master of quickly reading and fulfilling people's needs—especially women. The women who happened into his life couldn't get enough of Darren. Because of his immaturity at the time, he couldn't comprehend the consequences of his unique talent. Unable to understand or handle the praises bestowed on him by the throngs of grateful women, Darren assumed their words of praise were empty because, in his mind, the women were no different from his mother. So his trust in women plummeted even further.

What was it about Claudia that allowed him to drop the wall that protected his heart from further injury? I guess you could say, "There was something about Claudia." Somehow, she slipped under his protective wall and planted a seed of trust. Using empathy as a fertilizer, Claudia forced the seed to germinate. She watered the fragile plant of trust with her wet kisses and it slowly began to grow. Protecting its delicate foliage with her words of reassurance, it developed into a beautiful groundcover, a foundation for their love. Eventually, it grew tall and became dense enough to hide Darren's old baggage under its petals of trust. With his childhood baggage out of sight, and a strong foundation of trust, he pledged his unconditional love to Claudia. They married and produced two beautiful children.

Unfortunately, Claudia forgot to weed the groundcover one day, and a very old, aggressive, and deadly plant found its way back home—a plant whose roots can be traced to Claudia's childhood. This weed's poison was as deadly as the hemlock. It was an heirloom weed, passed down from the previous generation, ready to destroy Claudia's foundation of love and Darren's groundcover of trust.

The weed matured and all hell broke loose in the garden of Darren and Claudia. The only woman he has ever trusted betrayed him completely and she did it in the worst possible way—by "doing" *another man* . . . in his *house* . . . and in his *bed*.

What makes this the worst-possible way to betray a man? If you subscribe to the popular belief that women have sex to get love and men give love to get sex, then it follows that men view having sex as love, while women view sex as an expression of love.

Using that belief, it's logical to conclude that men are physically oriented when it comes to love, whereas women are emotionally oriented.

Stretching my neck out further on the academic chopping block, we can say that men get hurt when the woman they love physically connects with another (has sex), while women get hurt when the person they love emotionally connects with another (falls in love).

Please bear in mind that this is my own psychobabble bullshit theory, based on the popular belief I mentioned above. I don't have a shred of research or evidence to back it up, other than my years of working with couples and reading the thoughts inside their journals.

Something else about Darren's journal entries was that they were replete with instances of "he" or "him." He used these pronouns whenever he referred to Claudia's lover. I didn't have to ask Darren why he did this; it was a safe place to direct his anger. "Him" allowed Darren to vent all of his anger onto this non-person instead of onto Claudia. This convention of "him" was most effective in averting the anger that *could* have pushed Darren to physical violence.

One day Darren overheard a conversation Claudia was having with a girlfriend about "him." The conversation was about the welfare of her former lover. Claudia wondered if he was doing okay, if he had stopped drinking, and mentioned how much she missed him. Darren told me that when he heard Claudia express her concerns about "him," the movie screen within his head went pitch black and the only thing he could see was his heart being completely drained of trust. In a voice as cold as death, Darren said, "That was the darkest moment of my entire life, Jean-Paul."

I was quite concerned when Darren talked about this "darkest" moment. My concern turned into fear when he reiterated the statement during our next three sessions. Incidentally, I was seeing Darren four to five times a week during the first month of our sessions, just to get him stabilized after finding out about "him."

During one session, he verbalized the five-alarm phrase that every abused spouse is taught to listen for: "If I can't have her, then he won't either (no one will)." As I probed deeper, to better understand his statement, I realized he wasn't talking about taking Claudia's life—he was referring to "him." When I read the section of his journal entry about the heart operation on Mr. Singer, it confirmed my suspicions: he was going take the life of Claudia's lover.

Darren was about to cross the fine line that separates genius from insanity. It would have been the worst thing he could've ever done to his children and himself. Nervously, I questioned him about the five-alarm statement and what he intended to do. Darren told me he had gotten the phone number of Claudia's lover from her cellular phone billing. He tracked the number until he found the first time it appeared. Scraping his palms over his face as if he were desperately trying to remove the skin, he told me the first time the number appeared on her cell phone was 9:32 A.M. on Valentine's Day.

With the help of a private investigator, Darren got the home address and phone number, place of work, and "his" daily routine. Darren so much as told me that he had intended to perform a single bypass on "him" with the aid of a rather large-caliber projectile.

His response brought me to within one nervous grunt of a case of colitis. I canceled the rest of my appointments and spent the remainder of the day with Darren. We ate lunch, walked through Hart Plaza, drove through the tunnel into Windsor, Ontario to gamble, took in a movie, and ended our day at an all-night greasy spoon truck stop under the Ambassador Bridge for supper. As I nursed a cup of coffee that had become lukewarm hours ago, I searched every file cabinet in my brain for a quick fix—anything that would prevent the nasty "surgery" Darren had scheduled for "him."

Have you ever been hurt by a loved one so deeply that you begged for the pain to be taken away even if it meant taking someone's life? In light of the above, do you have a deeper understanding and greater appreciation of the term—crime of passion?

My father was a man of passion and he was no stranger to the pain of love. He understood better than I did at the time, and for that I am forever grateful that he intervened, and stopped me from committing murder.

As I listened to Darren go on about "him," a strange thing happened. It was as if someone turned my head and made me focus on the short-order cook's "Mom" tattoo. Instantly it hit me! I delivered a guilt trip that stopped Darren's gruesome train of thought.

I borrowed an infamous line from a seasoned strategist. A person who had a tried and true record for stopping Darren dead in his tracks. I asked, "This is how you repay your mother, after all she's done for you?"

He looked deeply into my eyes, probably remembering the silvered-hair woman's face, blinked once, twice, and started to cry for the first time in three weeks. For once, I was grateful that his mother had in-stilled this guilt device in Darren's conscience.

There are a few more points in Darren's journal that I would like to discuss before moving onto the difficult task of deciphering Claudia's thoughts.

Darren's journal entries revealed a behavior that most people ex-clusively associate with females. Because his self-esteem was at an all-time low, Darren began to question his desirability as a man. He won-dered why Claudia's lover was desirable to her as a man. He compared himself to this man with no name, no face, no body, and no personal-ity. He asked himself questions that most-probably will never be answered.

In a manner very much like that of his female counterparts, Darren asked himself the following questions: "Does he look better than me? " "Does he dress better than me? " "Does he smell better than me? " "Does he taste better than me? " "Does he make love better than me? " "Does he make more money than me? " Then the ultimate question, the male's equivalent to a woman asking about breast size—"Is his penis bigger than mine? "

Another hurdle that Darren had to clear to reclaim his peace of mind was the blaming of himself for Claudia's indiscretion. Darren needed to realize that he had nothing to do with Claudia's decision to seek someone outside their marriage. There wasn't much more he could have provided financially, spiritually, or emotionally for his family or his wife. Even if Darren would have been around to, as Claudia said, "do me more," it still wouldn't have made a difference. Her infidelity wasn't about his cocksmanship. It was all about her.

Darren's only fault was ignoring the truth that came from Claudia's eyes. He didn't heed the words of the silver-haired woman soon enough. Darren wasn't an ideal spouse: they don't exist. No one can provide one hundred percent of their partner's wants, needs, or desires; but Darren came damned close to being an ideal husband.

The most difficult task I had to perform was to get Darren to put this painful incident behind him. He had to carry on with his life, with or without Claudia. I wanted him to reframe the way he saw Claudia so that he could get past the anger he had buried deep within his heart of hearts for her. I wanted him to see Claudia not as an evil and scheming jezebel, but as a needy person crying out for help.

Despite it all, I could support Darren only while he waited for the pain to subside. None of the techniques I learned in school, or any of the tricks I had developed and kept stored up my sleeve would speed Darren's healing process. As in the case of Dominique and Christian, our next couple, only the passage of time would put this terrible incident in proper perspective for Darren. Time will minimize the hurt and pain within his heart of hearts. Time will ultimately be the most effective doctor.

I could give Darren only one guarantee concerning this situation— the memory of this incident *would* resurface for the rest of his life. When it does, it will cut into the massive scars on his heart as a painful reminder: "Never ... forget ... to ... remember, believe only the words that come from a person's eyes ... they never lie."

The tragic irony of Darren's situation was that, as a cardiac surgeon, he repairs human hearts with his gifted hands, but he was unable to mend his own heart of hearts.

Finally, what about the statement: "Sleep has become my only source of comfort"? For Darren, sleep was the only place left where he could become Claudia's *all and everything* once again, even if it were only in a dream.

Anger is a mask that people wear to conceal their true emotions. In her entry, Claudia expresses herself angrily whenever she thinks about

Darren's teary eyes. She blames him and his teary eyes for bringing back the painful memories of her past. What was the hidden emotion that was responsible for such enraged statements as, "Those damned eyes of his!"?

Was it sorrow? Could it have been fear? Was it the powerful emotion of hate that spawned these angry remarks? What specifically agitated Claudia whenever she looked into Darren's tear-filled eyes?

Claudia, as you may have gathered, wasn't one to reveal her feelings easily. Our few sessions together were much like her journal entries, helter-skelter. When she talked about her *affaire d'amour,* she would jump from one seemingly unrelated thought to another within the same breath. For instance, she would start talking about Darren in the present tense, then suddenly interject the past regarding her father, then swiftly return to the present to blame Darren for both her mother's abandonment and her father's inability to express love anymore. Confused? I was, and imagine how dazed and confused Darren felt, trying to deal with both Claudia's irrational train of thought and the pain within his heart of hearts.

Several questions came to me as I untangled Claudia's diary entry. In one of her entries, Claudia mentioned that she had had several other liaisons during her marriage to Darren. What basic need was she trying to satisfy by weaving one man after another among the matrimonial fibers connecting her and Darren? What root emotion was she hiding behind her mask of anger? What factor prevented her from leaving Darren and taking off with one of her lovers? Why was she caught this time and not before? What virtue forced Claudia to leave the incriminating evidence that allowed Darren to discover her unfaithfulness? Before answering these questions, let's take a moment to briefly discuss the reasons for Claudia's adulterous behavior.

By the way, Claudia's affair was exposed because of her sloppy housekeeping. When making the bed after her afternoon delight, she missed an opened condom wrapper that had become wedged between the mattress and the leather-covered headboard. As luck would have it, the evidence was left on Darren's side of the bed. Accidental? I think not.

What about you? Have you ever left something out "accidentally" and gotten caught? Sure you have, even if it was only cookie crumbs on the floor in your bedroom—where eating was not allowed. Forensic experts believe that even the best criminals always leave at least one clue at the scene of the crime.

"Could the condom have been Darren's? Did he consider that a possibility?" These seemed like logical questions for me to ask after she made that statement. I remember the word *stupid* flashing brightly in my mind like a neon Vacancy sign at a sleazy roadside motel when she said, "Darren had a vasectomy after our thirteen-year-old was born." Surely, after all of her years of fooling around, Claudia knew to double, triple, and quadruple check for tell-tell signs. But, then again, she *was* foolish enough to allow her lover to "do her" in her own home.

What made Claudia look for love outside her marriage? How could she overlook Darren's love? What kept her from finding that love she longed for in the arms of at least one of her lovers? It was her inability to get out of her *own* way. That's right. It wasn't the sight of a handsome face. It wasn't animal magnetism. It wasn't the power they wield or their positions in life. It wasn't the size of their feet or hands that made Claudia open her heart and legs to them. Claudia was stuck in self-indulgent pity. She didn't know how to let go of her mother's physical abandonment or her father's emotional abandonment.

What Claudia was trying to find was the love her mother took from her and the love her father used to give her. She was unaware of her reasons for the affairs. Her needs, wants, desires, and behavior were out of her conscious control—all of her actions were being dictated unconsciously. Claudia was frozen in time. She was stuck! That's why she couldn't get out of her own way, and that was the reason for all of the affairs.

Everyone gets stuck emotionally; that's how we develop our personalities. We get stuck because of a psychological wound we receive as children. The wound is the result of a significant incident that we witness or experience in our childhood. Our parents or parental substitutes are, for the most part, the instruments that inflict this accidental wound; the reaction we have to this traumatic incident is the substructure of our personality.

Remember the wounds that made Dex and Epiphany ideal parents?

Better yet, what about Darren? Think about the wound his mother inflicted on him that led to his distrust of women. What about you? Who inflicted your wound and how did it dictate the outcome of your personality? What about your significant other's wound?

Before you tell me I'm wrong, before you blame your parents for screwing you up, allow me to finish. The traumatic incident is not always heinous. Most of them are simple mistakes made by our loving amateur parents. Except for abuse, molestation, incest, or other wounds of this type, most wounds are bad only because of the immature perceptions we had as children. If these same wounds were inflicted on us as adults, our experiences would allow us to evaluate the comment or situation, and respond accordingly. Our sensory acuity, an emotional microscope, increases with our life experience.

For an explanation of the term *sensory acuity*, imagine this joke on the movie screen in your head: A five-year-old walks in on his parents while they're making love. Running down the stairs, he screams to his brother and grandfather, "Come quick! Mommy and Daddy are fighting!" His fifteen-year-old brother makes it to the bedroom first, looks, and says to his brother, "They're not fighting; they're making love." Their seventy-seven-year old grandfather arrives behind the older brother, and with a look of disgust says, "And they're doing it rather poorly, if you ask me!" The ability to make finer distinctions (through sensory acuity skill development) increases with life experiences.

What is the treatment for these parental wounds? If the child has parents who are average or above average in their emotional health, the parents will recognize that a wound has been inflicted, help the child to understand and make sense of the incident, and reinforce the love they have for the child. This child's degree of "stuckness" in life will depend on how well the parents explained the situation, how well the child understands, and how much of the reinforcement is absorbed by the child.

If the parents are unhealthy emotionally, the child has to do the best he or she can, seeking or fabricating answers to survive the ordeal. If the wound is very extensive and the child fails to make sense of the incident, the degree of stuckness of this child in life is analogous to the feet of a fly stuck to flypaper—stuck for life.

This stuck child becomes a stuck adult. This stuck adult is the one who has strong issues that prevent them from enjoying life to its fullest. This stuck adult child, often makes life difficult for the people with whom he associates—especially his loved one. When you hear someone who consistently repeats such statements as . . . "I'll never trust a woman again!" "All men are controlling!" "They never stay." or "I want what I want!" it's a good chance they're emotionally stuck to some degree.

To put it in very elementary terms, if you don't recover from the emotional wound or wounds inflicted by your parents (remember, most parents are good and well-meaning) you'll get stuck in an emotional time zone. You'll respond with a childlike immaturity in situations similar to the one that caused your childhood wound—you'll run from the emotional wound (your core fear). Unless you face the wound issue, it will never heal.

The above explanation is an extremely simplified model of how our personalities are determined and shaped in life. This "crystal ball" book was not intended to be a textbook. However, I have listed nine universal core fears (sticks) and their corresponding desires (carrots) at the end of this chapter. These fears and desires are the engines that power your actions and reactions in life. The degree to which they dictate your life's dramas depends upon your degree of stuckness.

If you subscribe to this childhood wound theory, then you can see that affairs rarely have anything to do with the spouse of the adulterous person. The one committing adultery is running away from the old emotional wound of childhood that has never healed. Adultery is an effort to recover the losses that occurred because of the wound. Unfortunately, because the loss is outside of the adulterer's conscious awareness and controlled by the unconscious mind, the adulterer will blame this unfaithfulness on his spouse. Until he becomes aware of the real problem and corrects it, the adulterer will continue to have affairs for the temporary fix they offer.

I would like to point out that adultery is just one of many destructive behaviors used to heal childhood wounds.

In Claudia's case, her parents inflicted two emotional wounds—the wound of being abandoned by her mother and the wound of feeling forsaken by her father. Because Claudia identified with, and was influenced more by, her father, she became more stuck on the wound of being unwanted.

Claudia was looking for this lover, as with the others, to tell her she was worthy of being wanted and loved. I don't believe Dante was with Claudia just for sexual fulfillment; he believed he had found the love he was deprived of when his wife died. Claudia told me that whenever he got drunk, which seemed to be quite often, he would make statements such as "You remind me so much of her."

Without a history on Dante, it's difficult to pinpoint the incident that inflicted the wound of being unfulfilled or deprived. But when the stuck state revolves around being unfulfilled, the person usually wants that which they lost to be given back tenfold. They become gluttonous, thinking that receiving what they need tenfold will assure that they will never again be deprived. "You can never have *too* much *x!*" often comes out of their mouths.

Neither Claudia, nor her lover was very healthy emotionally. Despite his failed attempt to puncture the aorta of Claudia's lover, Darren was the healthiest one inside this triangle. Unlike "him," Darren wasn't trying to get over another woman by loving Claudia. Unlike Claudia, he overcame his childhood wound of distrust and conditional love. Now Darren had to deal with this new wound of infidelity—a wound that is difficult, but not impossible, to heal.

Claudia had numerous affairs because none of her lovers could heal her old wound of feeling forsaken. Each affair was doomed before it started, because her lovers didn't have a clue about what Claudia needed. They thought she wanted a better sex life. When they failed to make her feel wanted and loved, she dumped them and started the cycle all over again. She will continue to have affairs, looking for Mr. Right the rest of her life, unless she receives the proper "medication" to heal the wound.

Claudia stayed with Darren because he was like a rock. She knew he would always be there for her—faithful and unchanging. He was one of the few consistent things she could count on in her life. Because of his rock-like quality, Darren eliminated her lesser wound of being abandoned. He was the cure for the security wound inflicted by her mother when she left for the good life. However, he couldn't "fill the prescription" she needed to make her feel wanted and loved. Although he was her "all and everything," while growing up, he didn't have a model from which to emulate the warmth associated with love. As a result, he wasn't as warm and expressive as Claudia's father once was.

His mother was a conditional giver of love with a body temperature close to that of liquid nitrogen. He learned what little he knew about hugging, kissing, spooning, and all the other warm feelings associated with love by reading how-to books and from what he saw at the movies.

Why didn't Claudia teach him the fine art of loving? She certainly knew how to rock a man's world. Claudia didn't know she was missing the warm feelings associated with love. She was consciously unaware of the wound that deprived her of Daddy's warmth and love. Remember, Claudia is stuck. Claudia just knew that something wasn't right, that something was missing when they made love. Claudia wanted to make it to the mountaintop, but something was preventing her from reaching it.

About Claudia abandoning home to be with one of her lovers—she never left because she loved, adored, and worshiped her children. Knowing the effect it would have if she left, Claudia stayed because she didn't want her children to grow up in a broken home.

Despite the joint sessions in which I revealed Claudia's wound to her and Darren, as well as the recommendations I made for healing it, she couldn't stop fooling around on Darren. She would not "see" the wound. It's scary to revisit something that has hurt you—it could hurt you again.

Because of her stuckness, Claudia realized her greatest fear about three years after our last session together. Darren divorced her and won sole custody of their two children. He remarried after the children graduated from college and is extremely happy in his new relationship. The woman Darren married is very capable of keeping his childhood wounds medicated, as well as soothing the wounds inflicted by Claudia's infidelities. He married a psychologist who specialized in childhood development.

I've gone on at great length about Darren's and Claudia's journal entries. That's because it's difficult to understand the reasons a loved one becomes unfaithful. It is a subject that painfully severs the loving heartstrings of too many couples. No one should ever experience a situation like that. If you encounter it, you will never forget the pain that it inflicts inside your heart, and you will never be the same again.

I'm going to read your mind right now, based solely on a few assumptions. Because you have read to this point, it means that you like having that special seat normally occupied by the proverbial fly on the (heart) wall, you feel a kinship with some of the patient's experiences, or you've gotten some insight into a situation you've already dealt with—or that you're dealing with now. With those assumptions behind us, allow me to read the world's ultimate computer, your mind. I bet you're wondering which one of us had the affair.

God, how I loved Simone! She was *my* "all and everything." I couldn't help myself. The love in my heart instantly turned into hate on the day I learned she was another man's all and everything, too. How could she do that to me? To us? To herself? Those were my initial thoughts. Then, my heart exploded, splattering painful scraps of love throughout my chest . . . the thought of her with another man overpowered my reasoning . . . the room darkened . . . I felt like a bull enraged by the swords stuck in his back to weaken him for the matador's blade of death, I screamed, "God, oh merciful God, what in the *hell* did I do to deserve this?"

When she cried out, "Jean-Paul, please forgive me!" I freaked out! I remember the razor-sharp words I spat out . . . "*Prostituée*! Bitch! *Souillion*! Whore! *Putain*! Hussy!" . . . and how I hoped my words would slash her black heart into bloody ribbons.

Blasphemously, I repeated this prayer each night for weeks: "May she suffer unspeakable tortures in the bowels of hell for the pain she has inflicted on me, and for betraying our love." I stopped saying that prayer when I remembered the words of Saint Thérèse: "More tears are shed over answered prayers than unanswered ones." I wouldn't wish this pain on anyone, especially my Simone.

Typing the first few sentences of this chapter, as you may have already guessed, unearthed a cornucopia of painful memories. The pain delivered by these images, feelings, sounds, and smells inside this horn of plenty ranged from that of paper cuts to ones that words could never describe. I put to rest these memories and the pain they caused many years ago, or at least I thought they were at rest.

When the worst memories sleeping inside my heart of hearts were awakened, the pain they released was so intense that I had to close my laptop and walk away. It didn't matter how far I walked. It didn't matter where I walked. It didn't matter how fast I walked, like leaches those memories clung to my back, taunting me as they did years ago.

It was difficult for me to write about Darren's and Claudia's conflict because of these horrid memories. My writing became as helter-skelter as Claudia's diary entries. On several occasions, I snapped and lapsed into my old stuck state. While I was stuck, just typing Simone's name made me cry.

When I cried in that stuck state, each tear seemed to stop momentarily on my bottom eyelid as if it were in deep thought. As if it were contemplating the value of its life before taking a suicidal dive onto my desk. I wondered was "it" a tear, or was "it" me?

Some sections made me bawl like a toddler separated from his mommy in a department store. The beginning of one section made my blood boil with hatred because of my Simone's infidelity, while the end of that section froze my blood with indifference to Simone's actions.

However, writing this commentary made me feel like Epiphany when she wrote "a wave of calm flowed over my soul." That calm moment gave me enough time to retrieve the reasons I forgave Simone. It gave me just enough time to remember her childhood wounds, her stuck state, how fear and desire dictated her actions, how she consciously tried to heal an unconscious childhood wound, finally recognizing that she was "needy," and that I could heal the wound by attending to her "neediness."

I forgave Simone because I loved her. It's just that simple. Simone was my best friend, the keeper of my heart of hearts, and the woman of my dreams. She was my lover, the morning sun that kissed me awake, and the huge August moon that softly lit my summer nights. Simone's every breath gave new meaning to my life. I forgave her because one day she would carry our bundle of united love within her womb. Simone *was* my all and everything. I couldn't walk away. She was my soul mate—we were destined to be together. Dexter was right, to love is our purpose in life, our reason for existing.

What made me react negatively after all these years? Every time I counseled a couple dealing with infidelity, Simone's affair would resurface, but not this strongly. Why was my reaction so intense this time? I am reminded almost daily of her adultery, yet it usually never brings forth these emotions. Why did I react so emotionally as I typed the words in this chapter?

Although I am a psychiatrist and I've had many years since the incident to mature, neither my profession nor time has protected me from the pain or the hurt. I reacted negatively because I'm human.

That incident crippled me for many years. I tried to act as if everything were okay, but I know Simone saw through the thin veil that covered the real me. Beneath this veil, I would blame myself for her actions, beg for her forgiveness, work too hard to show my love, and assume she was talking to "him" instead of me if she was late in calling me. I would also accuse her of wanting to be with "him" whenever she was emotionally down. I'd get pissed off whenever I thought about "him," and much more too embarrassing to mention. With time, we healed our relationship and had a wonderful, although short life together.

The only good thing that came out of Simone's affair was the additional love she brought back. I used to think of this extra love as the love she gave to him. The love that should've been mine. Every so often, we would bump into "him" at school during special events. I know this sounds childish, but it gave me great pleasure to let "him" see the love that was his holding my hand. It was also quite amusing to watch "him" and Simone acting as if they didn't know one another. I couldn't pretend. I just couldn't. How can you pretend not to know your best friend? Could *you* forgive an extramarital affair and continue your relationship with your significant other?

Following are the paired "sticks and carrots" I promised to list, for the curious few. You may want to read again the section in this chapter that talks about fears and desires, to refresh your memory about the whys, hows, and whats.

The core fears and desires that dictate the actions and reactions within our relationships are:

Fears	Desires
being unnecessary	to be essential
being superficial	to be insightful
being undesirable	to be coveted
being immoral	to be virtuous
being forsaken	to be cherished
being unfulfilled	to be blissful
being dominated	to be powerful
being inadequate	to be competent
being isolated	to be harmonious

For a more detailed explanation, visit your local library or bookstore's psychology or self-help section for books on personality typing.

These core fears and desires are also known as "values." As you know, values function within us much like a traffic signal. They tell you when to go (green), proceed with caution (yellow), and stop (red) before someone rear-ends your heart—but only if you listen to that small-but-powerful voice coming from your heart of hearts.

Which pair dictated Claudia's actions? If you were to choose one of the pairs above that dictates your significant other's actions, which would you pick? What about you? Which stick and carrot best dictate the actions and reactions of your relationship dramas?

There is a saying that is *apropos* of this chapter's ending: "If you pay attention to what a person pays attention to, then you will know how to attend to that person." I would like to modify this statement to assist you if you ever need to heal a loved one's wound or even your own. If you pay attention to what a person says (negatively) about himself or herself, then you will have a better insight into the childhood wound (fear) that controls their actions. With this information, you can work on applying the correct medication, to aid in healing that wound.

4

Dominique and Christian

We promise in proportion to our hopes,
and we deliver in proportion to our fears.
> —FRANÇOIS, DUC DE LA ROCHEFOUCAULD,
> *Moral Maxims and Reflections*

Dominique—February 14

Why does the thing that brings me joy also bring me pain?

I wish Christian would stay. It's as if he's upset with me for choosing how I want to live the rest of *my* life. He was to be my friend for life—at least that's what I thought. A friend who could share in the new-found joy that has come into my life. He deserves to see me happy, especially after the horrible times he has seen me through during the past three years. But he has decided to abandon me. Why, Christian?

He'll leave after his house overlooking the river Seine is sold. I recall those awful nights in his living room when I'd cuddle in his lap like a frightened child, desperately trying to count the lights on the Eiffel Tower to keep my mind off the events of the past three weeks. Three hundred and seventy-two seemed to be the highest number I could ever reach, as I attempted to count the tiny lights that framed the wrought-iron tower. Each time I reached a certain height on the tower, the bright North Star would distract my eyes. I used to wish upon that star as a child and my dreams would come true. Then *Yves* took my wishing star and gave it to her. Damn that son of a bitch. That was my wishing star! I should have listened to my heart instead of my mother's foolish adage, "It's not a woman's place to question her husband's whereabouts."

It became too painful to look upon my bright star during those troubling times. That's why, whenever I reached the upper level of Eiffel's lighted tower, where God hung my bright wishing star, tears would well up and blur my vision. I was so thankful Christian was there to hold me whenever my bright star appeared. He just seemed to understand me without having to say a word.

Christian would let me cry until I could cry no more. Then he would dry the tears on my cheeks, chin, and nose with the "crying towel." The towel was soft and its rose-pink hue reminded me of the security blanket I had as a child. Christian's worn cotton afghan has dried many a tear over the years. It has even dried the salty liquid drops coming from his own eyes, on a few occasions.

After drying my face, Christian would gently stroke my hair with his large fingers and sing his American blues to me. "Is You Ever Seen a One-eyed Woman Cry?" was his favorite ballad to sing right after I finished crying. Somehow, that song always made me realize that my situation could have been worse. At the very least, the song made me grateful I had two eyes.

Christian was the only support I had during that terrible ordeal. I don't know how I would've made it through without him. Now this happens.

Whenever he spoke, I could hear the quiet power in his deep voice. The inflection of his voice, his presence, and his undeniable love always made me feel insulated from the pain of my nervous breakdown. Heaven knows I've been traumatized from that awful nightmare, but Christian made me feel like everything would be all right one day. That day has finally come and he's not here to partake in my happiness.

Christian shouldn't leave the city of love; Paris was built just for men like him. It is the most romantic place in the world. He is without a doubt the most thoughtful, loving, and romantic man I have ever known. Christian's loyal and unselfish heart is a graduate of an elite university. As a student of Eros, Venus, and Kama, Christian's heart was well-schooled in the art of love and romance.

Christian, it's as if they fashioned your heart just for me. I placed him on a pedestal to show the world that men are capable of expressing love. You were created to love me. Damnit Christian, I'm here waiting for you. Take me! Break your damned promise. Can't you see how much I love you?

He shouldn't leave Paris . . . and he shouldn't leave me.

With the living trust Christian set up for me, I was able to lease a loft in Montmartre. This area of Paris has retained many of the characteristics of the France of yesteryear. Montmartre, known for its rustic cafés, old windmills, and Bohemianism, is in a perfect location for me. Because it is the highest elevation in Paris, I have a good vantage point for painting my landscapes. Montmartre is the perfect place for an artist to live, work, and play.

I remember returning home after a short holiday at my grandmother's house in Versailles to find red-and-white rose petals tracing the path from the street to the front door of the renovated warehouse. I thought it was a little strange, but I quickly chalked it up to some eccentric artist making a statement about some social injustice. As I opened the building's front door, the petals scattered into the foyer—at least I thought they were the same ones from outside. Shaking my head in disgust, I wondered why someone would destroy such a beautiful flower just to make a statement that wouldn't change one single thing.

I started up the stairs after collecting my mail addressed to *Occupant*. Much to my surprise, the red-and-white petals didn't stop in the foyer. They trailed up the stairs and under my door. Sticking the key in the lock with a combination of wonderment, excitement, and fear, I entered my loft. My mouth flew open, and the air passed through my vocal cords as I tried to scream—but like a mime, not a sound escaped my mouth!

I couldn't believe my eyes. Next to the tall windows that overlooked the countryside was a gilt antique wooden easel. On top of its worn wooden clamp were two long-stemmed roses, one scarlet, the other the purist white I had ever seen. Their crossed stems pointed out and upward, while each blossom rested on the canvas below. A stick figure of a woman lounging in a bathtub with a big bright star above her head had been sketched on the rose-framed canvas. The next morning, when I critiqued his caveman-like artwork, Christian assured me he wasn't going to quit his day job to pursue an art career, at least not just yet.

He wasn't a master artist like Michelangelo, but Christian is the only artist of love and romance I have ever known.

I had admired that easel a couple of months ago when we were window-shopping in the Beaubourg art quarter. Most of the gold leaf was missing and its wood was splitting from age, but to me it was magnificent. It also happened to be way out of my price range, so I quickly dismissed the thought of ever owning such a fine piece of art. Over the past two years, I have finished most of my gallery pieces on that easel.

Oh Christian, you were such a comfort to me during my troubled days. Please come back. I want to share the good fortune you have helped to create in my life.

A ceramic table, which I had seen in the Needless Markup catalogue, replaced my cracked vinyl card table in the kitchen. Christian told me this store's entire marketing strategy, is geared towards the rich and foolish, who thrive on conspicuous consumption of outrageously priced items. My gracious Madison Avenue attorney can be quite sarcastic at times. He thought I needed to consume conspicuously at least one time just to get it out of my system.

Gathered about the table, replacing the plastic folding chairs, were two wrought-iron bistro chairs with cappuccino muslin cushions. The centerpiece of the table was a beautiful Lalique crystal-handled vase, filled with several dozen red and white rose petals.

Oh Christian, couldn't you break the promise for us?

The *pièce de résistance* in my loft was the metamorphosis of my used hotel mattress. Where it once lay on the floor, a new mattress now lay on a brown-speckled, wrought iron, four-poster bed. I once asked Christian why he preferred a queen size to a king. Without a moment's hesitation he said, "Domi, I never want you to be more than an arm's length away from me." My heart raced. Tears of joy came to my eyes, while a warm wetness ran down onto my thighs.

Christian was my slice of heaven.

Fastened to the ceiling over the bed, was an ornate medallion. Through its center opening flowed yards of creamy silk, which completely surrounded the bed and puddled on the floor all around it. The bed seemed to be resting on a fluffy cloud. I wish my angel would stay and make those clouds dance again.

Christian, please stay!

When I entered the silk enclosure, there among a dozen down pillows lay two long-stemmed roses. This was the second pair of roses Christian had placed on one of my gifts. I began to wonder if there were a hidden meaning, something I had missed. Why were they paired one red, one white? Why were there more red petals than white ones in the vase—or for that matter, coming up the stairs and outside the building?

A lacy cream ribbon bound a small envelope to the roses. When I opened it, I caught a hint of Christian's cologne on the deckle-edged paper. I can see those words even to this day:

Domi,

I hope the additions to your loft meet with your approval, sweetheart. We worked around the clock all weekend long. That's right; your man with the velvety soft hands was slopping paint, hammering nails, and carting heavy objects on his back up three long flights of narrow stairs! I knew there was a reason I went to law school, and this weekend made me remember why.

Darling, for so many years you suffered and struggled to make someone else's dreams come true, and then that person chose not to share them with you. I'm sorry things didn't work out the way they should have, but in time your wounds will heal and the North Star will once again shine brightly for you to wish upon.

I remember you telling me how your friends were making jokes about your mattress being on the floor—jesting that you could do no better. It's important to me Domi that you don't feel as if you're going backward. The future is waiting to bring happiness, peace of mind, and a million other joyous things to you, like the new look of your loft for example.

I know this is a little scary for you, being on your own and alone for the first time in your life. But I want you to know, as long as I'm around, you'll never be alone or lonesome. Domi, you can count on that promise.

Sorry I couldn't be there to witness your soundless scream (and I thought you only screamed like that when we made love). You did scream when you opened the door, did you not? I remember the most famous of all mimes, Marcel Marceau, saying, "Do not the most moving moments of our lives find us all without words?" I hope tonight has been a "most moving moment" for you, my love.

Sleep well, my darling, I'll pick you up in the morning around 10:00 for breakfast.

With adoration and much love,
Christian

P.S. The white rose epitomizes the purity of our relationship. The red, our eternal love. You were wondering about their symbolism, were you not, my inquisitive little mime. Goodnight, Domi.

Christian was the most romantic, thoughtful, and loving man I have ever known. But after a while, I started to feel smothered by his thoughtfulness. I know that when we first met, I was indecisive, needy, and weak, but since the divorce, I've grown much stronger. I simply wanted him to understand my need to be more independent, that I didn't need him to solve every problem or buy me things just because I mentioned they were nice. What he wouldn't give me was the thing I needed most—him.

Why didn't Christian accept my need to be "the one"?

Against my father's better wishes, I married Yves right after graduating from the university. Yves had women throwing themselves at his feet, willing to do whatever it would take to be his girl. At the time, Yves was the man, my romantic and sexy lover. He was all I could ever hope for in a man. That was the biggest crock of shit I ever swallowed. Not until Christian came along did I know what it meant to be with a *real* man. Damn you, Christian.

Christian and his damned integrity! Him and his damned promise! When will he realize he wasn't to blame?

Christian wouldn't break his "sacred" promise and I couldn't make that promise under the circumstances. He wanted me to be there when the time came. He wanted me to wait. I couldn't. I can't and I won't. For ten years, I listened to my husband's promises of a better future. I helped make his dreams come true, and then he divorced me. That bastard took *my* dreams and gave them to another woman. I can't risk losing them again—not to anyone.

I know Christian has worked hard to rebuild my confidence and self-esteem. He even managed to get my dreams back by restoring my childish belief that the North Star *is* my wishing star. But I can't afford to have my dreams taken away again. I couldn't bear to have my heart broken again. I can't, not even for my sweet Christian.

Christian knows the reason for my decision. We discussed it at length for many days and nights. It's as if he's fallen off the pedestal, hit his head, and damaged his memory and that wonderful heart *Eros* fashioned just for me. Why, Christian? Why can't you understand the need for me to be the one? I didn't hurt you.

Damn, I didn't realize it was so late. We're going to the opera house to see Puccini's *La Bohème*. I need to shower and dress, because Monsieur Henri, the stuffed shirt, is always on time. I'd better say goodnight, journal.

I hope Christian finds the strength to break his promise. I know he came from heaven to make some woman's dreams come true. Damnit, Christian, you were sent here for *this* woman! Break your promise and make Domi's dream come true . . . please.

Christian—February 14

I don't like this feeling of numbness inside of me, and I sure as hell don't like heights.

I never asked Domi to put me on that imaginary pedestal. I told her I was nothing special—that I'm just a man and—like any man, I would eventually do something to fall off her sacred dais. But she wouldn't listen. I fell and landed right on my *derriere*. Will she accept it that her Christian is human and not one of her mythical gods of love?

If I didn't keep my word, what kind of man would I be? What would Domi think of me if I were to break my word? Wouldn't she eventually ask, "How long it will take before Christian breaks one of his promises to *me*?" She's already been the victim of a broken promise and it almost wiped her out. I should think she would respect a man of integrity, someone she could depend upon. I suppose this is what I should expect from a woman much younger than me. Hell, I can't bullshit myself. Domi did what she had to do, and for that I respect her even more. But respect won't remove the numbness inside me that keeps me from feeling the passion jailed within my heart.

I was up-front with her from the start. Domi told me she understood everything and would stand by the firm resolve of my commitment. "I only need a friend. I can't handle anything more." was her reply when I told her about my situation. I suppose at my age I should've known better than to think we wouldn't take it any further. I needed a friend, but I also wanted someone to free the passion within me and burn away the numbness. I needed someone to share those days when life becomes too much of a hardship—to experience with me the days when life is one shade shy of phenomenal—who could help me make sense of it all. I knew that someone was Domi.

I knew she was fragile when we met, but I thought that if I could restore her confidence and self-esteem, she would be able to help me. That she would be there with me on those rare occasions when I'd wear the pain of the past on my shirtsleeve. I knew it was a foolish gamble, but I haven't made it to this point by betting conservatively at the crap's table of life.

I first saw Dominique one evening at a small bistro in the university district of Paris. She was sitting in a corner booth staring at a pile of crumpled papers. Not until I did a double-take to admire her beauty did I notice the tears streaming down her red cheeks. I watched Domi for several minutes as I contemplated whether I should ask if she needed a shoulder to cry on. Meanwhile, I recognized something rather peculiar about her dinner plate.

I thought it was a little odd that she was having breakfast. When I took a closer look, I could see the dried yoke from a partially eaten poached egg on her fork. The small glass of orange juice sitting next to her plate had separated into pulp and water from standing too long. Her knife had fallen onto the tablecloth, smearing a dollop of *Nutella* intended for her croissant. Her curdled *café au lait* had formed a brown ring inside the cup from sitting so long. Everything on the table indicated that Domi had been sitting there since breakfast. What happened? Why would she sit there all day long?

I walked over and asked, *"Vous parlez anglais?"* She replied, *"Oui,* I speak English." Although her eyes were bloodshot, they still twinkled brightly like the North Star. Little did I know that, just like the North Star guiding a ship to its destination, one day her bright eyes would guide my heart to do the right thing.

After several packets of tissue and two glasses of sherry, the stream of tears from Domi's eyes slowed to a controllable trickle. When the tears stopped, she began painting a picture of the tragic events that caused her depressed state. Her husband's attorney had served the divorce decree to her that morning while she was having breakfast. I remember Domi saying, "I sort of lost my appetite after reading the first sentence." I'm surprised she didn't lose what little breakfast she had gotten down. The first sentence of any legal document in which you are a defendant is quite offensive. Some person is alleging that you have wronged them.

It doesn't matter how the decree is served, whether it comes on a silver platter or if it's hastily shoved in your face by a New York City bike courier, the message that decree delivers *hurts*.

I told Domi about the trials and tribulations of some of my business clients who had gone through divorces. I told her how each of them felt their pain in a different way. Whether it was the pain of losing their spouse, knowing they were no longer wanted, being wrecked financially, or being separated from their children—there was always some degree of pain for each of them.

Domi talked about the struggle and sacrifice she made as a young wife so her husband could attend medical school. During the day, she taught at the university; her evenings were occupied giving private art lessons, and she waited tables on the weekend just to keep them afloat. Domi willingly denied herself new clothes, vacations, movies, and even lipstick to pay for Yves's schooling. Domi gave up these things without hesitation, because it's what one does when one is in a loving relationship. Therein laid the problem—Domi was the only one in love.

Domi leased a cheap apartment to cut down on living expenses and continued to live in that wretched apartment for six months after the divorce, partly because she had to pay the student loans she took out for Yves, but mainly because she wanted to be self-sufficient. Her stubborn streak and foolish pride kept her from accepting my help. Not until someone broke in and trashed her place did she agree to move.

To avoid making her feel like a kept woman, I had a living trust drawn up so Domi could withdraw money from her "savings account" whenever the need arose, without feeling like a gold digger or a codependent. Although we're no longer together, I have continued to fund Domi's trust. That's partly because it's my fault that her living expenses are more than she can comfortably handle, but mostly—because I love Domi. I wanted her to live out the wish she made upon the North Star. Unfortunately, she refuses to use the trust because of her foolish pride.

It's ironic how Yves took everything and gave her nothing, while I've given her everything and taken nothing from her—yet she still has the same issues.

We talked through the evening and well into the night. We talked until her tears stopped. We talked until we ran out of words. I had never talked so openly or freely in my life as I did that night. It felt good talking to Domi. It was as if I was talking to myself. I liked the way she made me feel about myself when I was with her. I believe she felt the same way—at least I hoped she felt that way.

After we parted, I couldn't get that wonderful feeling of being with her out of my system. She awakened the emotions sleeping inside my heart. Domi opened the locked jail cell that had imprisoned my passion for the last ten years. She guided those feelings out of the dark cellblock with the twinkling of her North Star eyes. Domi was gorgeous, attentive, and intelligent: qualities that any man would desire in a woman. However, it was her passion that counteracted the numbness within me. The passion was so strong within her that night that I could feel it despite of the thick blanket of pain surrounding her heart.

After the incident, I had given up hope of ever feeling passionate again. That night, my hope was renewed.

I knew what I was doing was selfish, but I couldn't risk losing her or the euphoria she created in my heart. Whenever she needed me, I made myself available. If she wanted something, it became hers. We were together as much as it was humanly possible and I loved every minute of it. I was determined to relieve her suffering in every way possible. I only wish I could have taken the pain out of her delicate heart. But only time can take away the pain inflicted by a loved one.

Within a short time, I became addicted to both Domi and that euphoric feeling she induced in me. I was like a junkie. I had to have

my Dominique fix at least four or five times a week. I had to be in
the presence of the woman I loved. Was that a crime? Am I not enti-
tled to life's pleasures like everyone else?

I believe it was this overly attentive behavior and my refusal to
break *that* promise, which toppled me from Domi's pedestal.

Early in the relationship, we came extremely close to making
love. I told her it wasn't a good idea. I didn't think she needed to
deal with the strong emotions associated with making love just yet. I
thought she should allow herself some more time to sort through
things—reexamine her emotions and real desires. I also didn't want
to take advantage of her delicate emotional state. Greater than all
the reasons I gave her for why we shouldn't make love was the
Number One reason—I was scared.

Although it had taken a couple of months, we had finally counteracted Domi's bad feelings with a multitude of good ones. I didn't
want to risk a setback. Besides, I know that love relationships
started in highly emotional states rarely ever last.

Was I being too cautious—too virtuous? Was I full of shit?

It had been a while since I had slept with anyone, but I knew this
wouldn't be right. I must admit, my smaller head did present a con-
vincing case to me for why we should make love. However, I knew
her heart needed more time to deliberate on her true feelings. Then
my one-track smaller head tried plea-bargaining to a lesser act of
oral gratification. However, my heart, acting as judge in this trial, rejected this cunning-linguistically contrived motion. Without warning, two days later, my little head locked out the judge and jurors
and convinced me that Domi would be okay. It was time to get busy.

Why didn't I heed my own warnings? What made me break
down? How could I give in so easily?

I know I shouldn't have broken my word; after all, it is supposed
to be my bond. Nevertheless, I did. I broke the promise I made to
myself. It was a promise of insurance. A childish promise to never
hurt again. I promised to never fall in love again. I broke it and I
fell, and I fell hard. It felt so damned good to love and be loved

again. There is a truth my great-grandmother told me, one that cannot be denied:

> When love decides, you can't hide; you can't even run
>   away.
> You have no choice my dear; you must let it stay.
> Because, in the end, love always gets its way.

I didn't have a choice. Love made me break my idiotic promise—love always gets its way.

I wanted—no—I *needed* Domi. We didn't have a choice; we *had* to make love; and sweet love we did make. The way Domi moved her hips gave new meaning to the term French *roll*. I can't begin to describe all of the things we did, the way we did them, or the pleasures that came as a result. But in the past ten years of having sex, this was the first time I had made love. Hell yes, I broke my promise and I don't give a damn.

If I break the other promise I made ten years ago, will I soar with the eagles again? But what about the accident?

I didn't mean to push him, but he kept swinging that damned racket at my head. I was only trying to protect myself, but I lost my composure and pushed the son of a bitch! I wanted a goddamned explanation. I damned well deserved one. I didn't see her standing behind him or I never would've pushed him in that direction. But, I *did* shove him, and when he stumbled back, he knocked Ellen down the stairs.

In a flash, everything I saw, heard, and felt went into slow motion. Her arms instinctively covered her head, trying to protect it from injury as she began her inevitable plunge down the stairwell. She was wearing a straight mid-calf-length dress that kept her from using her legs to slow or stop her fall. Her left foot lodged between two steps and twisted her ankle back on itself. Her fall ended when she landed on a crate at the bottom of the stairwell. That's when I heard a loud crack—like a piece of wood snapping. I thought it was the crate breaking from the speed of her fall and the weight of her body. But then, I heard that scream—the most God-awful cry I have heard in my life.

She didn't move. She didn't make a sound. She just lay there, a crumpled marionette, awaiting the puppeteer to manipulate her strings to move her—but he never came.

Domi says I shouldn't blame myself for what happened that night ten years ago—the night I anesthetized my heart from feeling any more pain. The problem was, though, that the numbing that stopped the pain had also stopped any passion from entering or leaving my heart since that evening. That is, until Domi came along.

I left the house in the early evening on that Saturday ten years ago. I was meeting Kenneth, a new attorney in our firm, to make a last-minute change to his opening remarks for Monday's court date. I hate those frantic last-minute calls, but I was the only partner he could find. It really didn't matter; Ellen was getting a nail repaired and wouldn't get to the Weaver's party for another hour. It seemed as if she was always running to the salon for a repair or a color change. Ellen told me this salon was the best in our area for fill-ins. I was most impressed with their service. It didn't seem to matter what time of day she would call; they always accommodated her.

Kenneth was without a doubt the best litigator in our firm. He had a natural talent for getting a jury to see, feel, and understand his client's point of view. He reminded me of myself twenty-five years ago when I started the firm. I knew he would make partner in no time, and now, ten years later, Kenneth is a full partner. In fact, he will replace me when I retire next year.

When I entered the conference room, Kenneth looked at me as if I were the last person he wanted to see. I thought he was feeling bad for calling me on such short notice to review this case again. He knew how I hated to work weekends. I quickly dismissed his look and proceeded to read the brief. Suddenly, I heard banging down the hall.

I asked Kenneth, who was working in the office. He mumbled something and went back to reading the brief. I started reading again, but the noise became too much of a distraction for me. I decided to find the source of the pounding noise, and tell whomever it was to stop. I followed the sound down the paneled corridor, toward the Madison Avenue side of the building.

The noise was coming from Lloyd's office. He was trying to make partner at the firm, so he often worked late except on the evenings he played tennis. I figured he was hanging another one of his damned tennis plaques. It sounded as if he were driving a big tenpenny nail into a piece of knotty pine. As I opened the door to the office and stepped in, I received a numbing blow.

He *was* pounding a nail, but it wasn't into a piece of knotty pine that he was hammering it—it was Ellen.

Ellen has been a paraplegic ever since she fell down the stairwell ten years ago. I know it wasn't my fault, but if I hadn't lost my cool, Ellen would be walking today. She still blames me. She cheated on me, humiliated me, and broke my heart, but she blames me.

I won't forgive her for breaking my heart, because she broke our promise of "till death do us part." But, I also can't seem to forgive myself for causing her injury. Did I purposely push Lloyd to knock her down the stairs, or was it really an accident? I can't seem to forgive anyone connected with that dreadful night.

My broken heart healed with time, but her severed spine will never heal.

How can I leave her? There's no one else to care for her. Lloyd left the firm and moved out of town shortly after the accident. Ellen hasn't heard a word from him since that horrible night. I feel so guilty and so responsible for her condition, and Ellen knows that I am guilt-ridden. She uses it to her advantage. She made me promise never to divorce her. It may sound stupid, considering what she did to me. But how could I divorce her after destroying her life?

How do I get over this useless and devastating emotion we call guilt?

I sometimes wish the fall had killed Ellen; the guilt would still be there, but at least I would be free. What a cowardly statement; I have the power to set myself free right now. Am I too much of a coward to break the foolish promise I made to Ellen—a promise based on deceit and guilt? Does my love for Domi outweigh my guilt obligation to Ellen?

It will cost me a fortune to divorce her, not to mention that I've already paid her a king's ransom and I'm still not free of the guilt. Still, I would willingly give up everything to spend the rest of my life with Dominique.

I should be with the woman I love—the woman whose eyes twinkle like the North Star.

As I read the thoughts in the journals of Dominique and Christian, the floodgates to questionland opened and the interrogatories rushed out, demanding to be answered. I wondered—if I were a woman, could I have walked away from a man like Christian? Would you have turned away from him? If a Christian materialized before your eyes as the almost perfect package, would you turn away because of his old baggage? Did Dominique think Christian was too good to be true? After all, how many times will she meet a man with the means to satisfy her every whim and whimper financially, and the ability to support her emotionally?

An excellent example of Christian, as the almost-perfect package, was the living trust prepared at the Paris branch of his law firm—the trust he funds, even now. How many men will she encounter who are willing and not afraid to openly express their feelings of love? Christian's mannerisms, class, and unique ability to be sensitive and strong are quite rare. To quote a gen-Xer, "Boyfriend got it goin' on!"

I'm sure most women would love to have a Christian. But *not* every woman is capable of dealing with or appreciating a Christian. I'd love to have a female version of Christian. It would be nice to take a breather for a while . . . to have someone in my life who would take away, or share some of the responsibilities, instead of my being responsible all of the time. Ah to dream!

The questions wouldn't stop. It was as if I had struck black gold and they gushed out in a steady stream one after another. Could he continue to satisfy her every dream? If so, would she eventually take him for granted? Did Christian break his promise to Dominique, or did she make it impossible for him to keep his promise to her? Did he really smother her with his affections, or was she the type of person who needs conflict in her life? Did Dominique decide that she no longer needed him, now that she was back on her feet again?

Did she leave because the wound Yves inflicted was more serious than either she or Christian imagined? What dreams was Dominique referring to when she wrote, "For ten years, I listened to my husband's promises . . . took my dreams . . . can't risk losing them again—not to anyone." What dreams could Christian possibly take away? He made her dreams come true, did he not?

What made Dominique change her mind and insist that Christian break his promise? I understand the need to be one with the other, as in marriage or living together, but his marriage was only on paper. I'm sure there are many of you right now who are saying, "That's what they all say!" but Christian was with Dominique twenty-four seven. He was there emotionally, romantically, financially, and physically. It doesn't matter why he loved Dominique, but it was obvious from his actions that he did indeed love her. What gives?

Would you be willing to accept the limitations of their relationship? Did Dominique take advantage of his kindheartedness? Did he take advantage of her weakened state of mind? Did she leave Christian because he wouldn't commit to a permanent relationship with her? What was the real reason that prevented Christian from breaking the forced commitment he made ten years ago?

Dominique's opening journal entry, "Why does the thing that brings me joy also bring me pain?" is intriguing. It is one of the few thoughts in her entries that require an explanation. Her opening statement also contains the answer to most of Dominique's problems. It contains everything she needs to become unstuck and live her dream to the fullest.

When you think of the word *joy*, what images, feelings, and sounds does it conjure in you? Do you immediately think of things that make you feel good? Stop for a moment and let your mind ponder the meaning of joy as it relates to you.

I'm willing to bet that most of you had several pleasant memories fading in and out of your mind, maybe some warm emotions stroking your heart, or the words of an old song playing in your head and the titillating effect that has on you. It certainly is a good feeling, is it not? Now move onto the other side of joy, and let your mind ponder the meaning of pain as it relates to you and the events of your intimate relationship.

When you think of the word *pain*, it usually doesn't take much effort to invoke the associations one makes with that word. I'm willing to gamble once again and say that most of the words, feelings, and visions that you had were not pleasant. What if I told you that pain has another meaning, one with a very different purpose? I would like you to temporarily drop the bad associations you have with the word pain, and consider the following. If you choose not to embrace this new perspective regarding pain, you can always revert to its more familiar and dismal meaning.

I believe joy and pain are opposite sides of the same coin—the coin that's used in sporting games to determine possession of the ball, or the one some people use to determine the fate of their relationship, "Heads he stays, tails he's outa here!"

Joy lays face up in the coin collector's cabinet where everyone can view its shiny face. Joy gets all of the attention and has an incredible view. Her sister, Pain, lives on the other side of this coin. Pain spends her life face down in the collector's display case, destined to lie against the cold glass shelf, doomed to a life of darkness, isolation, and loneliness.

Joy is the Siamese twin to her sister, Pain. The twins reside within the same heart, perhaps in your heart, and are joined by the wall that divides the heart in two. The twin Joy approaches life, love, and happiness with an optimistic attitude. Why? It's because her half of the heart receives the blood that has just been freshly oxygenated. Her twin Pain views those same three—life, love, and happiness—with a troublesome attitude because of the carbon dioxide-rich blood that she receives. Pain's outlook is pessimistic because of the headaches and nausea caused by the depleted oxygen supply in the blood she receives on her side of the heart. Pain's despairing life is complicated even more because, despite the weakness and fatigue she experiences during every heartbeat, she still has to pump the used red liquid into the lungs to keep the body, hers, and her twin sister's alive.

We have a tendency to view pain as a bad thing, but if you change your perspective, pain can also be good.

Emotional pain is your heart's way of letting you know that something isn't quite right. It is a signal for you to stop, evaluate, and resolve the issue or conflict at hand. Once the physical reaction to pain settles down, pain is the heart's greatest teacher. It deepens your understanding of love and strengthens the values that govern your love life. Remember the sticks (pain) of motivation discussed in Darren and Claudia?

On a more global level, pain was and still is the composer of the greatest love songs. For instance, one song that has given hope to many broken hearted people is "A House is not a Home." The paintings and sculptures of the great artists, such as Michelangelo's *Pietà*, are inspired and created from a deep well of pain. Pain is also responsible for the countless written works of arts, with their messages of hope for a better tomorrow.

Pain was the internal editor that helped me write down my life's experiences and coping mechanisms within this book. I feel the same intense pain to this day because Simone whispered, *"Please forgive me . . . I have . . . and . . . always will . . . love you . . . and only you . . . Jean-Paul!"* in my ear as she died in my arms. That pain . . . the one I will never be able to resolve because I wouldn't respond when I had the opportunity! If I had only told her the truth, my heart would have been spared the additional pain I carry today. If I had only given her the chance, I know Simone would have said, *"I forgive you Jean-Paul."* It's too late now. I hesitated, and as it is said of all those who do so, "He who hesitates, waits and waits and . . . "

I have talked about reframing as a method of viewing situations from a different perspective, one that could give you a better understanding about a conflict. I want you to see pain in a different light. I want you to view the pain in your life as an emotion of empowerment. Pain is like an empowering wrecking ball that knocks down the paralyzing emotions within you and makes room for more positive ones. I don't want pain to cripple you as it might have in the past, or set you up to get stuck like Dominique. Pain can be either friend or foe; it all depends on how you view it.

When you read the passages above regarding pain, did you find yourself feeling a little more understanding, maybe even a little more compassionate about pain? Were you able to comprehend the alternative reason for its existence? Can you view pain as a friend bearing bad-but-beneficial news? If not, then keep your old views of pain and let it continue to gnaw at your heart of hearts—beat by beat, year in and year out.

Dominique had to deal with the horns of a dilemma: the uncertainty of her future with Christian. Will he really go away? Will he go away and never return? Was I wrong in asking him to choose between Ellen and me? Was I too demanding in wanting to be, the new "Mrs. Christian?" Was I better off to have him in my life without the piece of paper legalizing our relationship? Maybe I shouldn't have listened to my friends when they told me, "If he really loves you, he'll divorce her and marry you!" Maybe they were envious and didn't want me to be happy. Maybe . . .

Dominique's dilemma was also future-oriented. As a result, she suffered from one of the two most-controlling emotions we humans have—anxiety. The other is guilt. Dominique concerned herself with a future over which she had little or no control. Yet *none* of us can control the future. We can put things in motion that will help to shape the days, months, and years to come, but we *cannot* control the future. There is one exception, however. You can control your earthly future by committing suicide but, on judgment day, you still have to deal with the consequences of killing yourself.

To ensure maximum control over her stuck state, Dominique's unconscious added another emotion to go along with her anxiety. That additional component was fear.

Rather than enjoying the present and simply planning her future, Dominique wanted to control the future—today. Her future orientation was responsible for many of the panic attacks she experienced after Yves left, as well as those she experienced toward the end of her relationship with Christian. Because of this future-oriented state of mind, she destroyed her precious present.

How many of your friends desperately attempt to control their future? Have you been a victim of, "I want, I wish, I desire" syndrome? I'm not talking about planning or predicting a future trend based on the past. Nor am I talking about praying for guidance or asking for abundance in the future. I'm talking about going into your future and saying, "I want what I want, and damnit, everything will be exactly as I say it should be!"

Remember Claudia's queries, "What about my needs? My desires? Darren is always working. We have enough money to last us a lifetime. He's so damned worried about securing our future, that he never took the time to secure 'us' in the here and now." Claudia was talking about the loss of their precious present.

When a person lives in "futureland," they reduce the attention and focus they need to function in their life today. They not only lose their precious present by hanging out in the future, but they also can't prepare or shape their immediate future, tomorrow.

During the sessions we had together, Dominique repeatedly talked about two seemingly different, painful thoughts regarding her life. Although she presented them as being different, they were in fact the same thought. What were the two thoughts? Dominique was afraid Christian would never divorce Ellen so that they could get married, and also that Christian would leave her as Yves had. She was frightened to death of being alone.

To control her future, she gave Christian an ultimatum to use the pot or get off it. This ultimatum came because Dominique was a *counterphobic*. Counterphobic? For example, if a bull were to charge a counterphobic person, that person would anxiously respond by running head on to meet the bull. They would do so to more quickly end their anxiety about the bull gorging them to death. Dominique charged her anxiety head on by forcing an answer from Christian about their relationship.

Unconsciously, it didn't matter if Christian stayed or if he chose to leave; it only mattered that Dominique have an answer. If he said yes and stayed, it would eliminate her anxiety. If he said no and left, it would still eliminate her anxiety. In either case, she would know today, what the future held for her. If Christian stayed, she wouldn't be alone, or if he left, she was free to find someone who would stay.

Dominique wasn't very open about her childhood, and our sessions rarely involved any discussion about her parents. I suspected there was emotional abandonment somewhere in her past that could possibly explain her extreme fear of being alone.

After Christian left, Dominique transferred the fear, the anxiety of her uncertain future with Christian into anxiety about whether he would ever come back. I suspect she will continue this pattern of going backward and forward until she has another life-changing experience that breaks this ping-ponging of her anxious nature. Who knows, maybe Yves will come back into her life and beg her forgiveness for running off with the young head-nurse-in-search-of-a-doctor-husband. Yeah, right.

There were a few questions I wanted to ask Dominique during our final session, but I knew they would open a can of worms and I can't stand those slimy little critters. What would Dominique have done had she known Christian was selling his house and moving back to the States only because he was complying with her wishes? Could she date another man so soon after Christian? How would she have reacted, if she knew Christian hasn't dated anyone since she asked him to leave six months ago? Isn't it usually the other way around?

According to most women and statistics, the fact that he hadn't dated anyone since their breakup is phenomenal. Most women would expect Christian to be walking at the top of the Champs Élysées, where twelve avenues converge toward the Arc de Triomphe, wearing a big sandwich board advertising ... ROMANTIC RICH GOOD-LOOKING MAN AVAILABLE RIGHT NOW ... while shouting, "Next!"

Christian *also* had to deal with the horns of a dilemma: he suffered from the other controlling human emotion—guilt. Unlike Dominique's anxiety about the future, Christian's guilt, as with any form of guilt, has all of its meaning in the past. It's the "I shoulda, woulda, coulda done things differently" syndrome. Sound familiar? How many times have you heard your friends utter the " ... da's"? Have you ever run back in time to beat yourself up over a conflict that left you feeling guilty?

Maybe it's the memory of your high school boyfriend, who absolutely adored you—the one you lied to about being sick, then went to the movies with his best friend.

Guilt, like anxiety, is a control emotion. It reminds you of something you should not have done. It keeps you wallowing in the past, stuck and suffering. We must also give equal controlling credit to guilt's faithful sidekick—shame. After all, it isn't enough just to feel guilty; let's really screw ourselves up and feel ashamed of what we did as well.

The Paris branch office of Christian's law firm handled the closing of my mother's estate. After Simone made her transition, his firm advised me on setting up the Simone Lefervre Foundation. Simone was a great advocate for disadvantaged children with alternative learning preferences (ALP).

Our daughter picked up the bad genes on my side of the family, which resulted in her becoming a child with ALP. I'm dyslexic but she was more like her uncle in that she was extremely dyslexic, and she also struggled with attention deficit disorder (ADD). Simone spent most of her free time and our disposable money working with her and other ALP children, because no one else would.

I visit the foundation several times a year to check in on Simone's Kids, and to reminisce. It was on a return flight from one of my visits that I happened to learn more about Christian.

I always thought Christian was a little distant because he was an attorney. But as time progressed and our friendship grew, it became apparent that the distance was not due to his training, but to some painful past experience. It was on this flight that Christian opened up and told me a little about himself and Dominique. I suggested he make an appointment with me as soon as possible so we could work through his dilemma. I also suggested we include Dominique in some of the sessions.

As usual, I asked both him and Dominique to write down their individual thoughts from the beginning of the relationship to the present. During his private sessions, I discovered one of Christian's dark secrets. Guilt, consumed Christian's life. In the past he had to deal with the articles in the *New York Times,* and the scandal sheet headlines . . . "New York City's Wealthiest Attorney Tries to Kill Adulterous Wife!" "He

Couldn't Satisfy My Rich and Lustful Needs!" "Wife of Prominent NYC Attorney Paralyzed for Life!" The combination of public ridicule, pressure from Ellen's family, the ACLU, and feminist lynch groups forced Christian to seek asylum in Paris until things settled down.

I had some questions regarding two thoughts Christian mentioned in his journal entries: Why did the numbness wear off when he met Dominique? What fortune is Christian referring to when he talks about divorce and Ellen?

What was it about Dominique that brought him out of his ten-year numbness? Was it really her North Star eyes? Was it her "French roll" that jolted his sympathetic nervous system into action? What really took the numbness away?

Maybe the numbness left because the kindness he showed Dominique was, in his mind, retribution . . . a repayment of sorts that eliminated his guilt for not being able to help Ellen, especially because he believed he wronged her much worse than Yves wronged Dominique. What do you think?

I wish there were a long explanation to justify such a worthy change within him, but it's very simple. Christian shifted—displaced—the feelings and desires he had for Ellen onto Dominique. Christian's unconscious mind allowed him to bring his strong feelings of love out of storage, and attach them to Dominique. That is why his numbness wore off so quickly. It was also one of the reasons he fell in love so quickly and completely with Dominique. Christian's other-than-conscious-mind had convinced him that Dominique was just like the Ellen he fell in love with twenty years before.

There was one more reason he fell in love with Dominique, but I will allow one of Christian's toughest sessions to reveal that jewel.

Displacement is one of the defense mechanisms your unconscious mind uses to cope with the perils of life. These mechanisms protect our egos from shame, anxiety, loss of self-esteem, conflict, or other unacceptable feelings or thoughts.

Remember what Claudia's lover said about the love he had lost, "You remind me so much of her." That was displacement. Dominique had something within her that allowed his heart to transpose the love he had for Ellen onto Dominique. With the love he had for Ellen transferred to Dominique, he could safely express it again. Christian's heart was free to feel again. I don't know if it was Dominique's physical features, a look she may have given him, the sound of her voice, a touch, or her North Star eyes, but something about her clicked inside of Christian's heart of hearts.

The second point I would like to cover is regarding Christian's closing statement, "It will cost me a fortune to divorce Ellen, not to mention I've already paid her a king's ransom and I'm still not free of the guilt." When I first read this thought, it seemed innocent and straightforward. It was a simple metaphoric sentence. As I read it a second time, it brought a question to my mind: cost him a fortune?

Why would a man worth $250 million concern himself with the cost of divorcing his wife? There was a prenuptial agreement disallowing all financial rights should she commit, among other things, adultery. If she did get a substantial financial settlement, it wouldn't matter. Christian told me that he lives off the interest he earns from his investments, and he doesn't spend all of that income. Money wasn't the issue.

Perusing the thought for a third time, I eliminated some of the sentence. I distilled it, leaving only the most crucial words of this entry. At our next session I wrote the distilled words on a sheet of paper and gave it to Christian:" ... paid ... ransom ... free ... guilt."

With a bewildered, look on his face, Christian asked, "Jean-Paul, what is this? What does it mean?" I told him it came from his journal, and that he already *knew* what it meant.

I have found that if a person is totally uninhibited and writes truthfully in their journal, they will eventually write one thought that sums up the internal conflict created by their childhood emotional wound— the same conflict that rears its ugly head over and over unless or until it is resolved.

Do you remember the movie, *Three Days of the Condor*, where Robert Redford worked for the CIA as a bookworm? His job was to uncover and report any plots, schemes, or other covert actions hidden in the pages of novels, that the CIA deemed a threat to national security. Writing in one's journal, openly and truthfully, will eventually reveal the major threat to a person's emotional security.

I asked Christian if he knew anything about the language spoken by his unconscious mind. With a confused look on his face, Christian nodded as if to indicate "yes" while saying, "I have no idea Jean-Paul." The mixed response he gave me wasn't unusual. Almost everyone will respond incongruously when wrestling with a decision. How many times have you witnessed a person indicating "no" by shaking his head from side to side, but "yes" with his words? Words represent thirty percent of our communication, whereas body language makes up the other seventy percent.

My mentor had a great example to define a mixed emotional response. He said, "Jean-Paul, it's as if a person has one hand beckoning you toward himself, while the other hand is signaling you to move back. Verbally it converts into, "Go away closer."

I told Christian that the unconscious mind speaks in symbolism—a language that communicates through images, pictures, and dreams that appear unconnected, discombobulated, and make no sense whatsoever, but are somehow meaningful to the situation. I finished the explanation by telling him that the other-than-conscious part of the person pieces the "symbols" language together like a puzzle. The result is that an answer, solution, or missing piece is revealed, or a secret file containing the answer to whatever was troubling the person is unlocked. Dreaming, hypnosis, and meditation are ways to bridge the chasm between the conscious and unconscious minds.

I sent Christian home with the four words I had written on the scrap paper, and asked him if he would give some thought to them as they related to him and Ellen.

Three weeks passed before I heard from Christian again. He scheduled an appointment for the following week. Christian walked in with a sparkle in his eyes, pep in his step, and standing a few inches taller. I asked, "So, Christian, what's been happening?" With an excitement in his voice that I'd never heard before, Christian responded, "It's the craziest thing, Jean-Paul. I woke up one morning and everything made sense. My self-imposed guilt, not Ellen, made me promise I wouldn't divorce her."

I interrupted his train of thought to make what I considered an extremely important point. "Christian, ninety-nine percent of the guilt in your life is self-imposed. You have the choice to accept the guilt or reject it. Your choice depends on many factors. The most influential determinants are how you were 'guilt trained' as a child, and how well your bullshit-detector works."

Pausing for a moment as if to compose his thoughts, Christian continued, "The greatest *fortune* I possess in the world is the family name my father passed on to me. You see, Jean-Paul, I didn't want to taint his . . . our family's name by breaking my word. Father would always tell me, 'your word and honor are your bond, son. That's the only thing I can give you that nobody can ever take away—carry it with pride.' It's so childish, but a part of me thought if I divorced Ellen, I would've broken my word and disgraced my family name."

I was curious about his family name and its perpetuation, because he and Ellen didn't have any children. When I asked, Christian talked about Ellen's infertility and how she objected to adoption or to a surrogate mother carrying their child.

Christian felt sad that his family's name would die with him. I pointed out that he was still a young man and that men much older than he was were still fathering children. I told him not to rule out the possibility of having children one day.

Christian sat silently in his chair, staring at the ceiling. He seemed to be reflecting on something. I assumed he was thinking about the words I had just spoken, or that he had made a new connection regarding the situation. Moments later, in a very solemn voice he continued, "My father and mother sacrificed everything to put me through law school. Dominique wasn't too unlike them in the way she sacrificed for Yves. That thought had never crossed my mind, Jean-Paul."

Eagerly, I asked, "What thought?" He replied, "The fact that Dominique was just like my parents. You know, sacrificing and everything. I understood what she went through to put Yves through school. I understood because I knew how much of a struggle it was for my mother and father to put me through school. I know how painful it would have been for my parents had I disowned them after law school. My mother would have cried just as Dominique did, and it would've killed my father's spirit. I loved Mom and Dad for . . . what . . . they did . . . for me." His sentence sounded more like a question than a statement, which I took to mean he was questioning his own statement.

There was a pregnant pause before Christian spoke again. I wondered if his revelation would bring him freedom and happiness, or doom him to be numb forever. The silence was broken with the deep "quiet power" voice Dominique had described in her journal.

"Jean-Paul, could that be the reason I fell in love with Dominique?" This time the question sounded like a statement.

I answered with, "I think you already know Christian, do you not?"

I got lucky. Christian solved the problem he had been struggling with over the past thirteen years. Christian realized he wouldn't be disgracing his family's name by breaking his promise to Ellen. Because of this awakening, he was free to marry and spend the rest of his life with the woman with the North Star eyes.

I pointed out to Christian that although Ellen's injury was most unfortunate, it was an accident and *not* his fault. He might have been the force that started the chain reaction that knocked her down the staircase, but her adulterous behavior and Lloyd's attempt to do Christian bodily harm were the catalysts that brought about her physical impairment. Christian was only defending himself from the volley of Lloyd's racket attack.

The last point I made to Christian regarding his revelation was concerning Dominique's state of mind. It was important for him to understand her stuck position, how she got there, and what they needed to do together for their relationship to work.

Before I discuss the issue of Christian as Dominique's knight in shining armor, I would like to share the tip that might have enabled Christian to make the connection between his conscious and unconscious minds.

I knew that Christian was a visual person. I hoped he would translate those four words into pictures that would represent his relationship with Ellen. I was also hoping that the part of him that was responsible for piecing together the unconscious's symbolic language would utilize some information I had offered. On the day I handed him the scrap of paper with the four words (paid, ransom, free, and guilt), I also handed Christian an envelope with instructions to open it after he had reflected on those four words for several days. The envelope contained a cheat sheet with the following written on it:

paid, *verb*: To give recompense for; *a kindness that cannot be paid back.*

ransom, *noun*: Theology. A redemption from sin and its consequences.

free, *adjective*: Not controlled by obligation or the will of another: felt free to go.

guilt, *noun*: Self-reproach for supposed inadequacy or wrongdoing.

Proverbs 21:18: **The wicked become a ransom for the righteous, and the unfaithful for the upright.**

It has been my experience that people often have the wrong "definitions" of the problems they're trying to solve. If you have the right definitions, half of the problem is already deciphered.

The last question I asked myself regarding Dominique and Christian put me into a reflective state of mind. Was Christian the wish Dominique asked the North Star to grant, or was he merely her transitional man?

Have you ever had or been a transitional man? Do you have a need for one in your life right now? What about a transitional woman? Have you found yourself in this role? Most everyone at some time and to some degree has acted as a transitional person.

A transitional person is one who happens, serendipitously, into a person's life after a crisis has occurred. Generally the crisis will create a major change in the victim's life. The catalyst that created the major life change could be the loss of a loved one through death . . . losing the hope of ever being loved, but most often it is the emotional trauma suffered when an intimate relationship has ended tragically.

By chance, the victimized person stumbles upon a transitional person tailor-made for them. The transitional person assists this individual as they pass through their pain and grieving until the person makes it back to stable and often better ground.

The transitional person (TP) assists the person suffering through the major life change in a variety of ways. The TP will help the individual get through their initial devastation, the rocky period of recovery, the strengthening stage, and finally as they metamorphose into a new and better person. Eventually, the person emerges from their cocoon as a magnificent butterfly, anxious to try their new wings. Many times they will fly away, leaving their TP behind, and never come back.

Sad? Heartwarming? What do you think? How would you feel if you were the one who suffered the loss? What if you were the TP? How would you feel watching the beautiful butterfly you nursed and, for lack of a better word, mentored, fly away? After all, it was your choice to become their TP, was it not? Maybe it wasn't your choice. Maybe it was your destiny, your purpose in this life, to help this individual.

Some people are better suited to be TPs than others because of their personality type—just as there are those more likely to become a casualty of love than others. Of course, for a TP to exist, the victim must be willing to accept help.

When I spoke to Christian about the concept of the transitional person, he closed his eyes, sighed, and shook his head. He felt as if he had been a foolish old man, playing a knight rescuing a damsel in distress. I told him he shouldn't feel foolish; what he had done was a kind and noble thing. With all due respect to women's equality, we could use more chivalrous men in our world. After all, chivalrous is the word for a gentleman who has an exceedingly courteous and generous nature.

To alleviate his solemn state, I related an incident that had occurred in my life. With a look of disbelief, Christian told me he couldn't believe that I, a psychiatrist, could be as foolish as he had been. I explained that my degree didn't make me immune to acting on my emotions, just as his law degree wouldn't keep him from being sued. If anything, my training makes me more vulnerable because of my desire to help, my understanding of human nature, my ability to heal wounds, and my underlying need to be needed.

For a transitional man to exist there has to be a female in distress. Her profile is usually that of a very strong woman who has been dealt an evil blow in her love life. She may be going through a divorce or getting out of a bad relationship. As a result, her heart is dying a slow and painful death.

Because the situation has taken her by surprise, or because she has been ignoring the obvious, her state of mind weakens. Instantly, the doldrums set in: dejection, low spirits, depression, gloom, and the blues. With her judgment and outlook on life impaired, she gives up and succumbs to the horrors of her falsely perceived reality. She pines and wails over her broken heart, broken dreams, and the love she has lost. As if that isn't enough, she's left with most of their bills, but she has only her half of the money. She allows fear to enter her world because he left her with all the financial responsibility; she covers her fear with a mask of anger.

Her iffy friends will begin the misery-loves-company routine. "How are you gonna make it?" "He wasn't shit to begin with!" "You better move back into the city . . . you *know* you can't afford to live in the 'burbs anymore!" "You ain't gonna find a man who wants you and your baby *too!*"

Burdened with what she perceives as too much responsibility, no money, and, heaven forbid that she has a child, she'll break down, unable to maintain the facade that everything is okay. At this point, she begins to wear the hurt and pain on her sleeve in public.

With her heart on her sleeve, desolation on her face, and the occasional outbreak of tears, she might as well wear a billboard that proclaims **Help!** Her guardian angel arranges for her to bump into her rescuer or savior (TM) while she's drinking her lunch, at the ATM withdrawing the last of her reserves, or grocery shopping.

As she stands in the checkout line counting her money to make sure she can pay for her groceries, she can't help feeling someone staring at her. Turning to see who is watching, her elbow bumps the magazine rack, she drops her coupons, and stares as they cascade towards the floor.

Falling to her knees, she sweeps the coupons into a pile with her gnawed-off fingernails. The last coupon she scoops up slips not once but twice out of her shaky hand. Slowly, tears well up in her eyes and, no matter how hard she tries to hold them back, they begin to drop, one by one. Just as guilt has shame as its sidekick and anxiety has fear, soon her tears are accompanied by their cronies—the sniffles. On her third effort to pick up her canned bean coupon, a beige Bally loafer containing a naked foot, steps on the coupon. As she follows the linen pant leg upward to confront the ill-mannered owner of this shoe, an opened packet of facial tissue interrupts her train of thought.

Bending down, he says, "Go ahead . . . take one."

As she pulls a tissue from the cellophane packet, the owner of the shoe kneels down and looks directly into her steel-gray eyes. He picks up the elusive coupon, hands it to her, and says, "The prices in this store are enough to make anyone cry." She stares into his kind eyes as he helps her up, tilting her head up to maintain eye contact as he rises a foot above her. He offers another tissue and asks, "You would feel better crying over a cup of tea or coffee, wouldn't you?"

Her rescuer, her knight in shining armor, her earth angel, her transitional man has arrived.

For those of you who might be thinking, "why do men always think women need rescuing?" not all of us think that way. In fact, we ask similar questions when women say, "He just needs a good woman, that's all!" Being "rescued" isn't about sexism; it is an innate wish every human being has when facing insurmountable circumstances. Haven't you ever said, "If I could just find a bag of money, all of my problems would . . . " or "If somebody could explain my situation to them—I know they wouldn't be so . . . " or "If I just had someone to talk to, I . . . " These wishful statements convey the same message. They say "save me!" and both men and women make them.

I believe men and women are more *alike* than different. Men have the same desires, wants, and needs as women; both want to love and be loved in return. The only difference is that females are fancy on the inside and males are fancy on the outside. *Viva* to that difference!

Her new friend, like Christian, fit the perfect profile of a transitional man. He was sympathetic, had disposable income, was a widower, classy, sophisticated, into pleasing, in need of being needed, and he was lonely. Although it isn't necessary to be handsome, he was, if I might toot his horn.

The cups of tea and coffee arrived while they shared a plate of *petit fours*. He made small talk about everything except her tears and the broken heart on her sleeve. She admired him, not because of his charisma, but for his inner beauty. She believed he respected her because he never once pried into her business while they were dining.

She asked, "Did you ask me to have dinner because you felt sorry for me?" He stared at her for a moment as if he were dissecting her question, looking for some hidden meaning the way psychiatrists do. He finally said, "No." Turning the delicate porcelain cup in his tanned hands until it had gone full circle, he continued, "I eat alone almost every night, and the thought of eating by myself again was a little more pain than I could handle this evening."

A kindred feeling turned the corners of her mouth upward, creating a kind of smile—a smile that is common to those of us suffering from the pain of a broken heart or loneliness.

Suddenly, he leaned forward. There was a seductive look in his eyes, which made her uncomfortable. Her hands became clammy as his romantic stare turned into a hedonistic glare. Inwardly, she badgered herself; I'm not ready for this! I can't handle this right now. I knew it was too good to be true. He's probably a member of the 4F club, "find 'em, feel 'em, fuck 'em, and forget 'em." Damnit Chaundra, here you go again, stepping into the lion's den!

As he moved closer, his head stopped directly under the table's crystal chandelier. The light cast a shadow down upon his face, and changed his seductive look into a sinister one. With a Cheshire cat grin on his face, he purred, "Plus I wanted to know how you saved twenty-seven dollars on an eighty dollar grocery bill." Unable to contain herself, Chaundra laughed out loud with every part of her being.

As with any good TM, he provided her with a shoulder to lean on, a perfect ear for listening, his backbone while hers was out for repair, and a piggy bank that filled the gap between paydays. He offered a safe haven where she could be herself without the fear of being judged, and he lit the end of what once appeared to be a bleak and never-ending dark tunnel.

Several months passed, and Chaundra was feeling secure within herself again. She began to develop feelings for her no-sock-wearing TM. In time, and with her TM's help, she recuperated from the financial straits of her divorce. While Chaundra didn't like being dependent on her TM, she loved the peace of mind he carved out of the chaos that once enveloped her. Her TM created a picture-perfect road map that would direct her back to her hometown—Independence.

Eventually, with the assistance of her TM, Chaundra got back on her feet again. She reclaimed her independence. She loved being in total control of herself, her finances, and her life again. As with any species of animal that has been caged, she wanted more freedom, more choices in her life. She often remarked, "I just want to see what's out there, that's all. I've missed out on a lot this past year." Her TM knew what was going on; he was trained by his mentors to predict future human behavior based on information gathered from their past.

Chaundra became angered and eventually enraged over a quote she accidentally happened upon one day. Accidentally? Nothing happens by chance. There is always a reason or purpose behind every chance encounter. Chaundra eventually began to view her TM not as the rescuer or earth angel he was when they first met, but as a controlling and manipulative man. In fact, in her mind, he was starting to act just like her former husband. The quote had obviously triggered the wound that led to her divorce, a slow-healing wound that needed more time to close completely.

The quote? One day Chaundra found a romantic era art book on her TM's nightstand when she stopped by on her way home from work. She was thumbing through the book and happened on some lecture notes. The first page started with a quote credited to George Bernard Shaw, and seemingly was for some seminar called *Cross Roads: Follow Your Heart*. The quote read, "The only way for a woman to provide for herself decently is for her to be good to some man that can afford to be good to her." Obviously, without the context in which the quote was used, it could be, and was, misconstrued.

Her well-trained TM understood. He recognized the warning

signs while they were having dessert with their coffee and tea that day over a year ago. I knew better, but, as I tried to make Christian understand, my degree doesn't keep me from getting lonely. It had been a while since Simone made her transition, and I knew it wasn't healthy for me to live in the memory of the only woman I have ever loved. It was time to let go and move on with my life. But I also knew that no one would ever take Simone's place in my heart of hearts. I knew that any woman with half a brain would eventually realize this truth as well. I always told them up front: I could never love another after loving Simone.

I couldn't have a woman in my life who wanted me to say, "I love you" or promise I would be hers forever. I only wanted the company of a soft, warm, and willing body to eradicate the loneliest of my lonely nights. I needed an occasional pillow pal on those rare nights when Simone's memory couldn't take the edge off my loneliness.

I have always carefully chosen the women I would rescue. I didn't want them to get hurt; it's much too painful. They would always be women who only needed a friend to be there until they could gather themselves and go on with their lives.

That type of woman was perfect. I knew they wouldn't stay, and that was exactly what I wanted. I needed a woman to come into my life for a season. I needed someone with me in the spring, when the pink-and-white apple blossoms open. I needed someone to go antiquing with me in the fall. I needed a woman to come into my life for a reason . . . someone to laugh with, cry with, or just hold. What I didn't need was a woman to come into my life for a lifetime. I have already walked down that path, and my everlasting love for Simone will not allow me to do it again.

This kind of woman always leaves. She has to leave. Like the character Vivian in the movie *Pretty Woman,* this kind of woman wants the whole fairy tale. I could only function as their fairy godfather. I resigned myself to watch as they rode away in a horse-drawn carriage, or floated away on a cloud of fairy dust. I could only wave goodbye and wish them well. It was not my destiny to walk down that path *with* them.

For those of you with a logical, analytical, or Detective Columbolike mind, I want you to know that I didn't transfer my feelings of Simone onto Chaundra or any of the others, the way Christian displaced his feelings of Ellen onto Dominique. I'm very conscious of my actions. There is no denial, displacement, identification, projection, repression, or any other defense mechanism going on within me. I'm simply waiting for God to call me home so I can be with my Simone for all eternity.

Cruel? Cold-blooded? Calculating? No. Those words suit Ellen better than me, because of the way she used her knowledge of Christian's values against him as guilt. I would be cold if these women walked away with less than they had when we first met. I'm left with the same loneliness that I brought to the table, while they have all walked away with much more than they brought. They walked away having been put back together again—including the lost, broken, and stolen pieces of their dreams. It has been a win-win situation for them and for me. I avert the loneliness for a while. They get their secret and sacred wish fulfilled—their desire to be rescued.

I knew better than to think that Chaundra would stay. I knew it was a dead end street before I signaled my intentions and turned onto that boulevard. Nevertheless, I was and still am lonely.

You do know how it feels to be lonely, do you not? Have you ever reached over to touch that someone special during the night just to connect, or to hold them just in case the bogeyman returns the same night—but all you contact is a pillow? Some of you are lonely at this very moment, aren't you? You are lonely, even though a warm body is sitting or lying next to you—right now. You *do* know what I'm talking about; do you not?

My experience with Chaundra is why I could truthfully say to Christian, "It isn't foolish to love; it is only foolish to deny love." At the end of their relationship, Christian denied himself and Dominique the love within his heart. I do not deny the love I have for Simone. Like the words to an old song, I could never love another, after lovin' you . . . and to this day Simone, I haven't.

Transitional people are not gender bound or exclusively hetero-sexual. They aren't limited to the old and wise or even the old and foolish, nor are they restricted by nationality, race, religious belief, or skin color.

What *is* important regarding TPs is their ability to see past the suffering caused by a love loss, to see the good in the person's heart, to see their potential, to see the talents they possess, and that they have the skills and desire to get that person back on track with their lives. A TP doesn't have to be romantically involved like Christian to be effective, and it isn't necessary for a TP to have disposable income to support the person.

Functioning as a transitional person may be nothing more than being a big brother or sister to a person in need. Remember, our divine purpose for being here, is to love one another.

5

Blair and Marcy

*The true index of a man's character
is the health of his wife.*
—Cyril Connolly,
The Unquiet Grave

Blair—January 7

When will she learn?

Damn, I wish Marcy wouldn't press me so much. She knows it only makes her situation worse. What would she do without me? Who else would put up with her? Hell, this is probably the reason her first husband divorced her. She's constantly nagging and nipping like that little mutt Fluffy she used to have.

Every time it happens, I feel helpless to do anything but keep her under control. Afterwards, I feel so guilty, but there's no other way to get her to understand. I always feel like I have to apologize after her episode is over. The therapist gave her some pills to help relieve her uneasiness, but they don't seem to work very well.

It seems I attract women who just don't understand. Why me, Lord? I've always provided the basic comforts and much more, but that never seems to be enough. My women never had to work; they didn't even have to leave the house. I did the grocery shopping. I would call or stop by the house during the day, just to make sure they were okay, and they never had to want for anything. No matter how much I would do for them, they still didn't get it.

I warned Marcy about gossiping on the phone to her so-called friends—the same friends who seduced her into believing that things should be different, better for her. Where were those meddling friends when I had to straighten things out? I'll tell you where they were—behind closed doors passing judgment on me!

Maybe I am overprotective, but I only want to safeguard my Marcy from herself and from those men who wish to use her for their own selfish reasons. My father raised me to believe a man should protect and defend that which he owns—his family. It's the foundation of this great country we call America.

Her sister and friends tell her I'm just too jealous. Doesn't anyone understand the second Commandment given us by the Almighty? "Thou shall not have any Lord other than Me, thou shall not bow down before any others, for I am a jealous Man, punishing those who disobey Me, and not keep My commandments." I provide her with everything she needs, wants, or desires. What's wrong with me being a little resentful of her so-called friends and family invading our haven? It's her safe haven and my house, isn't it? You're damned right it's my house and her safe haven from the cruel world outside!

My father was a real man. He knew the Bible backward, and was our church's best elder. I can remember to this day how he showed us why it was necessary for him to be so strict. Right after the last confrontation, the one that occurred because my mother pressed my father into arguing, he got knocked out with my baseball bat. She left him and us, and never came back. Oh boy, did we ever pay for her sins! I learned a valuable lesson—obey your Lord and Master, and everything will be all right. It was easy to see that, after she left, Dad became a much calmer man. He said it was easier on him because he didn't have to keep Mom in line anymore. He said keeping us on the straight and narrow was a piece of cake.

Well, it's getting late, and I've got to meet the deadline for my Sunday article, "Life, Love, and Choices." I'd better kiss my Marcy goodnight, and reassure her that everything is okay.

Even though no other man would have her, she's still the woman I want. She's mine forever.

I hope she'll forgive me again. She knows I'm only trying to help her, but, under her breath, she insists the only thing that can make everything all right and set her free is this Silent Witness cult. The only silent witnesses she needs is God and me! God will set her free if she'd only listen and obey me.

Marcy's no Virgin Mary, and I know she's crazy as hell, but, I still love that little half-breed.

Marcy—January 7

Am . . . I . . . really . . . crazy?

I don't think I'm crazy, but what other reason is there for staying with him. I do love Blair, and that is the only reason I'm staying. I know he loves me. He tells me all the time, that is, until I . . . make . . . a . . . mistake. I know one day he will change . . . at least I pray he will. I've tried so hard to understand him and his needs. I've tried even harder to follow his rules, even though he continues to change and add new ones each week.

I don't call my friends very often, and I never call them while he's at home. I stay in the house while he is at work, except when I go out to get the morning paper. He likes me to read his column and tell him how . . . well . . . he writes. He needs to hear me say how . . . good . . . he is every day, kinda like a little boy, who wants his mamma's praise. I read his column repeatedly every day so I can tell him how . . . good . . . he writes.

Not too long ago, he found out the paper boy wasn't a boy at all; he's twenty-something. Blair saw him one day a couple of months ago when he came home early. Blair comes home without notice a lot, almost like he's trying to catch me breaking one of his rules. He came back to get a rough draft off his desk, and saw me wave at Tim, the paper carrier. It was innocent. I meant no harm. But I knew better. I shouldn't have been on the porch any longer than it takes to get the paper.

Blair has warned me about being outside. He has told me many times before, and it really is true; there isn't a need for me to leave the house. He does all of the shopping, and takes care of the chores outside of the house. The only time I need to go out is when we go to church on Sunday morning. He was right about Tim. It was my fault; I should've come right back in the house instead of lingering on the porch . . . but sometimes I get so lonely. I promised Blair I would never do it again, but he didn't believe me, so . . .

Yesterday Blair called from his car while I was in the shower. I didn't answer until the fifth ring, because I couldn't hear the phone with the water running. When I answered, he screamed at me. He said I took too long to answer. I should've taken the portable phone into the bathroom, as he always tells me to do.

I'm trying to follow the rules . . . it's just getting harder to do lately.

When he got home, he saw the unopened newspaper on the coffee table in front of the sofa. He flew into a terrible rage at the sight of the paper, just because it wasn't open. Blair said I had enough time to read his column this morning, and he knew the reason I hadn't opened the "damn paper." He accused me of taking that shower because I had "been" with Tim. The fierce look on his face and the anger in his eyes frightened me more than ever before.

Glaring at me with his cold, dark eyes, he screamed, "Marcy, your sins cannot be washed away with soap and water. Your body and soul must be purged by the burning light of God!" He didn't want to do it, but he had to enforce God's rules. Besides, it was my fault for not answering the phone after the first ring. The burns always heal fast, especially if I use cocoa butter.

Later, he wanted to know what unnatural sex acts I performed with Tim. I told him I could never be with another man, because I loved *him*, and besides, no other man would have me but him. He made me strip and then slapped me onto the floor. He made me crawl naked on all fours towards him. Then he howled, "Crawl to me, you little cunt. Crawl to me like the half-breed bitch you are," then he . . . he . . . marked me. It was the most degrading thing he has ever done to me. Even now, just the thought of it makes my skin crawl.

Whenever I think about that night, the smell and the taste of his urine as it splattered onto my face makes me want to throw up. No man would want me now, not with the . . . stench . . . from his urine still on me. He forbade me from showering that night or the next morning. He wanted Tim to know I was his property, and his alone. God, what did I do to deserve this kind of punishment? I *am* crazy.

This afternoon I asked Blair if he wanted me to leave because I am always making trouble for him. His voice was soft and calm as he said, "I can't live without you, Marcy." Then his voice changed. It became brutal. It was barbaric. His eye left twitched as he savagely said, "And if I can't have you Marcy, no one else will!" I knew what he meant. I'm not *that* crazy. I have to get away. I can take the beatings, the tongue-lashings, and the other horrible things he does, but I can't let him take my life.

I don't care if nobody wants me. I will live alone. I just don't want to die like my Fluffy. Each time I think about her, I start crying. Blair hates it when I cry too loudly. He says it disturbs his quiet time. So I try to cry softly, but it's difficult to do, because it hurts so much when I think of her. Fluffy gave me hope, the way she wagged her tail, and cuddled with me. After Blair kicked Fluffy down the stairs, she cried out for me to help. Blair wouldn't let me go down to be with her . . . she cried all night long . . . it was a horrible cry . . . a cry of death . . . a cry that says hope is gone . . . she died alone . . . now . . . I can't get the sound . . . of . . . her . . . painful . . . whining . . . out . . . of . . . my . . . head.

They helped me make an escape plan at the shelter a few months back. Susan told me if ever there came a time when I thought he was going to kill me, I should use it to get away. I never thought I would have to use it . . . I thought he would change. I hid it under the middle drawer of my dresser. Maybe I can get to it before my eleven o'-clock curfew . . . oh no, he's coming!

Is he coming to kiss me goodnight the way he does every evening, or is he coming to beat me . . . the way he beat my Fluffy to death? Oh God! . . . Please! . . . No! . . . I want to live!

It is my hope that what you have read up to this point will disturb you and make you do something—something that might help one person you may know or one you've never met before to stop being domestically abused.

Do you know of someone who is in an abusive relationship? Do you know that physically attacking a mate is just one form of domestic abuse? Have you ever had first-hand experience with domestic violence? Are you a person who suffered through a childhood of abuse? Are you afraid to get involved, again?

In the conservative all-American Midwestern state of Michigan, home of Mom, cherry pie, and automobiles, there is, on average, one domestic-abuse homicide every five days.

I've included the thoughts of Blair and Marcy to increase awareness of domestic violence. I want you to know the profile of a batterer, the countless reasons they abuse, and the techniques they use to gain their victim's confidence. I want you to understand the victims and how they endure and why they stay. How much do you know right now about the heinous crime of domestic violence?

Action! I want you to act. After you finish reading this couple's chapter, I want you to get up and do something. Call someone. Talk to your coworkers. Pull someone's head out of the sand and let them know that hiding isn't going to make this horrible form of oppression go away. If you prefer to be passive, fine, write a check for ten dollars to a shelter or an organization that truly helps the victims of domestic violence. Money does make a very strong statement, does it not? Do something! Do anything you can, short of abusing the abuser, to reduce or end domestic violence.

Ordinarily, I would not have seen this couple. This type of case requires someone who specializes in abusive behavior, someone who can remain emotionally detached from the situation. Because I volunteer one weekend a month at the free clinic, I agreed to be the stopgap therapist until the clinicians from the Domestic Violence Center could work this couple into their overbooked schedule.

In domestic violence cases, it takes time for the abused mate to trust the counselor, and the battering mate will not stay in therapy unless the courts have ordered him, or her, to do so. At best, I could only hope to be a part of Marcy's support system. As for Blair, well . . .

The knowledge I have acquired about abusive behavior has resulted from the cases of Post Traumatic Shock Disorder (PTSD) that I used to treat. PTSD is not very different from what a battered victim goes through during the cycle of violence in domestic abuse. Someone very close to me at one time suffered from PTSD because of being tortured as a prisoner during the Vietnam War. Because of the devastatingly painful experience I had with this POW, I chose not to treat patients who are batterers.

My encounter with this man was physically painful, but the emotional pain I suffered was a thousand times worse. It still lingers within me. As a result, it's impossible for me to keep my personal experience of abuse from tainting my professional treatment of abuse. I know that sounds horrible, that I should follow the adage "doctor, heal thyself," but I'm human and I accept the limitations I have placed on myself. That's why I refer all cases of physical abuse to the free clinic or to my colleagues.

I didn't work with Blair and Marcy for very long. I was able to get Marcy to write in a journal that she hid at the bottom of a box of sanitary napkins, a place where Blair—and most men, for that manner— would never look. Blair wrote one entry and refused to write any more, claiming that this entry told it all. He was right. There was nothing more he could write. He had nothing more to write, because the pattern of his violence was always the same. The only thing that changed were the excuses he used for abusing Marcy. Sick son of a bitch!

Rather than go line by line dissecting their journal entries, I would like to reverse the process. I'm going to give you specifics regarding abusive personalities and domestic violence; then I want you to go back and identify these items in their journal entries. I will interject portions of their journal entries on occasion, to emphasize certain points.

Abusive partners look upon their battered mates as their personal property. Just as it's okay to bump their car door, trash the house, break a chair, or throw a book into the fireplace, it is okay to beat another piece of property—their partner.

Batterers have no remorse in their souls for their abusive behavior. Their ability to emotionally feel anything, diminished with each blow from the hand of their own childhood abuser. They have *no* emotional sympathy.

Abusive partners have a frightening and rather extreme type of jealousy (known as morbid jealousy). As you know, jealousy has absolutely nothing to do with love; it is in fact a sign of emotional insecurity.

Like everyone else, batterers need affection, but they're unable to ask for it because of the abuse they suffered as children. They can easily be hurt emotionally, but can't allow themselves to be seen as such and would never admit the hurt to their partner. Batterers also hurt from a lack of love; but when they receive genuine love from their partner, they can only criticize it.

The batterers who demonstrate morbid jealousy and are obsessive about their partners are more likely to kill. Do you remember how Blair reacted to Tim, the paperboy?

Batterers who have abandonment fantasies (abused partner leaving him) or suicide fantasies (killing himself because their partner tries to leave) are more likely to kill their partners than batterers who haven't had these fantasies, or have not developed these fantasies to the extreme. This type of batterer believes his abused partner has no right to live a life separate from him. This batterer will make the five-alarm fire statement, "If I can't . . . no one will!" which can lead to him living out his abandonment or suicide fantasies, and killing his abused partner and himself.

Batterers are often very charming, seductive, and gregarious. They come on hard and heavy to their potential victim, and want them to get involved as quickly as possible. A batterer will approach their victim with an almost desperate plea, pushing the potential victim to commit quickly to a serious relationship with them. They will become indispensable to their victim, by at first being the perfect partner. Once the potential victim is seduced into their web of desperation, they reverse and become the perfect abusive machine.

A batterer will always blame their abused partner for his feelings. Then he'll use these feelings to manipulate the abused partner into feeling guilty and making the victim believe they have done the batterer wrongly. "You hurt me by not doing what I told you to do." "It's difficult for me not to be mad." "You make me feel good!" are a few statements the abusive partner will use, but these lines always mean the same thing—"Abused partner, you control how I feel . . . and right now you're making me pissed off enough to kick the shit out of you!"

Batterers are not limited to heterosexuals; there are gay and lesbian batterers as well. Batterers are not limited by socioeconomic factors or religious beliefs. Batterers are like the colors in the spectrum of light—they go from white to black, with every color in between. They are not limited to blue- or white-collar workers. There are practicing psychiatrists who treat patients by day and beat their partners at night.

Abuse is not limited to battering. Emotional, economic, sexual, and verbal abuses are some of the other weapons of destruction used by abusive personalities.

As I gained Marcy's trust, she offered tiny bits of information about Blair that were almost textbook perfect. For example, when you read Marcy's journal entry you can safely assume that she was the offspring of a bi-racial couple, because of Blair's use of the derogatory term, *half-breed*. Marcy told me that whenever he called her a half-breed, he would add other words that were hurtful to her. This is classic verbal abuse. What do you think those words may have been?

Abusers use several derogatory words to verbally violate their victims. The ones that are most frequently used to demean their partners are: *bitch* and *whore*. When they want to totally mortify their partners they will call them a *slut*, or *cunt*. These are woman-hater words that refer to a female who is supposed to be sexually "loose." The abuser uses these words because he fantasizes that his partner is sleeping around behind his back. In the abuser's world, a female is either a good girl (Madonna, the good mother) or a bad girl (a loose woman unworthy to be called a mother).

I'd like to make one final comment regarding Marcy's journal entry, but first I want to talk about the why's and how's of the victim's responses.

What makes a victim of domestic abuse stay in the relationship? Why does she stay, knowing that she's going to be beaten again? Some stay because they are hoping that better times will come soon. Another set stays because they begin to identify with their batterer and become sympathetic to the batterer's cause. This phenomenon, the Stockholm syndrome, is named after an incident that occurred in 1973 in Stockholm, Sweden, where a hostage in a bank robbery became romantically attached to one of her violent captors.

Other victims stay because the fear of running away and the harsher punishment meted out for running away is greater than the fear of their next beating. This conditioning is the same one used during slavery, where a slave's toes on one foot would be cut off for "running." If he ran a second time, they might castrate him. If he ran a third time, they would kill him; he was bad for the morale of the other slaves, and was costing his owner more money than he was worth. The batterer is just as cruel to his partner as the slave owner was to his slaves—the only difference being that it wasn't against the law to kill a slave. Sick sons of bitches!

How are these victims able to make it through an attack from the batterer? The strategies used by both battered women and children to endure their beatings are unique. The most interesting one is almost metaphysical. It is akin to the new age astral projection phenomenon, in which a person sends their spirit to a different plane of existence (another planet) while the body remains on earth. Battered women survive the beatings at the hands of their mates by dissociating themselves emotionally during the incident.

Some women become, figuratively, a fly on the wall (they dissociate) and "watch" themselves being abused. Without a body to feel the physical pain, the victim feels safe emotionally. Of course, once the attack is over, she immediately "checks back" into her body (associates) and the pain from the attack is there, eagerly waiting to greet her.

Here is the final comment I want to make regarding Marcy's journal. When Marcy wrote the entry "I can take the beatings, the … but I can't let him take my life!" she was at a pivotal point in her life—Marcy had become more afraid of dying than of being beaten or abandoning Blair. This pivotal point came about when she recognized that Blair actually thought of her as his property, just as he had viewed her dog Fluffy. It was only logical for her to take this "property view" to the next level. … "When will he decide to kick me down the stairs and leave me to suffer and die—alone?" By the way, from the age of five I have never trusted people who were cruel to any kind of animal.

I don't know what happened to Blair or Marcy. The appointment she had waited for with the therapist at the clinic became available, and I never saw them again. I believe Blair was too entrenched in his behavior to ever change, and for this reason I would have preferred that Marcy leave him for good.

To help someone who is the victim in an abusive relationship doesn't take a great effort. You can do a world of good for an abused partner if you would:

- tell her she's not alone
- tell her she has nothing to be ashamed of
- tell her she's not to blame
- tell her that she has shown great courage by speaking to you about the problem—her talking to you breaks one of the batterer's cardinal rules and puts her at a greater risk for more battering for exposing his abusive personality
- let her know you are available if she needs you
- let her know her secret is safe with you … that you will not tell anyone unless she asks you to

- make sure she has an escape plan for herself, her children, and even the pets
- make sure she knows the location of a shelter, and that she has the necessary telephone numbers to call for help
- let her know that you can only be supportive, and to remove herself from this type of relationship, she'll need professional help; give her the number for the local United Way for their referral list of free clinics
- learn more about domestic violence yourself
- pray

If by your actions, sending a check, volunteering at a shelter or being a friend, you can prevent or free one person from being abused, you will only need to perform two more miracles before being canonized as a saint.

During the last year of my residency, I had to prepare for my board and licensing exams. As you may already know, these exams are no walk in the park. I became a recluse—an evil one, to boot. My temperament was less than desirable and I resented anything or person that would interfere with my limited study time. Even my Simone had to suffer the rath of my fury—a rather large mistake on my part, one that I would regret for a lifetime.

The final straw that sent me into a complete rage occurred four months before the exams. At the time, I had an old beat-up Renault that burned more oil than gasoline. It had served me well through med school and my residency, but it eventually gave up and sputtered its final puff of white smoke four months before the exams. I knew that in four months the banks would be willing to loan me bags of money, but right now money was a big concern—we didn't have any.

This loss cut us down to one car to share between the two of us.

However, that wasn't the problem. What was the problem? Simone worked on the opposite end of town from the hospital and our schedules overlapped, making it impossible for us to carpool every day.

Simone wanted to take the bus, but she had to travel through some rough neighborhoods along the way, so I rejected that possibility. Then it occurred to me that Luc had to pass our apartment on his way to the city, as well as her office building on his way into school. It worked out perfectly. He taught at a trade school not far from her, they both got off work about the same time, and it was the perfect solution to our problem. Besides, Simone has always enjoyed Luc's company ever since they were attending the university.

God was I ever burdened with studying for my boards. I spent every waking moment I wasn't seeing patients with my head stuck in review books. On one of my rare off-days, I got up early hoping to surprise Simone with breakfast in bed. I was hoping this pitiful offering would let her know that I was still the man she fell in love with and not the evil ogre I had temporarily become.

Simone didn't have much to say while we were eating; it was almost as if her body were here with me but her mind was somewhere else. I took her silence to mean she was upset with my "Dr. Evil" behavior, and that it might take a little time for her to warm up and forgive me. As I dried the last dish from breakfast, I mustered up my sexiest and heaviest French accent and made my move. "Sweetheart, would you like to . . . meet me at the Kasbah . . . to enjoy a little quality time, eh?" She jerked away almost as if my movement had surprised her, as if she were afraid of me. She passed on the quality time.

Simone was kind enough to tell me that her refusal had nothing to do with me. Almost in an apologetic manner, Simone told me she wasn't feeling well. It was time for her redheaded aunt to visit and the cramps were getting the best of her. I told her she didn't have to apologize for inheriting Eve's curse. Besides, I was happy to know that her aunt *was* visiting; the last thing we needed right now was a little Simone or J-P Jr. crawling around. She forced a halfhearted smile, touched my cheek with the palm of her right hand, and headed toward the bathroom.

I rationalized the rejection by telling myself, "With my tired ass, I probably couldn't have gotten it up anyway." As she walked down the narrow hallway of our tiny apartment, I sensed something else was going on with Simone and it didn't have anything to do with me. Within moments, my mind was flooded with questions and possible explanations regarding her behavior. What happened to make her act like this? Could she be irritable because of her period . . . but didn't she just get her period a couple of weeks ago? Was there a problem on her job? Had I been that much of a bastard these last four months?

I decided to probe a little to see if I could latch onto a reason for her behavior. I knocked on the bathroom door and waited for a response. I knocked again. She didn't answer. Concerned, I walked in.

Simone had shed her papaya-colored nightgown and was straddling the *bidet*. She just sat there, staring into space with a blank look on her face. I asked twice if she was okay, then I touched her shoulder to wake her from her stupor. Like a frightened cat, she sprang up and stumbled backwards. Her complexion paled. I wondered what I had done to scare her so badly. Crossing her arms as if to protect her breasts, Simone trembled, dropped her head, and hunched her shoulders like a scared puppy. I slowly extended my arms and waited for her to enter.

I could feel Simone's body trembling; her breathing quickened and her heart pounded like a newborn's when she finally bound her body tightly against mine.

After a few minutes, when I thought she felt safe enough, I whispered in her ear, "It's okay Mone, it's just me . . . it's okay, baby." I didn't think of it at the time, but it was odd that she didn't make a sound until she was safe within my arms. She didn't go into hysterics when I touched her shoulder, but I knew she was terrified. Still, she should've been screaming like a banshee based on her physical reaction to my initial touch.

In the safety of my embrace, Simone began to weep. Then she broke down and cried. As Simone's warm tears soaked my nightshirt, a cold sweat covered and chilled my brow. Why was this happening?

I held Simone until she calmed down, then I draped her grand-mother's antique brocade robe over her shivering shoulders as I had done many times before; but somehow, this time was different. This time she couldn't stop shivering. While fastening her robe, I noticed some new red bruises scattered among the older purple ones. As we left the bathroom, I couldn't help asking myself, "What in the hell is going on?"

Simone was clumsy all of her life. She was constantly tripping, falling, bumping into doors, tables, open cabinets, and slipping on wet maple leaves during the fall. I was used to seeing her with bruises on her arms and legs, but these bruises were different. They were larger and uniform in shape, and they weren't on her legs or the usual places she bruised in the past.

We had a wonderful day at the *Musée de Louvre*. We walked, talked, and relived the first day we met at the romantic gallery in the *Musée*. During dinner, I asked Simone again about the bruises. She jokingly told me how she had tripped over her chair at work and fallen onto the copy machine. When I questioned her again about the fall, I could tell she was getting nervous, so I joked about her having two left feet and went back to stuffing my face with the gour-met meal she had prepared.

I finished my studies a month ahead of time and there was only one thing left to do—pass the boards. The thought of buying a house and a new car was the only incentive I needed to ace the exams. When I told Simone the good news, she was overjoyed. She immediately asked if I could drive her to work now that my sched-ule was back to normal. I still had my resident's duties to perform on Tuesdays and Thursdays, but I told her I would love to take her to work on my free days. I guess Luc's war stories were becoming too much for her delicate ears.

With my workload reduced, I could spend more time with Si-mone. I loved being with her, listening to her as she laughed or watching her sweet lips as they curled upward, forming that wonderful smile of hers. Simone was indeed my soul mate.

During the next month, I noticed a decrease in the frequency and days we made love. Instead of our usual four or five times a week, we were down to twice a week and the days were always the same—Sunday and Saturday. Simone also seemed to be bruising herself more, and again they were on odd parts of her body, her back, shoulders, and about her breast. Once again, I asked Simone about the bruises, and once again, she gave me several lame excuses.

Then one day it hit me.

The bruises were always fresh on the days that I didn't take her to work. It was Luc. The bastard was abusing my Simone. When I confronted her, she broke down and bawled as if her world were ending. Simone confessed. She said Luc had been abusing her, but she didn't want me to find out because she knew what I would do. She was right. With a grip of panic, she held onto the back of my clinic jacket, trying to stop me as I charged like a raging bull toward the car.

As I drove with reckless abandon towards Luc's house, I screamed, "Why didn't you tell me? I'm gonna kill that sick son of a bitch!"

Despite the rage boiling inside me, I realized that my actions were upsetting Simone. Calming myself as much as I could, I told her, "It's okay, Mone, it's not your fault. I just never thought he would ever do that to you. It's all my fault, I knew what he was capable of doing, but being tortured doesn't give him the right to abuse anybody, goddamnit!"

My rage escalated with each red light. Too much time had already lapsed—the first time he hit Simone, he should've been killed.

Crashing through the front door, I took three steps at a time up the spiral staircase that led to Luc's room. He was lying on the bed. I grabbed the wooden chair next to his desk. Lifting it above my head, I screamed like a madman, "You sick son of a bitch!" and brought it down hard across his chest. Picking up the splintered legs, I beat him again. I beat him until blood gushed out of his nose and mouth. I stopped momentarily when I heard a familiar voice, raw with terror, cry out, "J-P stop this! Stop this right now!" Turning a deaf ear to the voice, I started beating him again until I felt a pair of strong hands pulling me away from my semi-conscious victim.

My rage grew stronger at the thought of someone trying to abort my fratricidal mission. The fact that some idiot was trying to rob me of my savage right, my instinctual right, to kill the beast that defiled my woman, enraged me even more. The idea of someone trying to save this worthless piece of shit fueled my hungry rage to the kill-or-be-killed level!

Turning about, I readied myself to mutilate this would-be defender of Luc. With blinding speed, my hands gripped his neck, while my left foot swept his legs from under him. As he fell to the floor, I pounced on him like a panther—readying myself to rip out his throat. Suddenly, his face came into focus. God! I froze. I released my stranglehold, and watched as my father gasped for air.

With a hurtful look in his eyes, straining to speak, he said, "Stop."

In less than a second I went from being the savage barbarian who was hell-bent on killing his prey to an intimidated little boy.

With her head bowed forward, her arms and legs drawn into her chest, Simone rocked back and forth on the floor next to the door. My mother shook her head in shocking disbelief, stammering in a barely perceptible voice, "Why J-P? Why? Why are you doing this to your brother?" Staring at his broken, bloody, and battered body, I growled, "Ask Luc!"

Motioning toward Simone, Luc coughed and hacked as he spoke "Ask your whore . . . no slut gonna use me . . . tell me when she's had enough . . . that cunt was begging for a good fuck!"

"Jean-Paul, please forgive me . . . I love you . . . and only . . . you" were the muffled words that came from Simone's bowed head as she continued to rock back and forth by the door. Everything went black . . . there was silence . . . my life with Simone flashed before my eyes . . . the silence came back . . . the blackness returned . . . and nothing mattered anymore. Walking out of the room, my heart expired—and so did my love for Simone, and my best friend, my brother, Luc.

The issues I had to deal with at that time were Simone's infidelity, my brother's betrayal, the savagery I displayed in front of my parents, and the hardest one of all—the defiling and battering of the woman I loved.

Needless to say, I flunked the board exams the first time around because of this incident.

My brother was the POW I mentioned at the beginning of this section's commentary. Luc developed Post Traumatic Stress Disorder from being a prisoner during the Vietnam War. PTSD is a psychological disorder affecting individuals who have experienced a profound emotional trauma, such as torture or rape. It's characterized by recurrent flashbacks of the traumatic event, nightmares, eating disorders, anxiety, fatigue, forgetfulness, and social withdrawal.

When you have someone who has had early childhood experiences of some type of abuse and then experiences PTS, they can emulate, maybe even develop, an abusive personality. My brother was a prime example of this phenomenon, because of an incident that happened earlier in his life.

One day I mentioned to my mother that Luc was exhibiting the behavior of an adult, raised in an abusive home, as a child. That's when my mother told me about Luc being abused and molested by a janitor at a small boarding school.

When we were younger, I always thought Luc resented me. He used to tell everyone that I was the favorite child in the family, and he accused Mom and Dad of not loving him as much as they did me. It was a little strong, but it seemed like a typical case of sibling rivalry. I couldn't believe he would take it to the extreme and use Simone to seek his revenge.

I have never fully recovered. There is a part of me that won't let go. A part of me that still wants to avenge my Simone's honor. No one deserves to be defiled in that manner. But, Luc is gone, and along with his departure went the loss of my chance for revenge. He died from an opportunistic pneumonia infection years ago. My only solace was the painful way in which he died—he suffocated to death.

My parents were sympathetic and forgave me despite my attempt to reenact the Cain and Abel incident in the Old Testament. I surely would have killed him had I known he was also sodomizing Simone against her will. In Darren and Claudia I made the statement, "Do you have a deeper understanding and greater appreciation of the term 'crime of passion' . . . He (my father) understood better than I did at the time, and for that I am forever grateful." If it weren't for my father, I would be serving a life sentence or on death row—waiting the day they would extinguish my life.

It took several years of therapy before Simone recovered from Luc's abuse. Until the day she died, like any abused person or animal, she would always flinch whenever a sudden move or loud noise was made around her.

I never had the nerve to ask Simone if she loved Luc, if he was a better lover than me, or any of those things that Darren asked Claudia. I never asked because I didn't want to know, and probably couldn't have handled her answers. Had she answered yes, I would've been crushed. If she answered no, I probably would have doubted her answer, thinking she was trying to spare me. I told myself that a hundred years from now it won't matter—so why should it matter now.

How would you react, if a situation like mine confronted you? Would you become Conan the Barbarian as I did, or would you hold your head up high and walk away? Would you be able to forgive and forget? If you knew that the person who abused or molested your spouse or child suffered from a disorder that contributed to their abusive behavior, would that knowledge change your reaction to their crime? It certainly didn't change mine.

What action will you take to help the victims of domestic violence? It is time to act, is it not?

6

Charlie and Amileé

First love is only a little
foolishness and a lot of curiosity.
—GEORGE BERNARD SHAW,
John Bull's Other Island

Charlie—June 14

Why do girls say stupid things, and why do they ask stupid ques-
tions? Amileé is so stupid! I don't ask my dog if he likes me. I just
know he likes me, and that's good enough for me.

Amileé is real stupid. She's so stupid it makes me sick! She only
talks to me about girlie things. I don't want to play house, or play
with dolls. I'm a boy, and boys don't talk about or do girlie
things. We talk about comic books, play baseball, catch worms,
and cool stuff like that. Girls who don't talk about boy stuff to
boys are stupid.

Stupid Amileé!

I ran real fast today, and nobody could catch me. I like to run, 'specially when Amileé tells me that girlie stuff. Gees!

Girls, don't make any sense at all. They'll laugh at dumb jokes, but they get mad and kick you when you tell them a funny joke. I don't know why older boys like them. Maybe the girls start to act like boys when they get older.

Why did they make girls in the first place, and why does the gym teacher tell me we can't live without them?

Amileé is sorta cool, but she's still a stupid girl!

Amileé—June 14

Dear Diary,

Today, I told Charlie he was cute and that I like him, just like I did yesterday, and the day before. He turned red and ran away, just like he did yesterday and the day before that. Why did Charlie run away from me? Does that mean he doesn't like me?

Mommy tells Daddy she likes him everyday, and he doesn't run away. Mommy even tells Daddy she loves him, and he doesn't run away. I know Daddy likes Mommy and me, so that's why he doesn't run away like Charlie. I guess Charlie doesn't like me.

Maybe I should start doing boy stuff like Charlie told me. Maybe that will make him like me. But that's not fair. Charlie doesn't want to learn about girl things. He's not going to be a good husband or Daddy, if he keeps acting like this.

I wish I knew what makes Charlie act up, and why he calls me names that hurt my feelings. I'm not stupid! I just want him to like me, like I like him. Boys!

I know—I'll ask Daddy about boys. He was a boy when he was little. Maybe he can remember why boys act up. If anybody knows about boys, it will be Daddy. My Daddy knows everything.

Good night diary. Love, Amileé.

Do you remember your first love—you know, the little boy you kicked in the shins? Then you giggled as he jumped up and down for your enjoyment. Maybe he was the kid who sat two rows behind you in homeroom or the boy who wore the black-and-white saddle shoes and the high-water pants. The same one who passed you notes with his personalized love sonnets written on them: "Roses are red, violets are blue, I got a bulldog that looks somethin' like you!"

Perhaps your father was first your first love—or maybe you wished he had been your first love. Whoever it was, real or imagined, all of us have our first love tucked neatly away in our heart of hearts.

I remember my first love. Her name was Phoebe. She had the prettiest smile in the whole elementary school and she had the funniest-looking hat of any girl in our homeroom. It was flat on top like a crêpe and I used to tease her about it as I walked behind her on the way home. Phoebe kicked me in the shins just like other girls had done, except she kicked a hell of a lot harder. I often wonder what became of her.

What about you? Do you ever think about your first love? Have you ever wondered what would have happened if the two of you had remained lovers for life? I married my first real love, and I couldn't imagine loving anyone other than Simone.

Charlie was Amileé's first love. I remember the day she came into the office sporting a pouting upside-down smile on her face. I asked, "Why the long face?"

She put her hands on her narrow little hips, jerked her little neck and head to one side, and said, "I told Charlie he was cute, then he ran away! Does that mean he doesn't like me?"

I managed to keep the smile on my face from exploding into an ear-to-ear thirty-two-tooth grin and asked, "What do you think, Amileé?"

Amileé put her little elbows on the edge of my desk, rolled her eyes toward the ceiling for a moment, then surprised the hell out of me by saying, "I think he was scared! Boys get scared faster than girls."

"But sweetheart, do you think Charlie likes you?"

"Yeah, he likes me, just like all the boys like me. But they don't like me like Charlie likes me. He's cool!"

If I had to use one word to describe Amileé, I would choose the word *self-assured*. At ten she had already developed a strong sense of who she was, and wasn't afraid to let you know that she was Amileé. I will never forget the statement she made about Charlie when he ran away from her that day: "Daddy, he couldn't run very far. The playground has a fence around it."

You knew this little angel wasn't going to be a follower. Amileé was going to be a take-charge leader. She was charming, fun to be around, and always had a way of turning a negative into a positive. I remember what she told me during Simone's funeral, "There are more people waving hello, Papa, than there are waving good-bye." She was right. Amileé was and still is simply amazing.

The first time I saw her in the nursery, I knew she was special. As I searched the isolets, my eyes were attracted to a big-butt baby in the center row. Unlike the other newborns, this baby wasn't asleep or squirming around on her hospital blanket. This baby's head was up and her bright eyes were scanning the room as if to assess her surroundings—or maybe she was just being nosy.

Gowned, masked, and sitting patiently, I waited for the nurse to bring in our bundle of joy. Right when the nurse placed Amileé in my nervous arms, the world seemed to stop. Amileé was the most beautiful baby I have ever seen. Her gray-blue eyes were like the water in Cameroon's Bight of Biafra. Her pug nose was a perfect miniature of Simone's nose. Her skin was as smooth and soft as the words of a love song. The fine texture of my mother's hair and the sandy-red of Simone's mother smothered Amileé's tiny head.

Grabbing my little finger for support, Amileé began rooting. Moments later she opened one eye, looked up, and bubbled, as if to say, "Got milk?" A nurse averted our first fight by handing me a bottle of warm formula. Holding Amileé in my arms for the first time was the first of many milestones I was able to experience with her.

Milestone: *noun*, An important event, as in a person's career, the history of a nation, or the advancement of knowledge in a field; a turning point. I think of milestones as memorable moments—the kind I want always to remember—imprinted on the emotional canvas of our hearts and souls.

How many milestones in your life can you remember? Can you recall the ones you may have shared with a brother or sister, a friend, a

coworker, or a lover? If you add up all of the turning points and important events in your life, how many of them did you experience with
your father?

I believe that fathers are more influential in the shaping of their children's emotional makeup than they realize—especially in the emotional shaping of their daughters. For those of you who misread, or
who have opposing views regarding this statement, allow me to clarify
it. I said fathers are "more influential" in the emotional shaping of their
children *than they realize*. I didn't say they were more important than
the children's mother. To be effective, parenting requires the participa-
tion of both parents.

Did you have an absentee father when you were growing up? Such
a parent may have been absent because of limited visiting rights after
a divorce, being a workaholic, having a drug dependency—or many
other possible reasons. How do you think your life would have turned
out if your father had been more active in shaping the emotional part
of your life?

This chapter is included for the benefit of daughters who wanted,
but didn't have, a father to help shape them emotionally. I want you to
know that you were not alone. This chapter is also for the men trying
to break out of the macho-man father image thrust upon them by society. Finally, this chapter is included for mothers to use in awakening
their daughters' fathers, before their little girl grows up, and they miss
the opportunity to create some milestones in her little life.

The following pages contain several random but important milestones that I experienced, or helped create in Amileé's life—ones that
Amileé and I both cherish to this day. I hope that one of these milestones will inspire some fathers to become emotionally active in shaping their daughter's life.

The first memories in the milestone category were the father-
daughter dates we had every week. On Wednesdays, Amileé's responsibility was to decide what she wanted us to do for our morning or afternoon date. The activity would vary from week to week, and ranged
from dining out to trips to the racetrack at Bois De Boulogne Park. One
date that Amileé loved and put on her list regularly was the Musée du

Louvre. Her eyes would light up and she would giggle whenever we stood on the spot where I first met Simone.

The dates became less frequent about the same time she became interested in boys, but I loved and cherished every single date we had, including the seven-Wednesdays-in-a-row-ice-cream-parlor date. That girl could pack more vanilla ice cream away than Baskin Robbins could make.

One of the greatest milestones for me occurred on the day when Amileé became a woman. When Amileé first cycled into womanhood, she told Simone that she didn't feel like Daddy's little girl anymore. After Simone told me what was going on with Amileé, I went on a Daddy-to-the-rescue shopping spree, to buy a bunch of child/teen/ adult goodies for Amileé.

I purchased a large backpack and filled it with several items. Inside, there was a Raggedy Ann doll, a *What's Happening to Me* type of book, and some sidewalk/street chalk. A locket and gold chain encircled the doll's neck, and contained a picture of Amileé and me on the day she was born. There were also a ball and jacks, a diary with a lock and key, some pink-tinted lip gloss and clear nail polish, a spinning top, a gift certificate to the pharmacy (for her to buy, what she later referred to as, her unmentionables), crayons, and a Curious George coloring book. A small bottle of Channel Nº5 perfume, and a ton of other knickknacks that I can't remember. I have always loved to shop with and for Simone; now I could do the same for Amileé. I was having a ball.

I went to the card shop intending to purchase a Welcome to Womanhood card, but couldn't find one. It's hard to believe Hallmark doesn't have a card for that occasion; they seem to have ones to express everything else.

I wrapped all of the gifts individually, placed them in the backpack, and wrapped it as well. I found a blank card with a line drawing of a father and daughter on the cover that seemed appropriate for the occasion. Inside I wrote, "No matter what happens, Amileé, you'll always be my little girl!" I attached it to the package along with a rainbow of helium balloons.

I didn't want to invade her privacy any more than I already had. Like most young women when they start cycling, she was extremely self-conscious. I left the gift on the foyer table, where she could see it as soon as she came in the front door. Then I disappeared for the rest of the day and evening.

When I returned home later that night, everything I had placed on the table was gone. On the table, in the place where I had left Amileé's package, was an envelope. Written on the envelope with red, green, and blue-colored crayons was the word "Daddy." A kiss from a pair of small pink gloss-covered lips sealed the perfumed envelope. Inside there was a sheet of ruled paper with, "Thanks" written in calligraphic letters. It was signed "Love, Daddy's little girl."

Another milestone was her junior prom. She insisted that I go with her and Simone to help pick out a gown that would attract the attention of all the boys. I asked her what had she planned to do with her date, Charlie, if all the boys start talking to her. "I'll save the last dance for him." I prepared myself for the troubling teen years I would have to endure. Amileé was such a card.

A week before the prom I had the honor of giving Amileé her first lesson in how to read and predict what a boy (man) was going to do, before *he* even knows—I taught her how to slow dance. The lessons were going great until we had a dress rehearsal the night before the prom.

Amileé was radiant in her peach-colored gown and long evening gloves. She had on the pearl choker that Simone wore on our wedding day, and she looked just as beautiful as her mother did on that blessed day. I turned the stereo on and played "Smoke Gets in Your Eyes" by the Platters as Amileé slipped into her shoes.

I walked across the living room, bowed, and extended my hand, then placed my arm around her tiny waist. I took one step forward, Amileé countered by taking one step backward—and fell flat on her derrière. Thanks to her mother, Amileé has a healthy backside that softened her landing.

With a look of surprise on her face, petticoats twisted around her waist, and runs in her nylons, Amileé grabbed her tummy, and giggled as she rolled back and forth on the floor. I discovered the culprits that caused the downfall—her first pair of high heels.

As I helped her up, Amileé asked, "Why can't I lead?" I prayed for help. Lord knows I was going to need all of the help I could get.

The following milestones revolve around men, their hidden emotions, and my fatherly advice.

I always made sure I conducted myself in such a way that Amileé would have a model in her heart and head for the type of man who was desirable to have in her life. I didn't want to dictate or arrange the boys (men) she would date or marry; I wanted only to make sure she set a minimum level of acceptability—higher than rock bottom. I didn't want her to settle for any man just to have one in her life. I wanted her to be treated with respect and adoration. And I wanted her to see and appreciate how Simone and I interacted as a mature couple, as friends, and as each other's confidant.

I made it a point to always greet both her and Simone with a kiss, a hug, and an "I love you" each morning. When I had to go away, as I frequently did, I would call and express my love to them over the phone. The only exception to this routine would occur when I was staying in a third-world country with a lousy phone system. If I knew ahead of time that it would be difficult to phone, I would tuck little notes and small gifts in places where they would easily be noticed; just to let them know I was thinking of them. Finally, I would express my sentiments of love only when I could stop and give one hundred percent of my being as I said, "I love you."

I always told Amileé how beautiful she was to me. I opened doors for both of them, until women's lib came on the scene. Then I resumed after Amileé came to the realization that she has always been liberated—free to be herself. I asked Amileé for her opinion on important decisions regarding family matters, to let her know her ideas and preference were just as important as ours was.

It was important for me to let Amileé know, through my actions, that I wasn't superhuman. I wanted her to know that Daddy's (boys', men's) feelings get hurt, that I could cry, become depressed, and would have the same emotional reactions to situations that she and her mother had. I didn't want her to have this superhuman image of me (men) as all powerful and invulnerable, then watch her become frightened and get stuck when she saw me (her man) at one of those inevitable moments when I would hit rock bottom.

I wanted her to know that males and females are more alike than they are different—unlike the trendy belief marketed today.

I guess you can say I was writing, by example, a manual for Amileé: *How to Pick a Great Partner: Trusting Your Heart and Using Good Common Sense!* It seems to have worked; Amileé and Charles have been married for years and he has slept on the couch only twice that I know of. In the first several weeks of being married to Simone I slept not only on the couch, but on the back porch, in the doghouse, the car . . .

When Amileé started dating boys, I asked to be her first official date. We went to a restaurant where the bar was in the center of the room and elevated above the dining tables. I asked for a table that would put us in full view of the happy-hour crowd. After we ordered, I began my "You're pretty . . . Let me buy you a drink . . . Now let's go to bed . . . What do you mean I said I loved you? Good-bye!" "Next." "You're pretty . . . Let me buy . . . " lecture. It was the talk every father should have with his daughter about the thousand and one lies boys (men) will tell just to get into a girl's (woman's) pants. I know, because I told quite a few myself. If Amileé had been a boy, I would have said the same things, but obviously with a few modifications.

I asked if she knew why I had always told her I loved her, told her she was beautiful, hugged her, involved her in making family decisions, and why I always told her she could be or do anything she wanted— that all she had to do was . . . just do it. Of course, she answered, "No." I told her I had done all of those things so she could have ownership of those emotions, understand being respected, and distinguish between adoration and flattery. "Huh!" was the only response to my spiel. I prepared myself for a long evening.

I wanted Amileé to know she was her own person, that she didn't need a man to validate herself. I didn't want Amileé falling for those lame-ass lines that some of the women at the bar were going to accept as being real. I told her that some of those women will go to bed with those men—not because they wanted to, but because they hungered for attention, any kind of attention. I finished by telling Amileé that these women long for the kind of attention she has received all of her life from me. (To repeat, I believe fathers are more influential in shaping the emotions of their daughters, not more important.) "Uh-huh" was her reply when I asked if that explanation made it any clearer. I ordered two more dishes of vanilla ice cream and decided to try another approach.

I told Amileé that many of my female patients who had difficulties with their intimate relationships shared a similar central theme. When the patient and I traced the problem to search for its origin, in most cases it came down to the same thing. That was their having a father who rarely gave them the type of emotional attention they needed and desired, a father who didn't know how to express or was horrible at expressing feelings, or a father who seldom attended to any of their needs. As a result, they chose the first man to come along who paid more attention to them than their father did. I closed my eyes, cringed, and waited for Amileé's response.

"Uh-huh" quickly flowed from her mouth as she lowered her head to meet the spoon of ice cream in her hand.

"What? Are you sure you understand it?"

Flashing a smile of superiority, she said, "Daddy, all you had to say was, 'Don't give up the kitty-cat until you find and fall in love with someone who'll treat you the way I do.' Daddy, you always stretch things out too . . ." Before she could finish her sentence, Amileé broke into one of her giggling fits. She was such a joy to be around, despite the smart-ass remarks she would make whenever I stuck my foot in my mouth.

This milestone I should have patented. I started a tradition of giving Simone one small present as a token of appreciation for birthing our bundle of joy. The first present was a charm bracelet, and each year that followed, she received another charm. The charms always represented some milestone in Amileé's life; for example, the next year after her junior prom, Simone received a charm in the shape of some high-heeled shoes.

When Amileé got older, she took over the tradition of giving her mother a charm for the bracelet. I was a little surprised that Simone didn't buy a present for me on Amileé's second birthday. Usually, Simone was the first one to join in on any tradition started by our families. Still, having the two of them in my life was the best present I could ever hope to get.

One year, Amileé asked Simone why she didn't give me a present on her natal day. I don't know what Simone told her, but the next year Amileé bought presents for both of us for her birthday. My first gift from her was a one-minute egg timer. She wanted me to get my point across a little faster during our next "Daddy preaches, daughter listens" sessions.

The last present Amileé gave Simone before she made her transition, was a charm that said, "Grandmother." I was so grateful that Simone lived long enough to hold Amileé and Charles' little bundle of joy, Somali.

The milestone I'm about to mention is second in importance only to the day I first held Amileé in my arms. Every year on Simone's birthday and on the anniversary of her death, we'd meet at the mausoleum I built for Simone and me. Before entering, I would always read the words that Amileé used to console me during the funeral. The inscription above its entrance read, "There are more people waving hello than there are saying good-bye. You won't be alone, my love." We would place two long-stemmed roses, one white, one red, on her white marble *sarcophagus*. Sitting on the bench between the two *sarcophagi*, we would sing Simone's favorite song, "Smoke Gets in Your Eyes." Afterward, we would talk about the milestones created in our lives by Simone, over triple scoops of French vanilla ice cream.

Amileé has taken over as the Queen of Hearts in my life now—she's the only woman I have loved as much as Simone and the only one to reside within my heart of hearts, right next to her mother.

Which milestones do you remember? You did have *some* milestones while you were growing up, did you not?

7

Tyrone and Tyra

The real problem between the sexes is that for men,
sex is a gender-underliner, they need it for their egos.
We don't need sex to make us feel we are the person
we need to be.
—CAROL CLEWLOW,
Interview in *Observer*

Tyrone—November 7

Limp dick mothafucka'!

That's what I've become. It's been nine months since I've had a real good hard-on. They say at forty-five I'm supposed to be in the prime of my life. Hell, if this is prime, I'd hate to see what's gonna happen when I'm sixty. My dick will probably break off in my hands while I'm taking a piss!

All of this shit started when they gave Angus Lithgow *my* promotion. I worked my fuckin' ass off to become the regional division head, and now they want me to report to this little shit. Fuck that!

I knew about the "corporate glass ceiling," but, like the rest, I thought it would never happen to me. Shit! Why do I have to be ten times better than them just to be fuckin' equal. I labored for two years to make the Michigan plant profitable. A pat on the back, "Good work, boy!" and giving my promotion away is one helluva way to reward my efforts. When headquarters brought Angus in two years ago, I was assigned to train that flat-ass mothafucka.

Angus has a bachelor's degree from some little hick-town college, while my degree is from an Ivy fuckin' league school. You'd think my M.B.A. with honors from "Har-Vard" would count for something. Maybe I should call my homeboy June Bug down at the post office, and have him jack Angus up. On second thought, that crazy ass nigga' might go "postal" and kick my ass too.

Where in the *hell* did they come up with a goddamn name like Angus? And to think that they have the nerve to say us black folks make up strange names for our children.

I'm tired of all the tests, screenings, and doctors telling me not a goddamned thing about how to get my Johnson back up. Fuck some damned injections into my jimmy, or sticking an implant in my rod. The internist told me the high blood pressure medication isn't helping the problem. The goddamned blood pressure wouldn't be up if the fuckin' glass ceiling wasn't up. The second shrink I saw told me I'm suffering from performance anxiety. No shit, Sherlock. Let *his* dick hang like a wet dishrag and see how long it takes him to start asking, "Will this mothafucka' ever get up?"

To add salt to the wound, I've been drinking more. But sometimes a drink at lunch is the only thing that'll get me through the afternoon. Lately, I've been stopping by the Comfort Zone for a little happy-hour nip. It chills me out before going home to Tyra. I know the liquor adds to my joint problem, but what the fuck am I supposed to do to keep the thoughts away . . . the thought of being less of a man . . . of not being able to satisfy my woman.

About a year ago, I came home after a long day from work, tired as hell. Tyra was in the kitchen cooking dinner, and she was singing like an angel. I'm here to tell you, *gurlfriend* could put her foot in some smothered pork chops! Anyway, I went in to see what my nose smelled. My eyes opened wider than Buckwheat's, Stymie's, or Farina's all put together, when I saw Tyra.

Tyra was leaning over the island counter reaching for the meat tenderizer and all she had on was a pair of stiletto heel mules, white thigh-highs, a sheer apron, and a pair of white thong panties that disappeared down into the crack of the most beautiful ass in the world. Looking over her shoulder, Tyra held the mallet up and, with a wicked smile on her face, asked, "Do you want me to *beat* your meat and blacken it on my grille, or do you want me to smother it and . . . slow . . . cook it in my roaster oven?" Shhhhit, my dick shot straight up, damned near ripped a hole in my good pants, dragged me across the room, and charged, head on into the servant's entrance of Cupid's hotel.

Tyra tried the same thing two months ago to see if she could get a similar response. My eyes popped! My mouth watered! My heart raced! My blood boiled! But hangin' to the left, shriveled, and not the least bit interested was my goddamned dick.

Last night while I was packing my limp-ass Johnson into her *wet* pussy, Tyra looked back at me and said, "Tyrone, you fuck like a bitch!" She didn't mean it. I know she didn't, did she? Tyra had read an article in *Essence* that talked about how some men get turned-on when they get angry. Angry! Hell, after my dick shriveled to the size of a peanut, I broke down and cried "just like a bitch." The statement Tyra made was the truth—a bitch ain't got nothing to stroke with, and neither do I.

Tyra says she understands. I want to believe her, but it's getting harder to do so with each passing day. Harder! Yeah, that's what this limp-ass dick of mine is supposed to do—get hard. Sorry-ass mothafucka!

How could she go from getting eight inches of rock-hard dick every other day to a hangin' Johnny that I gotta pack inside her like sausage gets packed into a casing? How could she adjust so easily and accept the semi-hard dick she gets every now and then? She says she understands. I hope to hell she's telling me the truth.

A couple of weeks ago I was in our bedroom closet getting a flannel nightshirt off the top shelf. When I pulled the nightshirt down, a rolled up towel fell onto the floor. I wondered for a moment why it was here instead of the linen closet. Without much thought about it, I picked the black towel up by its fringed edge so I could put it with the rest of the towels. Something hit the floor with a thud. I turned to see what had fallen, and instantly knew I had been replaced. Lying there rotating and humming on the floor was a big black latex dick with vibrating rabbit ears!

I've been replaced by a battery-operated lover. Goddamnit! Why is this shit happening to me? I never got my forty acres and that damned mule. Asshole Angus took my promotion from me. Now a triple-D battery-powered coochie companion has taken over as my woman's pillow pal.

Will she eventually replace her toy with a real lover, when it can't satisfy her anymore? I can't stand the thought of some other man strokin' Tyra's sugar walls. I love her more than any woman I have ever known and not just because she is fanfuckintastic in bed, but because she believes in me. If she does take a lover, I couldn't and wouldn't blame her. She needs to get her freak on just like everybody else does. Tyra deserves to have a man, a real man, who can satisfy her sexually.

Will my shit ever get up again?

Sweet Lord Jesus, please deliver me from this living hell! Shatter that glass ceiling, and let the freedom bell ring. Let my nature rise . . . damn, I knew I shouldn't have skipped church last Easter . . . maybe on this coming Good Friday my dick will rise from the dead like . . . Lord, if You bail my ass outa this jam, I promise to . . . better stop, the last thing I need right now is to have a lightning bolt shoved up my ass for lying to the Almighty. I know damned well I ain't gonna sit up in church for four hours while my people sing, jump, and shout. I know God's hearing is perfect; so all that yellin' ain't necessary. I must admit, it does feel good to let loose every now and then when the spirit hits you. I wish the spirit would hit this dead-ass dick and make it jump for joy.

I hope this limp-dick shit ends soon. I don't want my condition to drive Tyra into the bed of another man. I can take being replaced by a vibrator, but being replaced by a warm body is more than this limp-dick mothafucka' can take. I know Tyra has always been faithful to me, but how much longer can she hold out before she needs some *GODHF* [Good-Old Down-Home Fuckin'].

Tyra—November 8

Daayumn! That was the shit!

I was climbing the walls trying to get him off me! One time I screamed so damned loud they probably heard me over in the next county. I couldn't catch my breath afterward, that shit was just too damn good! When he busted that last nut it was so delicious I wanted to slap my momma 'cause she never told me it was supposed to feel that good!

I get wet from just thinking about how damned good it was and how it was so different. I loved the way he darkened the room, lit several small candles, and told me, "When these candles take their last flickering breath, your coochie will be purring from pure pleasure." Then he lowered his naked hard body and started lickin' my toes . . . one . . . by . . . one . . . *very slowly* . . . over . . . and . . . over . . . until my coochie tightened up and soaked the sheets with my sweet love nectar.

Inching his way up, he alternated between, long licks of his muscular tongue . . . small wet kisses from his thick lips . . . and . . . blowing his hot breath all the way up my legs . . . *oh shit!* I had to bite my bottom lip to keep from cummin' too soon.

Looking down between my swollen nipples, I could see his eyes flirtatiously scanning my body. He looked up at me as if I was a slice of big-Momma's sweet potato pie that he was about to devour. His day-old stubble scratched my inner thighs as he drew his jaw along my trembling legs. Wedging his thick shoulders between my thighs, he slid his hot hands under my ass and squeezed each cheek firmly . . . *goddamn!* . . . then one of his hands finessed its way up and over my arching pelvis, until it came to rest on my silky smooth chocolate mound. He glanced up one last time, gave me half a wink, and then lowered his mouth onto my wet downtown gates.

Where did he learn how to do that? Who taught his tongue the lost art of going down on a woman? I want to thank her from the bottom of my . . . *oh shit!* . . . with a slow movement of his finger and thumb, he opened the outside gates that covered my juicy canal. Moving his mouth back, he blew a *long slow* stream of his hot breath onto my dripping inner doors . . . my sugar walls tightened once again, and released more of my sweet elixir for his taste buds to savor. Dr. Kegel would've been so proud of me.

Spreading my swollen gates further apart and pulling back the hooded cover, he teased my cultured pearl from its hiding place. Moving closer, he lightly tapped my pink pearl of pleasure with the tip of his skillful tongue, as if he were sending a Morse Code message . . . "Moan, scream, and purr for me Tyra."

Flicking his tongue as quickly as a humming bird flaps its wings, he . . . *no, not now!* . . . he caught me off guard . . . *damn!* . . . *no, not yet!* . . . I wanna ride the crest of this big wave just a little longer . . . stretch it out for as long as I can. I've never felt like this before and I wanna enjoy every sweet minute of this feeling. Suddenly every muscle in my body tightened . . . a warm sensation shot downward through my torso, and upward through my thighs . . . they collided at my sweet pot, and sparked a white-hot fire so sweet that my toes curled into tight little balls. It feels sooo damn good. Is heaven like this?

The tingling sensation is starting to . . . starting to radiate out to the tips of my fingers . . . it's red hot . . . *No!* . . . give me just one more minute before I reach the peak of this phenomenal feeling. *Shit*, he's toying with me. It's as if he's inside of my body and soul, feeling what I feel, knowing how far to take me before I explode, knowing just how much pressure to apply to bring me close—but not quite to—*that* point.

Sometimes his touch is so right-on, it feels like *I'm* touching myself, and . . . *no, not yet, not now!* It's like he knows just how far he can push my button without crossing my orgasmic circuit. He takes me within a curly hair's width of an orgasm . . . then he softens his licks . . . shortens his strokes . . . s-l-o-w-s his pace . . . and then . . . he starts all over again.

Suddenly I noticed something moving. I could see it out of the corner of my eye and it scared the shit out of me! Who was it? Jerking my head to the right, I saw our reflection in the full-length dressing mirror in the corner. I'll be damned if watching our reflection didn't turn me on even more. My fingernails clawed at the *chaise longue* in a desperate attempt to hold on. My straightened hair had reverted back into a tight 'fro. My toes quickly curled and uncurled with each stroke of his massive tongue. Hangin' in mid-air, completely supported by the palms of his hot hands, was my big black ass. My bent knees pushed out and back, rhythmically bounced off his shoulders with every sweet lick of his tongue. His bald head bobbed up and down like he was licking the last bit of cake batter from the bottom of a deep bowl. When I saw that shit, I got so turned on, I couldn't hold back any more.

I pushed hard against his face, flattening his tongue so it would cover more of my . . . damn, I can hear my sweet nectar sloshing against his tongue, every time he sweeps it over my pink pearl. It feels so good being satisfied this way.

Looking down, I see my pink pearl sticking out like a pygmy's Johnson. It's so hard, and so hot. I can feel it pulling back, moving back under its little hood . . . too sensitive to take this kind of tongue-lashing. Now, it's pulling back into its hiding place, safe from the cumming explosion, safe from the loud noise of my screams. "*Oh baby please . . . don't move . . . baby!* . . . don't change a goddamned thing . . . stay right there . . . right there . . . on Tyra's sweet spot."

"*Damn it's so good! . . . sooo . . . oh shit!* . . . I'm cumin' . . . no, not yet! . . . its gonna be a . . . a . . . hard . . . one."

Sucking in one last breath I prepare myself . . . *oh fuck!* . . . my whole body is tightening up . . . I . . . *ummm* . . . can't stop these spasms . . . *ohhhhh shit* . . . it feels so damned good . . . it's a sensation like I've never felt before . . . baby! Oh . . . baby! . . . I'm . . . I'm about . . . to . . . to . . . explode! Yesss! Oh, hell yesss! Unable to contain my self any longer I screamed . . . "Goddamnit *Tyrone*, eat it baby . . . don't stop . . . don't stop lickin' . . . I'm . . . I'm cummmming!"

We've been married fifteen years, and never have I had orgasms like the ones I've had over the last three months. Before Ty's problem occurred, he thought his big dick was the shit. He use to jump up and down on me for what seemed like hours, turning me every which-a-way but loose. The penetration felt good, but I was lucky if I had two or three good orgasms a week. Hell, just before his problem popped up, I mean before his condition occurred, I was only getting off once or twice a month.

I think he knew there was room for improvement in his lovemaking, but his damned male pride kept him from asking me how to do it better.

Journal, don't get me wrong, Ty was a pretty good lover before his condition occurred, but after he couldn't get it up, he slowed down, took more time, learned what turned me on, and learned how to do it. He's become much more romantic, attentive, and freaky ever since he started asking, "What do you want me to do, baby?" I also think he's trying hard to please me because he's worried, worried that I'll find another man to, as he says, "satisfy you sexually, Tyra."

I know the thing that made him feel that way was the "battery-operated lover" incident. Hell, he bought the damned vibrator a couple of years ago, to spice things up. He said the white boys at work told him, "Freakin' A Ty. My wife liked it so much that I started to use it on myself, bro!" He just happened upon the damned thing the day I used it to see if the batteries still had any juice . . . I mean power, left in them. Well, maybe I do miss the penetration of his thick hard juicy dick, but that vibrator is just a sex toy. It could never replace Ty.

This macho male bullshit of not getting it up is making him paranoid. I wish I could get him to understand that his Johnson is just one small—well it's not small—but it's only a small portion . . . no, a significant portion . . . of our lovemaking. Shit! Now I'm getting paranoid about the words I use.

Ty even fulfilled a long-time fantasy of mine, and believe me, it was well worth the wait. I've always wanted to watch him masturbate and have him cum on my breasts. Just thinking about the few times he's done it is turning me on. Ever since he became paranoid about me giving it up to another man, he's been willing to do just about anything, and, believe me, I'm gonna push him to the limit.

I wish he'd give me more credit. I don't want another man. Like the words to a song, "I love me some him!" If his dick fell off tomorrow, I'd still love him, I'd still respect him, and would be proud to say, "This is my man!"

No wife could ask for a better friend, provider, comedian, or a greater lover than my Ty. He believed in me when no one else gave a shit about my business. The initial success of my interior design business was largely due to his efforts, business skills, and charisma. He was responsible for most of the clients I worked for during my first year in business. He sold them on my concept of design before they ever saw any of my work. Now those clients are referring their friends and relatives.

Ty even financed my studio for the first two years, using his own money. He never complained about my long hours, or having to listen to my bitching every night about some of my fickle-ass clients. I must admit, there were only two assholes that I had to work with, but they were two very wealthy assholes who paid in advance. He never asked me to pay back any of the money he pumped into Affordable Elegance—Studio of Interior Design. What woman could ask for a better man? Hell, Ty is almost perfect, now that he—gives good lickin' and keeps Tyra's clock a tickin'!

Mmmm! . . . oh shhhhhit! . . . awww! . . . sweet flashbacks! Dayumn, I need a P.C. [panty change].

They say my Ty's not as good as them. That's bullshit! Ty has so many talents, skills, and abilities, he could start his own business tomorrow, and I guarantee it would be profitable within the first year. A "limp-dick mothafucka"? Hell naw! This is only a temporary condition that will be resolved when he breaks through that damned "ceiling," leaves that damned corporation, or breaks off his foot up in Angus' tight ass. When he does leave, my baby's Johnson will stand tall and straight, like the giant redwood it used to be. Then it'll be ready to give me some of that GODHF!

Journal, when Ty does get it back up, I hope he doesn't stop his fancy lickin'—cause Tyra loves Tyrone's tongue flickin'!

Whew!

Did you think Tyra was getting her freak on with another man—one who could get it up and keep it up? If you were thinking along those lines, what does that tell you about yourself? This isn't a judgment question. I merely ask for your self-discovery. What in fact would you do if you were in Tyra's situation? What factors would determine whether you'd stay or stray?

There is one important point I'd like to bring up regarding the quote that introduced this couple. It is the importance of sex and a penis to a man's perception of his personal self-worth. Here's that quote again . . .

> The real problem between the sexes is that for men,
> sex is a gender-underliner, they need it for their egos.
> We don't need sex to make us feel we are the person
> we need to be.
> —CAROL CLEWLOW, *Interview in Observer*

Like many men in the world today, Tyrone equated his manhood, masculinity, and sexual worth to his penis. To be more specific, Tyrone equated his self-worth to his penis in its erect form.

There are several reasons Tyrone believed the myth of "real big hard dick = real big hard man."

I discovered that his biggest problem wasn't the "glass ceiling" and the effect it had on his erectile difficulties. The biggest problems were actually his beliefs about sex and his attitude about lovemaking.

Unfortunately, like many men, Tyrone believed that sex, making love, required an erection. When I mentioned that to Tyrone he replied, "Shhhhit!" After wiping the tears of laughter from my eyes, I tried to explain what I meant by that. But he still found the concept difficult to accept. When he found out that nothing was wrong medically, Tyrone became hell-bent on the glass ceiling issue and the stress it caused. He wasn't ready to believe his difficulty in achieving an erection also had something to do with his beliefs about intimacy. Rather than fight his attitude, I started in on the glass ceiling issue, knowing that a window of opportunity would eventually open.

Tyrone had a lot of resentment toward corporate America and how it operates. If you could read more of his entries, you would know that he was more pissed off because of the way "they" treated him as an individual, and not so much because they had promoted Angus over him. It was safer for him to blame Angus than it was for him to express the real anger within his heart for corporate America.

What was the real anger? It was corporate discrimination, more commonly known as the glass-ceiling phenomenon. It pissed Tyrone off that he had all of the qualities they look for in a person for the higher management positions, yet was passed over for promotion. He was competent, experienced, effective, qualified, competitive, and equal to—and in most cases—better than the others who had been promoted above him. His question, "Why do I have to be ten times better . . . just to be equal?" was a strongly rooted conviction that I believed was keeping him from seeing the bigger picture and moving on to higher ground. That was the picture Tyra had vividly drawn for him two years before his erection problem ever started.

I learned that this wasn't Tyrone's first time being passed over for a promotion. This was the third denial in the past eighteen months.

I pointed out to Tyrone that although the glass ceiling phenomenon is unfair in the way it discriminates against minorities and white females, it still exists. Tyrone could have dealt with this situation in any of several ways. He could continue to belabor the point and remain in the same position until retirement. He could work within the system, conform, and do whatever he had to, to advance as far as possible. He could maintain what he calls his "ethnic integrity," fight, and possibly get fired. Finally, he could step into the big picture his wife had drawn—a picture worth a thousand corporations.

Tyrone certainly was qualified to do the same job as any of his non-black counterparts, but being qualified was just one of the many requirements needed to navigate the multilevel corporate labyrinth leading to the executive washroom. Some of the passages in the maze are easier to travel if an employee fits into the mold of the corporate cookie cutter.

The more an employee alters himself to fit the image, the closer he gets to the corporate brass ring. However, certain employees have problems conforming to that corporate image. Tyrone was one of those employees.

Tyrone was extremely articulate and was able to switch from his beloved ethnic vernacular to corporate America's perfect English. However, he resented that he must fit into the set box of brown shoes, brown socks, brown suit, brown belt, brown tie, white shirt, and "white face" attitude to be able to advance. Tyrone's cultural integrity—how he thinks, speaks, acts, and dresses, and his cultural roots—is very important to him. Being true to himself was at the top of his value system, and he refused to "sell himself out."

I can appreciate how important it is to not compromise your cultural integrity, but I also know that you can't have your corporate cake and eat it too. Unlike the other patients in this book, Tyrone wasn't wrestling with the horns of a dilemma; he was hoping for an outcome that was almost impossible to obtain. Tyrone was in a "Catch-22" situation.

Stroking his neck, Tyrone watched the ceiling fan jiggle in its socket, as it turned. After several strokes Tyrone said, "I got two goddamn Catch-22s, Doc."

"What's the second one?"

"My jacked-up Johnson won't let me satisfy Tyra. This shit is fucked up, man. It's all fucked up." The curtains parted and my window of opportunity opened. Now I could come back to the issue that most needed to be addressed.

I asked Tyrone if he thought discrimination was the stress factor that created his erection difficulty. Without hesitating, he said, "Definitely!"

I felt like a wolf in sheep's clothing as I manipulated Tyrone into answering my next question. I knew there was only one way he could answer this question because of his beliefs and attitude toward sex.

If you recall, earlier I mentioned the myth that "real big hard dick = real big hard man."

Well, Tyrone was a platinum-card-carrying member of that myth. He still believed the old locker room lawyers who exclaimed, "Man, you don't haf'ta eat pussy! Shit, it's them limp, pencil-dick mothafuckas that haf'ta lick a woman's carpet! If you got a big dick and you stroke that shit all night long, ain't no need to go down on a woman with yo' soup coolers! Shit man, I've never eaten . . . " I said a quick prayer, and then asked my question.

With a serious look, and in a concerned voice, I asked, "I'm curious, Ty, what would you do to satisfy Tyra if you didn't have a Johnson at all?"

His words were different from the ones I had in mind, but they had the same meaning. "Shit, what kinda man would I be if I didn't have my Johnson?"

"But just suppose you were a man without a Johnson. How would you satisfy your wife?"

"I'd find some way, but it wouldn't be as good as having eight hard inches of Dr. Feelgood, Dr. DoRight, Dr. DoAllNightLong Johnson broke off up in her sweet pussy!" Even he had to laugh at that line of pure locker room bullshit.

He laughed, but it was a nervous one. Anyone who has ever laughed nervously knows that it is a camouflage. What was he hiding? He was— pardon the pun—scared stiff. I wasn't a stranger to that nervous type of laughter. He was frightened to death that Tyra would take on a lover, a man who could give her what Tyrone thought she needed and wanted. Give her what Tyrone could no longer summon up.

Although Tyrone was very much in love with his wife, a great husband, companion, and friend, he was still hung up on his penis being the major source of sexual pleasure for Tyra. He really didn't know how to satisfy Tyra without using his "Johnson" and, sadly, he had never asked Tyra what turned her on and what would get her off.

Has your pillow pal ever asked you about your preferences, likes, and dislikes when it comes to making love or engaging in torrid sex? For that matter, have you ever asked your lover those same questions?

I related my personal experiences and told him how I had learned to use my entire body as an instrument for delivering pleasure to my partner, especially my mouth and its contents.

After much coaxing and reframing, I was able to convince Tyrone that the orgasms Tyra would derive from cunnilingus would be quite different from those of penetration. I placed heavy emphasis on the word *different*. I didn't want him to translate *different* into *better*.

I told Tyrone that when he mastered cunnilingus, Tyra's orgasms would be breathtakingly intense and multiple. His ears perked up when I told him that cunnilingus would give her more freedom to move and position his mouth so she could have several mini-orgasms. These movements would also allow Tyra to make fine adjustments against his tongue to obtain that "Don't move . . . stay right there on that goddamn spot, baby!" orgasm. Tyrone asked several questions, giving a good indication that he might give it a whirl.

He asked the most questions when I talked about positioning. I explained that if he were properly positioned, both of his hands could manipulate two more of her erogenous zones, which would increase Tyra's pleasure tenfold.

At this point, the information I had given Tyrone engaged his sense of touch, taste, smell, and hearing. I then introduced his last major sense: sight. I told him that he would receive double dividends by watching Tyra's reaction as he performed his "mouth music" concerto.

Watching Tyra would allow him to monitor her responses as he touched, stroked, and nibbled his way around her pleasure palace. Second, it would be a voyeuristic-like turn-on for him. I told him that most men are sexually stimulated by the sight of their woman as they turn up her erotic volume.

Do you remember in Darren and Claudia when I mentioned the belief that women have sex with men to get love, while men give love to get sex from women? I wonder what would happen to the world if both sexes knew how the other thought and functioned regarding love and sex. What would happen if we discovered we're more alike than different? Would the world be in a constant state of afterglow?

There's some real therapy possible in the prolonged spin-off effect of Tyrone watching Tyra . . .

The more excited she becomes, the more Tyrone will try to please her.

The more he concentrates on pleasing and driving her crazy, the less he will think about his "limp Johnson."

The less he thinks about his flaccid penis, the less he will concern himself with whether he gets an erection.

The less he concerns himself with getting an erection, the less he'll be hung up (pardon the pun) with performance anxiety.

The less anxiety he experiences, the more he can relax.

The more relaxed he gets, the more blood will flow into non-vital areas of his body—such as his penis.

The more blood pumped into his aroused penis, the more erect it will become.

The more erect it becomes, the more Tyrone will feel like a "real man" again.

The stronger his erections and the more he learns to "talk in tongues," the more he will become the gifted lover he was born to be.

The more he enslaves Tyra with his gigolo-like skills, the less he'll have to concern himself with thoughts of Tyra placing an ad in the Metro Times for a "coochie companion."

For obvious reasons, I didn't reveal to Tyrone all of what I have told you. If he were conscious of what should happen, Tyrone would stress himself out in anticipation, which could slow or prevent his recovery. I told Tyrone that this "therapy" would reduce his stress level considerably, because he would be satisfying Tyra. As a result of satisfying her, his fear of Tyra straying sexually would be reduced and he would eventually forget his foolish fear.

Tyrone asked me, "What makes you so sure she won't find someone else to stroke her sugar walls?"

Feeling my Wheaties, I told him, "Ty, if you become the dynamic lover I know you can be, and follow to the letter the techniques I've given you, Tyra *will* be faithful to you. I promise she will. Even if she does stray, she'll only do it once."

Tyrone logically asked, "Why only once, Doc?"

I told him, "Once she realizes how lame and selfish a lover 'WhatHis-Name' is compared to you, she'll run away from that ground round and never leave her thick and juicy Ty-bone steak again." That got his attention.

Tyrone wore a smile that wrapped around his entire head. I couldn't help myself. I had to mess with him a little. I threw my shoulders back and stuck my chest out, cleared my throat, and said, "That's right, Ty, your little lady will be by your side forever ... unless ... "

The smile faded from his face as Tyrone asked, "Unless what, Doc?"

"She may leave you, if the first guy she hooks up with is the one who instructed you in the lost art of 'lickity-split!' "

Like a true locker room lawyer, Tyrone laughed, grabbed his Johnson, shook it up and down at me while saying, "Hey Doc. Suck my ...!" That was a true gesture of endearment. I had won the respect of my gymnasium barrister.

If Viagra had been available at the time, life would have been much easier for Tyrone.

I would like to tidy up the loose ends surrounding Tyrone and the glass ceiling. Tyrone had overlooked one important fact concerning his performance under the glass ceiling. Tyrone had completely turned around the manufacturing plant in Michigan, making it a profitable division for the corporation. Tyrone needed to internalize the fact that *he* turned it around, not Angus, not the corporation, not even the almighty keepers of the glass ceiling. It wouldn't matter so much that the corporation hadn't acknowledged this achievement—if he himself could acknowledge it.

I asked Tyrone if he had ever considered doing consulting work or opening his own business. It was as if a light bulb flashed on in his head when I told him that he could afford to start his own business. I knew Tyra would be willing to financially support them, just as Tyrone had supported them when she started the interior design studio. Tyra believes in him. I believe in him. The question is: would he believe in himself?

Now I want to comment on a deadly entry Tyrone made in his journal. This entry more than any other charred my heart of hearts the way a white-hot branding iron sears the hide of a young steer. When he wrote, "If she does take a lover I couldn't and wouldn't blame her," I told Tyrone that he should never say that to his wife. My heart sank through the floor when he told me he had already mentioned it to Tyra. No one should make that statement to their spouse or lover unless they really mean it. With the uttering of those words, you could lose everything you've worked hard to establish in your relationship. It could be the most disastrous thing you ever did in your relationship. Your partner might take you seriously—and comply with your fear-ridden statement.

Is your man, significant other, husband, escort, sugar daddy, big poppa, Don Juan, couch potato, maintenance date, coochie companion, pillow pal, or lover that you "get jiggy with" limping? How is he dealing with this challenge? The problem is more common than either of you may think. Is his fear of not being able to perform turning into anger? Does he direct this anger toward you? How are you reacting to his anger? How do you feel about his erection difficulty? What about Tyra? What were her thoughts and feelings?

I loved Tyra's straightforwardness. She was a lovely, high-spirited woman with a great deal of sensitivity and love for her husband. She was so expressive that, when she talked about something, it was as if you were right there with her. In many ways, she reminded me of my Simone. Tyra wasn't afraid to open up and ask or say whatever was on her mind regarding their intimacy as it related to Tyrone's erection difficulty. Her ability to assimilate information and her openness made my task so much easier.

Whenever we had a session, Tyra would dive right in and search for any tidbits of information that she could use to help Tyrone. At first, we talked about the differences between sex and making love, interdependency versus dependency, and her views about men and their penises.

I still recall Tyra's response the first time I used the word penis. Fidgeting with her tennis bracelets, she looked at me and said, "Doc, it's okay to use the 'd' word if you want to. Penis just doesn't seem to do justice to my baby's big, fat, juicy dic . . ." Tyra slapped both hands over her wide-opened mouth. Her eyes popped open as her eyebrows shot up. She hit this incredibly high-pitched muffled scream, and turned two shades of burnt red. She couldn't stop apologizing for being disrespectful; I couldn't stop laughing because Tyra thought she was being disrespectful. If she only knew the real me.

During that same session, we talked about men and how some equate their Johnson's with sex and their manhood. Tyra smiled when I

referred to Tyrone's penis as a Johnson. I asked Tyra for the thought attached to her impish smile. "Doc, why do men name their stuff?" I explained that the more important a thing is to a person, culture, or
country, the greater the number of names it will have. Eskimos have
more than two hundred different words to describe the different types
of snow. Because they live, work, and play in snow for most of their
lives, snow is extremely important to them. I told Tyra that although I
didn't think Tyrone defined himself exclusively by his penis, it was extremely important to him concerning his self-worth as a man.

How many names did Tyrone have for his penis? To show you just
how important the male genitalia are to men in America, the following
is a tiny listing of the seven hundred fifty-plus names that have been
assigned to the male's sexual organ: cock, prick, phallus, peter, lead
pipe, tool, lance, purple-helmeted warrior of love, pud, banana, dipstick,
skin flute, heater hose, schlong, one-eyed snake, one-eyed stiff, reed,
trouser snake, wang, and salami. There are a few distinguished names
that if I didn't point them out, I would feel remiss in my duty as the
keeper of the penile name archives. There's the infamous "duck walk"
dancing Chuck Berry who sang about "My Ding-a-Ling." Do you remember Dexter and the reference he made about his "scepter" in
chapter 1? We can't forget the pet name given to little boys' privates,
by millions of well-meaning mothers, "wee-wee" hose. Let's not forget
the name of the big ones—Willy—and how they so desperately want
to be freed. Finally, there is secret—strong enough for a man, but made
for a woman.

I spent a few sessions with Tyra just talking about the demonic factors that induced or at the very least contributed to Tyrone's erection
problem. The number one demon on practically every list of medical
problems is **stress.**

Tension, depression, anxieties, self-doubts, performance pressures,
anger, alcohol, diabetes, high blood pressure (and medication), and relationship problems (infidelity in particular) are just a few of the conditions that can contribute to a man's temporary, or permanent, erection
problem. When these contributing factors grow in number and
strength, the man begins to spiral down like a plane that's about to

crash and burn. Unable to resist the overwhelming pressures, the man succumbs and follows the demons of stress downward.

I gave Tyra a scenario of what a man might go through when he first discovers the problem. I may have painted the scenario a little too realistically for her.

I explained that once he enters the abyss of sexual dysfunction—male hell—he'll cower in fear, fearful that when it's time for his manhood to rise, it won't. Engaging in negative self-talk, he inquires, "Will it get up this time?" He answers himself with a curt, "Probably not!" He pleads, "Please get up." The self-talk conversation ends abruptly with his final answer of "No!"

He will most likely refuse to discuss the problem with his lover. He'll become argumentative, and he may blame his lover for his unresponsiveness. Talking to himself, he says, "I'll snap out of it . . . things will get better." But things don't get better. It's not a slump; it's real.

He doesn't seek help because, for many men—baby boomer's in particular—it would be too embarrassing to discuss.

Drowning in the cesspool of ignorance regarding impotency, and besieged with negative emotions, the man doesn't stand a chance. Shame, disgrace, guilt, and self-reproach reinforce what he has already accepted: "You can't get it up!" "You're not a man!" "It's your fault!" "It's over."

When I finished the tale of male hell, I asked Tyra if she had any questions. She swallowed, then blew out a long breath. As I watched, tears trickled down her mocha cheeks. She sucked in a long breath, trying to get herself together. Her chin quivered, and before she could utter one word, she threw her face into her opened hands and sobbed. Between her gasps for air, Tyra wailed over and over, "Oh Ty!"

Tyra's painful cry made me flash back to a picture I had blocked long ago. It was the picture of the day I cried that way. Now I felt the pain from that day as Tyra felt the pain of her today. Oh God, that horrible picture . . . the picture . . . of Simone's face as she . . . took her last earthly breath. Unethical as it may have been, I held Tyra's trembling hands and quietly shed some tears of my own; salty ones, left over from that day.

Tyra talked about the "triple A" goal that Tyrone had set for himself. It was the same triple A goal that would often affect Tyrone's attitude, affection, and his love in a negative fashion. It was the goal to achieve, achieve, and achieve more. She had known it would eventually cause a problem, but she didn't have any idea that it could manifest itself in this manner.

Because Tyra was completely into her man, she embraced every suggestion and recommendation I made to pull Tyrone out of male hell. As a result, she never harassed him about his sensitive condition. She didn't accuse him, as so many women do, of losing interest in her because he was seeing someone else. She diligently worked on getting him to relax whenever he was in her presence, and never pressured him into having intercourse.

Tyra encouraged him to talk about his problem, and made a point to build up the positives, while tearing down the negatives that Tyrone would mention during their conversations. I told Tyra that she could make herself a big part of the solution by dealing with his condition as if it were hers. As it should be with every couple, it was a problem for her as well.

She was extremely cooperative whenever I suggested certain things that might entice Tyrone's penis out of hibernation. Based on the information I had secured from Tyrone about the things that turned him on, I was able to pass that info on to Tyra. While it didn't work the first time she tried, when she reenacted the "maid in the kitchen" role-playing episode six months later, it was extremely successful. For the record, I didn't suggest or agree with the "Ty, you fuck like a bitch!" approach. It only reinforced what he was already feeling.

I needed to emphasis two more important points to Tyra regarding Tyrone's erection difficulty. Like many baby-boomer men, Tyrone blamed himself for not being able to sexually satisfy his wife. However, unlike many of the baby-boomer boys, Tyrone didn't blame Tyra for her inability to arouse him. It's common for a man to say, "If you'd lose some weight, I'd get turned on again." "If you acted like you wanted some, I'd ... "

At one of our last sessions, Tyra brought up a statement I had made several months before. I thought she had forgotten about it, especially because it was during a period when she was quite despondent over Tyrone's condition. Wrong! Her steel-trap mind retrieved the statement, and repeated it to me verbatim. It wasn't a statement; it was a time bomb. It was about to explode in my face, and Tyra was the timekeeper.

During our first session, Tyra asked about the glass ceiling issue, and whether I thought it contributed significantly to Tyrone's condition. When I tell you how I answered, please keep in mind that Tyra is an emotionally strong, intelligent, empowered, classy, all-that-and-a-bag-of-potato-chips, take-no-shit-sista "gurl". I made the statement to point out that American males of African descent aren't the only ones scratching diamond cutters across the glass ceiling with the hope of slipping through a self-made opening. In fact, the descendants, the pride and joy of America's founding fathers, have troubles just like Tyrone's. I was okay up to that point. Then, just as my daughter says I do, I went a couple of sentences too far.

Here's my statement. "There's very little difference between the way black men and white women are treated in corporate America or in the American work force in general. White males and minority females are prime choices for positions of power, and positions of high-visibility."

"What did you mean by that statement, Doc?" was her question as she placed her thumb on the detonator of the bomb.

Tyra watched, even gloated, as I squirmed in my chair, trying to figure a way out of this dilemma. I gave her the standard shrink response: "I see that our time is up. Perhaps we can revisit that question at one of our next sessions."

At the front door, she turned and said, "I know you're not originally from here, Doc, but in this country they used to tar-and-feather folks for intimating that a black man and Mr. Charlie's prize possession were like each other."

I acknowledged her response and said, "Now they just put them in a corner office that has a glass ceiling."

"Which 'them' are you referring to, Doc?"

"Should it matter Tyra? We're all children of the Almighty, are we not?"

Tyra didn't say a word. She got onto the elevator, shot me a keep-your-mouth-shut look, then smirked as the doors closed.

I told Tyra that Tyrone's erection problem was only temporary and would resolve itself if he focused on what was important to him.

From reading Tyra's journal, you could see that Tyrone put his priorities in proper order. It has been seven years since he opened his management consulting firm, and three years since he purchased a failing manufacturing company. For the last two years, Tyrone's company, ARYT (Tyra spelled backwards) Manufacturing, has been profitable.

The erection difficulty turned out to be a good thing for Tyrone and Tyra. It confirmed his belief that Tyra would stick with him through thick and thin, especially because she had stuck with him through soft and softer. He also became much more intimate, romantic, and easygoing—qualities that most every woman desires and appreciates in her man.

Would you be willing to stick with your man through the trials and tribulations of an erection difficulty? Could you look beyond the accusatory statements, the rejection, and the drop in his sex drive? How would you fight the demons that are sure to attack you—the ones that may make you doubt your sexual appeal, feel neglected and rejected, wonder if he's lost his desire for you because he's met someone else, and finally, the one that makes you ask, "What about *my* needs?"

If your partner's erection difficulties aren't physical, and both you and he are willing to work together, in time a resolution will come.

Many years after Simone made her transition, my daughter badgered me to start dating. She used my "do you not?" approach and backed me into the only answer I could give. "Papa, you do encourage your patients to start dating as soon as they've gone through the grieving cycle, do you not?" Don't you just hate it when your child uses your own words and gestures against you? I couldn't argue with her, it *was* time to get on with my life.

Simone would've wanted me to go on with my life. She often told me, "Jean-Paul, when I'm not around, don't become selfish. Many women would love to meet and be with a man like you. Promise me that you'll make another woman's dreams come true . . . the same way you have made mine materialize. Besides, I know you'll get lonely. You know you can't stand being alone, Jean-Paul."

I would always answer, "I promise," but only after crossing my fingers. I knew Simone would be the standard I would use when choosing the women I wanted to date. That, of course, eliminated most of them as soon as they said hello. None of them came close to my Simone. She was the *précis* of womanhood—complete in every way.

Just as Simone had predicted, I eventually longed for companionship. I missed having intimate conversations by the fireside. I longed to stroll down the seaboard hand-in-hand with a woman, the way I used to with my Simone. I longed to have a woman's supple breast against my chest—you know—someone to cuddle with on those chilly winter nights. Yes, it was time to go on with my life. Loneliness was starting to torment my soul.

After several disappointing dates, I finally met a woman who excited and fascinated me. We shared many of the same life experiences: she had lost her husband; she had one child; she only wanted companionship, not marriage; and she was also in the medical field. I was actually enjoying myself. Like Christian, I had blocked out how it felt to experience life's little pleasures.

Things were going great until that unmanageable date . . . that date in which, a casual glance loiters just a little longer than usual . . . where each blink converts your sight into X-ray vision, revealing things you couldn't see before . . . where your "out of control" fingers explore each other's body, and where those naughty fingertips trace the bulges that suddenly appear under certain areas of your clothing . . . that date where an innocent hello kiss ignites and you lick your lips, desperately trying to douse the flames . . . where the slightest amount of perspiration releases an undetectable scent into the air, a potent pheromone: a unique scent, capable of freeing all of the imprisoned carnal desires and behaviors within your soul—the same behavior induced by Maia the nymph, the frenzied behavior of nympholepsy. That's right—that unmanageable date is the one where you're . . .

Caught up in the heat of passion,
  my clothes a flyin', her hips a thrashin'.
Moaning and groaning from sheer delight,
  but my Eiffel Tower wouldn't light up that night.

I hadn't had a spontaneous erection during waking hours since Simone died. I would wake up in the morning with the usual erection every man has when his plumbing is functioning properly; that told me it wasn't a physical malfunction. I could masturbate while fantasizing about my wild days and nights with Simone and maintain a firm erection during the process, even though the outcome was a less-than-satisfying "numb come." A visually sexy woman could pass in front of my eyes, and my manhood wouldn't acknowledge her with a quick salute. I knew exactly what was going on.

I was able to get a semi-firm erection on *that* date with Sybil, because she had both an internal and external sexiness about her. She had qualities that were similar to those of my Simone. I knew my erection difficulty stemmed from the issue of being with a woman other than Simone. Although she had made her transition, I still felt as if I was cheating on her.

Sybil was very sympathetic and understanding about my erection difficulty, and was quite willing to accommodate me to make that date a pleasurable one for both of us. (For the males who are reading this book, you should know that most women will be sympathetic and extremely willing to help you, if you ask.)

I was able to satisfy Sybil on that date because of the techniques I acquired while I was dealing with my first episode of erection difficulty. That's right; this wasn't the first time I had problems getting it up. When I was much younger, I went through several months of penile flaccidity. It was quite a humbling experience.

In Blair and Marcy, I told you how I had finished studying for my board exams early and, as a result, I wanted to make love to Simone all day long. Oh, how I wanted to make love all day long, but I would've settled for a firm erection for just thirty seconds. The pressure from studying for the board and licensing exams, combined with the long hours of hospital duty, trying to juggle time for Simone, and the damned car falling apart, completely stressed me out. I was concentrating so hard on studying that I hadn't paid attention to the fact that my penis wouldn't respond to the sight of Simone's naked body.

I thought I was just tired. Wrong! Like Tyrone, I couldn't get it up. Unlike Tyrone, I didn't have the good sense to seek help. Remember, going to medical school or being the doctor doesn't guarantee immunity from human frailties.

I didn't let Simone know that I was having problems with maintaining an erection during intercourse, or that the frequency of having an erection of any degree was decreasing. In my eyes, I was becoming less of a man.

As a result, I hadn't and wouldn't initiate or insist on making love to Simone. When I couldn't get out of making love, I would avoid intercourse and satisfy Simone in other ways. After she climaxed I would immediately fall off into a fake sleep.

After two or three months of avoiding intercourse and not cuddling with her during the afterglow, Simone grew suspicious. One night, after my dog-and-pony sex show, Simone confronted me and asked if I were having an affair. Because I was about to graduate from medical school, she thought I wouldn't want or need her anymore. She thought I had lost interest in her because she wasn't young and pretty like the nurses at the hospital.

I died a thousand deaths when she told me what she was thinking. It hurt me to know those kinds of thoughts were heavy on her heart. I loved Simone so much. I would never leave her for any reason, especially for another woman. I would've died for her without hesitation. But, at the time, dying for her would have been a thousand times easier telling her that I couldn't get an erection. Hard as I tried, as much as I tried, I couldn't open up and tell her. Big mistake!

I was stuck and in pain. As you might have guessed, the additional hurt and stress I absorbed because of her accusations made my situation worse. I had become, in Tyrone's words, a real "limp dick mothafucka'." It was another several months after that night before I was able to get some semblance of an erection.

Simone confronted me again the next morning at the breakfast table. It was the breakfast table, study table, dinner table, and on occasion it used to be the love table when I could get an erection. Anyway, after she attacked me at breakfast, I donned my mask of anger to cover my fear, and verbally attacked her. "I'm working my goddamn ass off so we can . . . and this is your way of . . . your gratitude. Accusing me of fuckin' around on you . . . sleeping with someone else just because they're young and pretty! I love you and only you, Simone. This is your dick for life and no one else's!"

Then I started believing my own bullshit and took things too far by saying, "Fuck you, Simone, and the goddamned horse you road in on!"

It was hard to believe that Simone would think I'd want anyone else. Then again, it was easy for me to believe because I *knew* she was totally unaware of what was going on. Poor Simone, she didn't have a clue, because I kept her in the dark.

If you think about it, our situation wasn't too different from the circumstances of Dominique and her husband, Yves. Both of us were in medical school. Our wives were footing most of the bills, and we were around the "young-pretty-nurses-who-were-looking-for-doctors-to-become-their-husbands" women, every single day. Yet there was one distinct difference between Yves and myself, his plumbing was working and mine wasn't!

I would never leave Simone. I definitely wouldn't take her dreams, no, *our* dreams, and give them to another woman the way Yves did. I would have gladly taken Yves' ability to get an erection. He took having an erection for granted, the same way I and countless other men took it for granted.

When Simone and I were in bed that night, I apologized for being such an asshole at breakfast. I tried to convince her that she should not worry. The last thing I said to Simone was the worst communication blunder I have ever made in my life. I said, "If we aren't making love as often as you'd like, maybe you should find something extra to satisfy your hunger." Big mistake!

Do you remember when I cautioned Tyrone not to tell Tyra that if she cheated on him, he would understand? Do you remember how my heart sank through the floor when I found out that he had already said that to Tyra? Well, when I said to, "find something extra . . . " I did exactly what I told Tyrone not to do. I meant that Simone might consider getting another dildo, vibrator, or some new toy from *Le Sex Shoppe* to hold her until I finished the exams and rotations, or until I solved my erection difficulty.

My word "extra" was vague and Simone interpreted it to mean a man. And because she thought I wanted her to take a lover, it reinforced what she had been thinking all along; I was seeing someone else and no longer wanted her. That's what set the wheels in motion for Simone's *Liaison Dangereux*.

It wasn't until I discovered the affair that I realized the magnitude of influence I had over Simone. She thought I really wanted her to find someone else. With that thought in her head—combined with being confused, scared, and lonely—it wasn't difficult for her to become vulnerable and succumb to the charms of a low-life, opportunistic two-legged dog. I just wished it hadn't been my brother.

Are you questioning or being a little judgmental right now concerning Simone's reaction? Perhaps you're thinking that no one is *so* weak as to act on such a foolish statement. Maybe you're thinking that no one could be influenced so easily. But think about it for a moment. Simone was afraid that I would leave her for someone younger, more shapely, and more exciting than her. If you were thirteen years older than your lover, wouldn't you be a little concerned, considering the circumstances? Simone had what I would consider normal, healthy doubts, especially when you think about my behavior.

Be honest with yourself. Haven't you ever loved someone so much that you would do anything to please them—to keep them in your life? Stop for a moment and think about that special someone—the one person who penetrated the vault that contains your heart of hearts—the heart reserved for the special love that comes only once in a lifetime. Do you remember that person? If not, your blessing will come one day, sooner than you may think. It only takes knowing what you want, seeing what you need, and trusting your heart of hearts to choose wisely.

I had that special someone in my life. When she was alive, I did many things to keep Simone in my life. If she were still here with me physically, as she is spiritually, I would do whatever it would take to keep her. Simone was my soul mate, life mate, and lover for life. Don't take love for granted. If you have that special someone in your life, do your best to keep them—you won't regret it.

When I look back at the situation, I felt horrible that Simone had to go through such an ordeal. She had to deal with the thought that I was having an affair. She thought I didn't want or need her any-more. She painfully complied with what she thought were my wishes. She got involved with my abusive brother. Then, to add to her misery, she had to manage all of that chaos amid her pain, suf-fering, and fear that she was about to lose me forever. That was all because I couldn't tell her about my penis and the limp state it was in at the time. What a foolish boy was I!

Even though I am sure you would never do anything like Simone did, put yourself in her situation. How do you deal with being inti-mate with the man you love while having sex with someone you've designated as your safety net? Now mix in your lack of love for this safety net, and the problem that he happens to be the brother of the man you love. How would you feel?

Let's make things a little messier. The safety net begins to abuse you verbally, emotionally, physically, and sexually. Now add in hav-ing to go home to: hide the bruises; fight back the tears that really need to flow; hope that the man you love doesn't see your pain; hope that he doesn't want to make love tonight; and pray that he doesn't discover your dangerous liaison.

Sprinkle all of that with the fear of losing the man you love be-cause you think you're too old and no longer desirable. Pour on the regret from the "worthless, painful, and demeaning affair" with his brother. Dread the thought that you may have to spend the rest of your life with this asshole of a safety net. Remember, when your hubby leaves, this man will replace him. How do you feel right now about your imaginary situation? Are you feeling confused? Are you feeling any pain?

You're not through yet. Consider the above as Simone's private little female hell. On the days when I could get an erection of sorts, Simone had to deal with her desire to make love to me, but her unwillingness to do so. Huh? Let me clarify that statement. Luc's sexual acts were along the lines of rape. Unlike a random incident of rape, where the victim has time to heal physically and emotionally before resuming sex with her loved one, Simone had to recover overnight to hide her "other life." Each time they were together, which was three times a week, Luc would rape her. She didn't have enough time to breathe, and no time to heal herself.

Now let's put the final nails in the coffin. Simone made love to me, in spite of the emotional pain inflicted by Luc, because she was still trying to keep me in her life. She didn't want me to leave her because she knew we were like swans—mated for life. Don't forget about the physical pain from Luc's beatings, and the façade Simone had to maintain at work. What are you feeling now? Are you feeling her pain? How well would you have functioned in this situation?

I have one word to say about this situation: Communicate. Open your mouth and tell your partner what's going on inside of you. Be extremely specific when you talk. Make sure that you understand your partner's words, and that your words are understood by your partner. If only I had opened up and let Simone know what was going on, none of the above would have happened. Big mistake!

My erection difficulty started to resolve about the time I took my board exams a second time. It came to a final resolution when Simone forgave me for not telling her about my erection difficulty. There were rough times during the resolution, and periods when I didn't think we were going to make it. But in time, and with the grace of God, we made it.

Just for the record, I resent the psychological terms impotent and frigid. Probably the same man who labeled men impotent, a word too often used to blame females for a man's inability to achieve an erection, also labeled women "frigid" to excuse away a man's inability to assist a woman to reach orgasm.

As men and women, we need to realize we are more alike than

different and stop hiding our frailties. We also need to stop blaming each other for our problems—particularly our sexual problems. What we need to do is open up, fix our problems, and go on with our life's purpose—to love and be loved in return.

8

Mark and Adrian

The body sins once, and has done with its sin,
for action is a mode of purification.
Nothing remains then but the recollection of a pleasure,
or the luxury of a regret.
—OSCAR WILDE,
The Picture of Dorian Gray

Mark-June 25

How could I have been so weak? So stupid?

We've been married for seven years now and Charlotte has never given me a reason to treat her this way. I didn't mean to cheat on her. I've been faithful to her from the day we became engaged—until tonight. What made me do such a horrible thing? I know my love for her has faded over the years, but I should still respect her as my wife and as a woman. What am I going to do now?

Hell, it was just a one-night fling. Maybe she'll understand, and forgive my sinful indiscretion. Who am I trying to fool? I screwed up and there is no mistake about what I did—one night or a thousand, I broke my vow of fidelity. Thank God, we don't have any children; at least we don't have to worry about what will be best for them. When will I tell Charlotte? How should I tell her? How did I get my ass into this mess?

I've seen it in the movies and read about it, but I never thought it would happen to me. Yeah, other guys I've known have gotten lucky, but not me. When I look back, it was several months after we started dating before I was comfortable enough to touch Charlotte in an intimate way. Hell, we were together for two years before she lost her virginity. She thought it was my strict New England upbringing that made me such an understanding and wonderful gentleman. If she only knew what was really going on in my mind.

I've never been one to do anything risky. I certainly don't know what got into me tonight. Well, I do know what got into me, but I didn't think we would go all the way. I've always been attracted to Adrian, but I have also always managed to keep our relationship on a professional level. However tonight, after a few drinks, things got out of control, and we started playing like little kids. We rolled all over the gallery floor, and almost knocked over the replica of Michelangelo's *David*. I was having the time of my life. I haven't had that much fun horsing around since my high school locker room days.

Suddenly the arm lock around my waist turned into a passionate embrace. Damn! It's been a long time since I've felt my body tingle from a simple embrace. I figured a few innocent kisses and my curiosity would be satisfied. Boy was I wrong.

It felt awkward at first. It was even a little rough at the beginning, but I like rough sex, which is one of the problems I have with Charlotte—she doesn't like it rough. After I relaxed and loosened up, it was damn good. Shit, it was some of the best sex I've ever had in my life. This is only the second time I've felt this way. The first time was college style during my junior year. I remember it took a couple of weeks to get over that feeling.

I thought I had lost all interest in making love. I thought I was frigid, if it's possible for a man to be that way. It's such a relief to know I still have it in me. Maybe I just needed the right stimulation to get me and my libido to finally come out again. But I still cheated on Charlotte and that wasn't right.

Could it be the memory of that college encounter that caused me to cross the line that separates fidelity from infidelity? Maybe *déjà vu* drove me into the arms of this brown-eyed man-lover in skin-tight jeans. I'm not sure what it was, but just thinking about the thrill I got on the gallery floor tonight negates the guilt of my infidelity. Well, maybe for a moment, but damn it was good.

Could it be love? Was it just animal lust? I know it's too soon to know, but I've never felt this free. One thing I do know—I don't ever want to lose this feeling.

I have always suspected it was in me to do something like this, but I never thought it would happen after I got married. As a matter of fact, it happened exactly like the fantasy I've carried around in my head since college. The same fantasy that I use while having sex with Charlotte. Frankly, it's the only way I've managed to have an orgasm with her lately.

How can I tell her she's been replaced? I know how I'd feel if the tables were turned. It wouldn't be an easy thing for me to accept, being replaced by another person, especially one who is much older, and so much different from me. Charlotte is too sweet for me to have done such a thing to her. It's not her fault. Damnit! Why is my conscience screaming in my mind, "You knew better!"? It's those damned ancestors of mine. Those puritanical, pilgrim assholes who came over on the *Mayflower*. The same ones who screwed the Native Americans are screwing me with their righteous guilt trips—four hundred freakin' years later!

There is also the moral consequence I must face. As a Christian, I will surely go to hell for this act: But it was worth every stroke of pleasure. The Moral Majority would have a scarlet "A" burned on my forehead if they knew what I have done. The *Massachusetts Monitor* would get great joy from unmasking Mark Darling, Object d' Art Gallery owner, as "The Freaky Adulterer."

That paper has been on my back ever since I brought Mapplethorpe's erotic photo exhibitions to town. "Artistic or not, abashed nudity will not be tolerated in this town!" That's the latest quote from Samuel Williamson. I wonder what the town would say if they knew about the *ménage á trois*, he had with his wife and their Swedish *au pair*. It's amazing how easily Ola let the cat out of the bag about their little triangle. Do you think it's because I'm the only one who speaks a little Norwegian in our town—*yä*?

Enough of asshole Sam. He's not worthy of a thought, considering the problems I've created tonight. What am I going to do? Should I tell Charlotte and break her heart? Should I keep it to myself and let this skeleton roam forever in my closet? After all, Adrian lives in New York, and comes here only once a month to pitch new exhibits. Charlotte is used to me being wined and dined by the art reps, and it isn't unusual for me to hang out until two a.m. on those nights. The likelihood of anyone finding out would be very slim. But can I live with a lie, knowing I have broken and probably will continue to break my vow of fidelity?

But what about me? Don't I deserve to be happy? Don't I deserve to feel good too?

I remember we talked for hours before things got out of control. We talked about my outlook on life, my marital problems, my business and lifestyle. We talked about the danger involved in living out one's fantasy. When we talked, everything made perfect sense. Before I knew it, we were bareback and a-bucking like wild stallions. During those moments of pleasure tonight, everything made sense, sounded good, and felt fantastic. But now, three hours later, I'm starting to doubt myself, questioning whether it was right. Doubting my feelings about this experience. Doubting my strength to control the hunger within me. The same hunger that at this very moment is begging to come out again.

I'm so selfish. What about Adrian? I haven't given one thought to the problems I might have caused as a result of wanting to live out my fantasy. How will Adrian handle all of this? Damn! Have I screwed up Adrian's life as well? What about Adrian's significant other, Todd? What about him? Will he bail out on Adrian? What have I done?

I've screwed things up for everyone, all for my Queen of Sheba. Just for a quick piece of ass.

Adrian-June 27

Finally!

I have wanted Mark ever since I set eyes on him last year. He finally gave in and let me have my way with him. My sympathetic line never fails. I love it when a man thinks I really care about the sad situation that exists in his home. How he's so misunderstood, unappreciated, and lonely. The best part is when I tilt my head slightly to the side, give him that wide teary-eyed look, and tell him how I wish I could take away his pain. Once I get inside a sensitive or weak man's mind and paint the right pictures, he's all mine.

It's getting too easy. Maybe I should raise my level of difficulty and fuck some high officials of the God Squad—the Moral Majority gold-card-carrying male members. I bet that would screw up their right-wing constitutions! Maybe then they would have some compassion for people like me, after being infected by my HIV-positive ass. That certainly would loosen up their tight assholes! Perhaps then they would ease up on us so-called hell-bent degenerates.

I feel so refreshed after having Mark I'm gonna pop a Crissy and hang out all night at the Vinyl Club, especially because I heard the Sneaker Pimps are playing this weekend. I need to celebrate adding his charm to my bracelet. Imagine that, tight-ass Mark finally gave it up! He even screamed my name out loud like all the other men-bitches I have poked in the past.

Goddamn! There's nothing that compares with the feeling of a straight man's cherry asshole, tightly wrapped around my rock-hard cock!

Ouch!

I have a hard time dealing with my internist's index finger when I get my yearly prostate gland checkup.

What did Mark mean when he wrote, "We've been married for seven years now and Charlotte has never given me a reason to treat her this way." I wonder, what could a spouse or significant other do that would make their partner break their vow of fidelity? If there could possibly be a reason, does that mean you should alter your values and morals to get back, get even, or show them? Would you speak up and voice your displeasure, as in the immortal words of my most colorful patient, Tyrone, "I ain't havin' that!"

By now you should know there is an unhealed childhood wound within Mark's being, which made him cheat on Charlotte. You should've also recognized that Mark thought, unconsciously, this brown-eyed man-lover in tight blue jeans had the healing ointment for his wound. As you also probably gathered, Adrian didn't have the ointment to soothe Mark's festering wound and he didn't give a rat's ass about anyone's injury—including his own seething childhood laceration.

I would like you to fully consider a question as we explore the journal entries of Mark and Adrian, and the alternative lifestyle they both embraced. Is Mark's act of infidelity the biggest problem? Or is committing the infidelity with another man even more of a problem? Certainly, in most women's minds it would be extremely difficult, if not impossible, to excuse away or forgive her husband's indiscretion when the other "woman" is in fact a man.

What would be your first reaction if you discovered your spouse was involved in an affair with a person of the same gender? What would you think? Would you sit down and talk it out? Would you say, "To hell with it" and walk away? If the two of you had children, how would you explain to them that Daddy was leaving them for another man? What would be your biggest concern after the initial shock wore off?

In Charlotte's case, as I suspect is the case with most women, the biggest concern would be: Does he have AIDS? Let me make something perfectly clear before every activist group jumps down my throat. AIDS is an immunological disorder caused by the HIV virus, and is spread through risky behavior. Sharing a drug needle or having unprotected sex where blood, seminal or vaginal fluid is exchanged between an HIV-infected individual and his/her partner is the most common mode of contracting the virus that causes AIDS. It is *not* a disorder exclusive to any one group's sexual orientation. AIDS has been around as long as any other human disease and, as with any epidemic, it's just a matter of time before a cure is discovered, I pray.

The real problem of Mark's infidelity wasn't that he cheated with another man, but that he cheated with someone who was HIV-positive. Mark put Charlotte at risk of being infected by his risky behavior of having unprotected sex with Adrian.

Charlotte, in my opinion, doesn't really have as big a problem to face as Mark does. Although she is the victim in this situation, Charlotte's femininity is not in question with this type of infidelity. Most women and men, when they discover that their spouse or significant other is involved with someone outside of the relationship, immediately attack themselves in particular as not being desirable anymore.

When Darren discovered Claudia's affair, the first thing he did was doubt himself: "I wondered if he was better looking than me. If he dressed better, smelled better, hell, if he tasted better than me. Yes, I even wondered if he was better endowed than me." In Charlotte's case, there was absolutely no way for her to compete with Adrian. He wasn't a female with whom she could compare herself. There was no way in which she could try to "improve" herself as a woman to get her man back.

A small group of women would be totally devastated, thinking their man turned to a male because she was not only an undesirable woman, but also so repulsive that she made her man turn to men. I know this sounds ridiculous, but some individual's self-esteem and self-worth are one toss away from the garbage dump.

Was Charlotte hurt? Of course she was deeply hurt, and for many good reasons. Charlotte was hurt because she had no idea the man she loved had a secret life. Not just a secret one, but one that was totally opposite of the value systems that attracted them to each other in the first place. When I spoke to her on the phone regarding the situation, her bottom-line reaction was, "He deceived me . . . I trusted him . . . I'm horrified, I could have AIDS . . . ."

The first question I asked Mark after reading his journal entry was, "Mark, aren't you the least bit concerned that, to Charlotte, your homosexuality is just as big an issue as your infidelity?"

Mark immediately responded with, "I'm bisexual, not gay!"

"Is there a problem with your being gay, Mark?" With the look a *pri-*

madona gives a conductor for implying that she didn't hit her note, Mark cooed flippantly, "Well ... no, there isn't a problem with being gay, but I'm bisexual."

"How do you know that, Mark?"

"What makes you think I'm not?"

"I didn't say you were, Mark, I only asked a question."

That statement was a good one on which to end that session. I wanted Mark to mull my questions around in his dressing room closet for our next meeting.

I believe Mark was in complete denial of his homosexuality. I also believe Mark was possibly using his claim of bisexuality as a transitional phase. He wasn't ready to come out completely, to stand tall and proud to be gay. Mark was a closet case, a homosexual who denies he's gay to keep it a secret from the world and, more often than not, himself.

I think the contents of his closet were a little too much for Mark to handle all at once, because of his childhood wounds. Although he was in denial of his latent tendencies, a part of him rebelled against being *in*. Mark outwardly protested his displeasure of having to hide in the closet by dressing and behaving in an androgynous manner. This was a safe way for Mark to be true to his inner self, if that makes any sense to you. For those of you who need a textbook explanation, Mark's sexual behavior (what he did) was different from his sexual identity (what he labeled himself as being).

When Mark wrote, "I like rough sex ... " I began to wonder if perhaps something in his background might have some bearing on his tendencies. Perhaps something he had blocked or pushed into the darkest corner of his closet.

The opportunity to explore Mark's old baggage presented itself during one of our sessions, when Mark brought up age regression and spiritual cleansing. He was a devout New Ager and was mesmerized when I talked about the karmic consequences of a person's previous existence. To be effective when treating my patients, I've discovered that it is absolutely necessary to talk in terms of their interest and beliefs. When you're relating to *anyone*, it is essential to talk in terms of his or her interest and beliefs. I did not say to mimic them, rather just put yourself in that person's shoes during your conversation. By doing this, you learn a great deal more about the individual and they appreciate you for being genuinely interested in them. You don't have to accept their point of view or beliefs, but it is important for you to appreciate, respect, and understand their perspective.

I asked Mark if anyone had used hypnosis to age-regress him, or if he had done it himself through meditation. After a brief explanation about the procedure, Mark consented to and was quite excited about, exploring his past lives. With his strong new-age beliefs and willingness to give it a try, it wasn't difficult to place Mark in a light trance where he could take a stroll down memory lane.

Mark was unable to regress beyond this life into a previous one, because of an old duffel bag he stumbled over at the corner of Childhood Boulevard and Forbidden Avenue. I asked him to tell me about the bag. He said it belonged to his mother's younger brother who stayed at their house whenever he was on shore leave.

"How old were you when you first saw the duffel bag?"

Mark thought he was between seven and ten years old when he first noticed his uncle's bag.

"Mark, do you feel comfortable enough to open it up? Is it a safe thing to explore or should you just throw it away?"

After a few moments he responded with, "No . . . it's not safe . . . but . . . I can't throw it away because . . . ."

"Because of what, Mark?" He started trembling and talked as if he were a child, " . . . 'cause he told me not . . . ." Unsure of what he was about to discover, but more important, unsure of whether he could handle the discovery, I used our safe word to snap Mark out of trance. Over the next several sessions, we visited the duffel bag, rolled it over, picked it up, and shook it before Mark untied the sailor's knot that has kept it closed all of these years.

The bag contained the memory of the horrid infliction of his childhood wound. A wound inflicted not by his parents, but by his uncle, who molested him. Before we could deal with his current issues regarding Charlotte and Adrian, I had to place Mark on a heavy dose of tranquilizers until he was able to destroy the duffel bag and store the traumatic memory in a secure place.

Please don't read more into what may have influenced Mark's lifestyle and assume this is how people become homosexuals. Yes, some men's and women's sexual orientation is influenced because of a childhood wound similar to Mark's. Others consciously decide to become same-sex oriented, and yet another group is theorized to be biologically predetermined through an insufficient or excessive amount of male or female hormones. I don't think it really matters what determines a person's sexual orientation; what matters is that the person is okay with who they are—not who others think they should be.

We were eventually able to address the issues Mark would have to deal with. Mark also had to deal with a host of problems as an individual. The biggest one was the realization that he was a homosexual and the ramifications associated with that lifestyle in this country—not his infidelity to Charlotte

I asked, "Are you prepared to make that lifestyle change? Are you ready to deal with the discrimination and social stigmatization associated with being a homosexual? If you claim to be bisexual, are you aware that not only will you be looked down upon by the homophobic heterosexual communities, but there's also a good chance you won't be readily accepted by some of the people in the lesbian and gay communities because you're straddling the sexual preference fence?"

It was most unfortunate, but after Mark came out, he was besieged with one misfortune after another.

What can I say about Adrian? Unbelievably, Adrian loved coming in for what he called his "talk show therapy." As you might suspect, Adrian was in a great deal of emotional pain for a number of reasons; the toughest one was accepting the fact that *he* was responsible for being HIV-positive. Our first session together was pretty much the way you might expect it to be, considering Adrian's attitude. At first, Adrian, literally tried to charm the pants off of me. Each time he poured on the charm or tried to steer me away from his core issue, I would ask the same question, "Adrian, why are you so pissed off with the world?"

I must admit that I got quite an education from Adrian. He translated many of the gay terms that Mark surprisingly used when writing in his journal and during our sessions. Adrian was extremely helpful in translating Mark's street jargon into plain English for me. I just thought it was odd that Mark, who was supposedly in denial of his homosexuality, was so well versed in the street slang of the gay world. Maybe he wasn't in as much denial as I thought.

I was surprised at how openly Mark's journal entries expressed his sexual orientation. If you recall, at the beginning of this book I included the cliché, "The truth has many wings" as a reminder that things are not always as they appear at times. If I had had the street slang terminology available before reading Mark's journal, I would have known what was going on from the beginning. Not until our third session did I know Mark was gay; before that, I just thought he was a male who was very effeminate. However, after reading his journal entries again with an enlightened eye, I saw how he explicitly detailed his alternative lifestyle fantasy.

After you read the next section, go back and read Mark's journal entry again, and see how "out of the closet" he was with the words he used. His journal entries were about being *out*. By the way, reading a person's personality considers their body language, the tonality of their voice, and their choice of words. Next time you talk to a lover, friend, or fellow worker, listen to (don't just hear) the words they use and the emphasis they place on certain ones—you'll be amazed at what they tell you about themselves.

Mark introduced us to his sexual orientation when he referred to having *college style* sex during his third year at college. He was referring to a sexual position in which a male could simulate sex with his partner without actually penetrating him anally. He would stroke his penis between the closed thighs of another male in close approximation to his partner's genitalia. In the fifties, it was a way of introducing a heterosexual male to the homosexual experience. During the eighties, it was reintroduced as a form of safe sex within the more daring faction of the gay community, to reduce the risk of contracting HIV.

Heterosexuals may recall college style as the "dry hump." In this instance, the dry hump wasn't a way to introduce a young lady to the sexual experience, it was a way to maintain her virginity, and it was *the* foolproof method of preventing an unwanted pregnancy.

The next reference Mark made in his journal is a widely recognized expression. He masterfully integrated it into the sentence in which he wrote, " . . . get me and my libido to finally *come out* again." As you know, this term is used to publicly declare oneself a homosexual.

Regarding Mark's reference to the "brown-eyed *man-lover* in skin-tight jeans," Adrian explained that, though the word man-lover generally refers to a young male who is sexually attracted to older men, it could also refer to gay men in general.

Mark mentioned that he had been fantasizing about having rough sex [with a man] while making love to Charlotte—not unlike heterosexuals who fantasize about the person of their dreams as they go through the motions of having sex with their spouses or significant others.

When he talked about his ancestors, " . . . puritanical *pilgrim* assholes . . . " the word *pilgrim*, coined in the sixties, refers to a male heterosexual who knowingly dresses in such a way that makes him sexually attractive to male homosexuals.

Mark's next clue revealed itself in the photo exhibits he chose to display in his gallery. He loved Robert Mapplethorpe's work. Mapplethorpe's photographs largely consisted of homosexual males performing sexual acts or wearing sadomasochistic paraphernalia. Much of Mark's gallery contained paintings, sculptures, and prints of erotic androgynous individuals.

Mark wrote in his journal about his uncertainty about telling Charlotte and being true to his sexuality, or as he put it, "let this skeleton roam forever *in* my *closet?*"

When he wrote, " . . . I was *bareback* . . . " he was referring to having anal intercourse without using a condom. He finished that same sentence with, " . . . and Adrian was *a-bucking* like . . . " *A-bucking* refers to a missionary sexual position that allows the homosexual partners to kiss, while providing a greater sense of intimacy as they engage in intercourse. When they engaged in intercourse, Adrian was the *topper*, the one who would penetrate.

When he wrote, " . . . Todd *bailing out* on Adrian?" he was referring to whether Adrian's lover was going to leave because of the tryst he enjoyed with Mark. Unfortunately, Adrian was a *bona fide* slut and Todd was just another *charm* that he added to his bracelet of conquests, the week before he deflowered Mark.

Last, Mark referred to Adrian's race when he wrote " . . . my *Queen of Sheba.*" Adrian was a *snow queen*, a derogatory term use to label black male homosexuals who date only white men.

I would like to introduce one more term that will later bear heavily in this chapter. The term is *facultative homosexual*. A heterosexual man in prison may become so desirous of sex that he may allow his homosexual tendencies to surface and even act upon them. He may do so by seeking physical relations with other men in the prison. He will return to a heterosexual life when he is freed, without ever having a desire to act on his latent tendencies again. Such a man is a facultative homosexual.

As with any secret society of the past or present, whether they are homosexuals, the persecuted Christians of Roman times, fraternities, sororities, Freemasons, or the Rosicrucian's, there are always covert words used to openly acknowledge one another in public without the fear of being exposed.

This couple had a most unfortunate ending, as you might expect considering the circumstances. Charlotte moved out. Adrian died of Kaposi's sarcoma, an AIDS-related skin cancer characterized by bluish-red nodules on the skin. As of this writing, Mark is in a hospice, waiting to die. He has contracted a pneumonia caused by Pneumocystis carinii, which, at this time, is the most common cause of death of people who have AIDS.

Mark didn't have any blood relatives living in the area to care for him. Everyone in the puritanical little town turned their backs on him except Ola, the *au pair* from Sweden. Old Sam did write a less than desirable article about Mark's affair, and Ola appeared on a local talk show the following week confessing her sin of the *ménage à trois* with Sammy and Mary. Ola hoped to invalidate Samuel's article about Mark with her confession. You could say it was Ola's poetic justice.

The one person who would have cared for Mark divorced him as soon as he *came out* and confessed his love for Adrian. She relocated on the West Coast in an attempt to escape the humiliation and shame she believed Mark brought on their marriage.

I want to make a final comment about Adrian and his sick mission in life. In each of the gay-slang dictionaries I read to better understand Mark and Adrian's journal entries; I found one definition that was intensely disheartening. It wasn't a derogatory term about gays; it was a humanistically repulsive definition that could be universally applied to any sexual group. It is a term that involves a person who blames the world for something they brought on themselves. These individuals want the world to pay because we did not protect them from themselves. That term is *AIDS terrorist*.

Adrian was an *AIDS terrorist*—a HIV positive person who purposely engages in unprotected sex with others to create the same horror, fear, and terror that they themselves harbor. You can replace the word AIDS with the name of any sexually transmitted disease, because the reason for the terrorism is the same—sick and senseless revenge. Be mindful. Be careful.

Sadly, the love that Mark had for Adrian, as well as the hate he harbored after discovering he had been purposely infected with HIV by his former lover, took me back to the day that we lost my brother Luc.

I had always loved Luc, but then a horrible incident had snuffed out any trace of love I had for him. I hadn't spoken to or heard from Luc since that dreadful day. Despite my Mother's desire to see our family whole again, she has always respected my wishes and never invited me over while Luc was in the house. Fortunately, she didn't have to juggle our comings and goings for long. Luc moved out of the house a couple of months after that day, then left the country a couple of years later. Mother would hear from him every so often, and that saddened her even more.

The fact that I never forgave him for his brutal treatment of Simone tore at our mother's heart. I tried and tried *hard*, but I knew my heart would never soften enough to let him back in, not even for my mother. It would have to come from a source greater than two of us.

One afternoon, Mother called and insisted that I get over to the house as soon as possible.

"Are you sick?" immediately sprang from my mouth, startling the butterflies in my stomach from their midday nap.

"No, Jean-Paul. Just get here. Bring Simone and Amileé." With that she hung up the phone, leaving me in a state of panic.

"Simone! Amileé! Come home quick!" were the words I shouted as I hustled across the deck toward the bedroom door. Simone had gone next door to get Amileé from our neighbor's backyard.

"What's wrong, Jean-Paul? Is everything okay?"

"I don't know, Mone. Mom just called and said to get over there now, and told me to bring you and Amileé."

During the short drive, I racked my brain trying to figure out what was happening. Mom was in excellent health. I knew because I'd read the results of her physical two weeks ago, just before we left for holiday. What? What was going on? Inside my head, I slammed the brakes on, as hard as I could, to stop the questions so I could gather all the things that I knew were concrete.

After a few seconds of sorting, it hit me. It was the *way* she asked me. Like every mother in the world, Mom had a sixth sense that kicked in whenever one of us was sick or in trouble. That was the voice I heard—one I haven't heard since. I remember her calling out in that same voice as I bolted up the stairs toward Luc's room. "No, Jean-Paul!" It was as if she knew instantly that I wanted to kill him.

That was the voice I had heard just moments ago. Something was wrong with Luc—her favored son.

What if I was right? What if Luc is the reason for her call? How will I react? Will I . . . what about Simone? Can she handle it? It's taken so many years for her to recover from the abuse she suffered at his hands. Even now, if the name Luc is mentioned on television or the radio, she recoils and sheepishly glances at me to see if I react. Can she deal with . . . everything?

The butterflies were fluttering helter-skelter in my stomach now.

I reached for the doorknob only to find it moving away from my hand. "Thank you for coming so quickly, Jean-Paul."

"What's wrong? Is it Luc . . . I mean Dad?"

Simone's eyes nearly popped out of their sockets when she heard me mention Luc's name. How could I have been so insensitive as to mention his name when I knew she was right behind me?

"Come, let's go into the kitchen . . . you too, Amileé." As I

mentioned earlier, we never excluded Amileé from any of our conversations unless they were too adult in nature.

Everyone took a seat except me. I couldn't sit. The butterflies
wouldn't let me; they suspended me in mid-air.

"I don't know how to tell you."

"Tell us what mother?"

"I don't know how to tell you . . . your brother is near death."

I was right. It was her favored son; he was the reason we were
here. I shot a quick glance at Simone to see her reaction as I put my
arm around Amileé to comfort her. Simone was still in shock from
the statement I made at the door about Luc. There was a distant
look in her eyes—the same spaced-out look she wore in the bathroom the day she had the nervous breakdown.

"Sweetheart, you'll feel better if you sit in Mommy's lap." I
picked Amileé up and put her in Simone's lap, hoping they could
keep each other on solid ground.

"What do you mean Luc's near death, Mom? What's wrong with
him?"

Mother had always kept me well informed about Luc and the
things he was doing, even though I didn't care. I would listen only
because I knew it made her feel better. She used to do the same thing
during his armed service tour and while he was in prison camp, but
things were different between us then, we were much closer. My
mother also did it thinking that one day I would soften and welcome
my brother back into my heart. She was hoping I would forgive and
forget his transgression of beating, cursing, threatening, and sodomizing my wife.

Hell no. Hell, fuck no! Even then, years later, I wanted that low-
life mothafucka' to burn in hell.

Mother sent me a passage through the mail one day, hoping it
would help me remove the hatred I had in my heart for Luc. It read:
"If thy brother trespass against thee, rebuke him; and if he repent,
forgive him. And if he trespass against thee seven times in a day, and
seven times in a day turn again to thee, saying, I repent; thou shalt
forgive him." Luke 17:3–4.

The only problem with the passage was—Luc never said he was sorry.

I wasn't an enlightened one who could forgive the individual and merely remember the crime. I was a stubborn buffoon who could neither forgive nor forget Luc for his crime against the woman I loved and cherished more than life itself.

"He hasn't been well in the last year, and now . . . he's hit rock bottom."

The butterflies in my stomach froze in midair and I dropped like lead into the chair next to my mother.

"Mother, are you alright?" She answered me with gigantic teardrops, and then bowed her head.

"It'll be okay, Mom. We'll get through this."

The word I left out of that statement was . . . somehow. The real question was: How *are* we going to get through it?

I grabbed the tissue box from the counter and offered some to everyone. My mother and Amileé took several sheets and started to wipe the liquid pain from their faces. Simone refused to take the tissue. Well, she didn't refuse, she just didn't respond. She still had that spaced-out look, even though her tears were now soaking the front of her blouse . . . just as they had soaked my nightshirt that morning in the bathroom. What's going through her head? *What can I say to snap her out of this dazed state? I need to get myself together. I need more time to think, but I can't ignore my baby, mother, and wife— not now. What would Father do if he were here? What would he say? Come on, Papa talk to me! Tell me what to say.*

Mother sniffed and continued, "Luc won't live to see another day . . . I know he won't. My son is going to die today."

If it had been any one of my patients saying something like this, I would have countered with one of a hundred questions . . . . *What makes you think that he won't make it? What if he does make it? Is that the only possible outcome? Is it possible he could pull through? You know miracles happen everyday, do you not?* Oh yes, I have all the right questions, but in all the years I have been with my mother, her sixth sense has never been wrong. Luc was going to die today— despite my questions.

The frozen butterflies slowly began to thaw—making me anxious once again.

"Luc wants to see Amileé and if Simone is willing, he wants to see her too. Jean-Paul, he knows you won't come, but he asked me to tell you . . . "

My brain started racing. On *that* day, I would have gladly taken a front row seat to watch him die. I would have taken great pride in making his last minutes on Earth the most miserable of his life, but now . . . "Jean-Paul, did you hear me?"

"No, Mother, I was thinking about something. What did you say?"

"Luc wants to see Amileé and Simone, but he knows you won't come, so he asked me . . . "

I interrupted her with, "Oh yeah, I heard that part, but you don't have to tell me what he said . . . I'll go, I'll see him. He can tell me himself."

My mother reacted as if she had seen a ghost. Amileé's face lit up as if it were Christmas Day and Simone snapped out of her self-imposed trance when I told Mother I would see Luc.

"Jean-Paul, are you sure you want to do that?" were the first words Simone spoke since we came through the front door an hour ago.

"I have to" came out so easily it frightened me.

"If you're willing to go . . . then . . . I'll go too." The shocked look on my mother's face instantly changed to one of joy. It wasn't hard to figure out why she was joyous—her family would be whole again.

Completely thawed, the butterflies resumed flying helter-skelter within my stomach—raising my anxiety level to an all-time high.

With tears streaming down her face again, Mother kissed my cheek and whispered, "You've made me so happy, Jean-Paul!"

I made my mother happy, and confused the hell out of myself. *What was this sudden change of heart? Did I intuitively know it would make Mother and Amileé happy if I agreed to see Luc? Was I trying to redeem myself in the eyes of the Lord for my attempted fratricide? Was it God's will? What in the hell is going on? Did the*

Devil make me do it? Have I put Simone in harm's way again with Luc? These were questions I couldn't answer, but at least my mother was happy.

"Give me a few minutes to get ready and then you can go see him."

As she scurried up the stairs, I tried to steady my nerves. Simone was re-braiding Amileé's hair, probably in an attempt to calm her nerves. I had to pull myself together. *What if I lose it and reenact that ugly scene? No, Amileé will be there and that will keep me civil—I hope.* With the veterans' hospital being a good hour's drive away, I would have that time to make up my spiel for Luc.

The butterflies went into a flying frenzy. Uncontrollably, I started trembling.

Coming down the stairs, Mother said, "Okay, let's go!"

"Let me get the car keys, Mother."

"Car keys? Why do you need your car keys Jean-Paul?"

"I'm not going to let you drive all the way to that hospital. Besides, you told me you've had some trouble with your car."

"Jean-Paul, Luc is upstairs."

One by one, the butterflies plummeted, crashing into the pit of my stomach like kamikaze pilots—determined to destroy me.

"What do you mean he's upstairs? What's he doing upstairs? I thought you said he was near death. If he is, why is he upstairs?"

It was as if the walls had closed completely around me. I was panting. My heart was racing in high gear. I thought I was having a heart attack.

"Calm down, Jean-Paul. Luc wanted to die at home."

"But . . . " Mother turned her head, locked her parental blue eyes on me and said, "Stop it right now, you're upsetting Amileé, Simone, *and* me!"

I felt a tug on my belt, and a little voice said, "It's okay papa. Grandmother is right there; *she* won't let anything hurt us."

Then Amileé grabbed mother's hand. A trembling arm gently wrapped itself around my waist and this time a bigger voice said, "It's okay Jean-Paul. I'm nervous too, and I'm scared, but we must do this."

Holding her hand that was around my waist, I took a deep breath, looked at Simone, smiled, and started upstairs.

I felt the last suicidal butterfly crash into my stomach's floor. My gut was calm—for the moment.

The last time I came to see Luc, I flew up this staircase. I was so agile. I adjusted my stride to the unevenness of each wooden step like a panther as it chases its prey through the rough underbrush of the jungle. One thought and nothing more was on my mind then— kill Luc. This time I crawled up the stairs at the pace of a slug, clumsily missing the edges of the wooden steps, tripping over my feet like a drunken sailor. One hundred questions jockeyed back and forth in my mind, each demanding to be answered.

The second wave of kamikaze butterflies materialized and flew down my esophagus at supersonic speeds, in a final effort to stop what was to be my last rendezvous with Luc. I was horrified.

As we neared Luc's room, Mother turned, gazed at me, and in a muted voice said, "He doesn't look like himself. He fades in and out of consciousness, and sometimes he talks out of his head. Try to be strong for him and yourselves."

Amileé clutched her grandmother's arm. Simone lowered her head and looked at the floor. Mother opened the door to Luc's dimly lit room.

I defended my stomach against the suicide squadron of butterflies, but they were too many, like the *Titanic*—I was going down.

"Where's Uncle Luc?" Amileé didn't recognize him. Simone never raised her head. I was shocked. He couldn't have weighed more than ninety pounds. His piercing blue eyes were set back so far they looked as if they were in a cave. He was very pale and his skin had a dark yellow-green hue. At the time, I had only seen photographs of the type of skin cancer that covered Luc's body. His skin had dozens of blue-red, raised patches. These were mainly on his lower body, but some were also on his chest, arms, and face. It's ironic, but they were about the same size and color as the bruises on Simone's body after he had beaten her.

Mother propped him up on several pillows to ease his labored and noisy breathing. She rubbed his back for several minutes to ease the pain. There was an IV drip on both sides of the bed. One bag contained morphine, the painkiller named after the Greek god of dreams; the other appeared to be an antibiotic. He didn't say anything when we first entered; he just stared at Amileé and smiled that crooked grin of his. Luc always had a way with children and they loved being around him. Amileé was no exception. She had enjoyed the times they played together when she was a toddler.

In a raspy voice, Luc called to Amileé, "How's the youngest Lefervre doing today, eh, my little princess?"

"I'm okay Uncle Luc. You don't look like you used to." He smiled. They chatted for several minutes while Mother adjusted his pillows and continued to rub his back. Mother softly hummed *Frère Jacques* as she massaged him. The sound of her beautiful voice took me back to my childhood days when she would wake me by rubbing my back and singing that very same song. My heart smiled, but only for a moment.

Amileé walked back, grabbed my hand, and pulled me over next to Luc. "Papa, say hi to Uncle Luc! He doesn't feel good. Can you make him feel better?"

I looked at him but he never took his eyes off Amileé. When I spoke, he didn't respond. I was trying, but as usual, he wasn't cooperating. Why did he tell Mother he wanted to see me? Maybe he didn't say it. Was mother up to her old tricks again?

Simone stayed in the back of the room near the door. I don't know if she didn't want to be bothered with Luc, or if she wanted to stay by the door to make a quick escape. Every so often Simone would tell me a little about how she had to sneak away from Luc whenever he started to drink. She told me that most of her beatings came while he was drunk. Even in his decrepit state, the emotional scar of his abusiveness toward her still makes Simone cower in fear. How can I possibly forgive him for the permanent damage to my Simone?

"Uncle Luc, I wish I could stay with you and make you feel better."

"Me . . . too . . . princess."

"Daddy says that little daughters make their daddies stay young.

I'm sorry you don't have a daughter to keep you young, Uncle Luc. Maybe you wouldn't be sick, if you had a . . . "

"Amileé, come here!"

Amileé skipped across the hardwood floor into the shadows where her mother stood. Moments later, in one of her happiest and loudest voices, Amileé cried out, "Papa!"

Luc turned his head toward her voice. That was the most he had moved since we had been there.

"Shhh, not so loud, sweetheart. What is it?"

"It's nothing, Jean-Paul." Simone jerked Amileé by the hand and took her into the hallway.

Luc soon fell off to sleep after Mom increased the drip rate of the morphine, to kill his pain. Mother quietly said, "He'll sleep for an hour or so. Let's go downstairs."

When we got into the kitchen Amileé asked if she could have some crêpes.

"Of course you can, darling. Will you help me?" My mother was like putty in Amileé's hands. Everyone was like putty in Amileé's hands. She was such a lovable little girl. She was the daughter I had always dreamed of having one day.

Later, I asked Simone why Amileé screamed out my name in such great joy. She told me it was nothing, just the childish notion that she keeps you young, and maybe she could keep Luc young if she . . . .

"Jean-Paul, your father is on the phone, he wants to talk to you."

"Let me talk to Dad and you can finish telling me about Amileé." I planted a kiss on the tip of Simone's nose and took the phone in the study.

After a brief conversation, I hung up and headed back to the kitchen. Just as I sat down, I heard Mom scream, "Jean-Paul! Jean-Paul!"

I bolted up the stairs the same way I did that day when I was looking for Luc. Little did I know that, this time, things would end the way I had planned for them to end on *that* day.

Mother was kneeling next to Luc's bed, sobbing, "No, please, not now. Not now!" Luc was gasping for air and holding his stomach as if he were in great pain. He was throwing up what looked like coffee grounds. I knew it was old blood. I turned him on his side so he would not breathe the sputum into his lungs. By that time, Simone and Amileé were at the door.

"Simone, take Amileé downstairs!"

"No, Papa I can make him feel better if I pretend to be . . . " I didn't hear the rest of her sentence because at that same moment, Luc started hemorrhaging from his nose and mouth.

I tried hard to stabilize him. He fought hard, considering his weakened condition, but he didn't make it. Mom was right—he didn't make it through the night.

Dad arrived home the next morning about nine. We talked for a moment, and then he took Mom to a friend's house. She needed to get away. Hell, *I* needed to get away. Those last moments with Luc reminded me why I went into mental health and not into any specialty that would require me to watch someone die or tell a family that one of their loved ones had passed away.

Moments before he died, Luc looked in my eyes, smiled his crooked grin, and squeezed my hand. Was that his way of saying, "I'm sorry" or was he giving the knife he and Simone embedded within my heart of hearts, one last twist?

The other thing I had to face with Luc's passing was the question of my mortality—one day *I* am going to die. We all will. The question is: Do you have enough time left to make a difference in the world? Can you afford to put "it" off until tomorrow? Will you put it off until the time is just right? Put it off until you look up and realize you're six feet under? You can make a difference. The only question is, Can you afford to wait? Time, unfortunately, isn't on our side, my friend.

My brother had made a great contribution to *my* world. It was my duty to make it greater. *What contribution will you make to the world? Are you up to the challenge?*

The butterflies gently floated to the bottom of my stomach after Luc's passing; a wave of calmness came over me. May both he and the butterflies rest in peace.

I mentioned how Mark and Adrian reminded me of Luc's passing. Now Luc's passing reminds me of Mark and Adrian. At the time of

Luc's transition, we didn't have a name for his condition. His death certificate listed the cause of his death as cancer-related complications. I now know Luc died of AIDS. Remember the blue-red nodules that I had only seen in textbooks? At the time, that was a rare skin cancer. It was Kaposi's sarcoma, a cancer very commonly found on people with AIDS.

Luc became a POW shortly after France and the United Nations declared war on Vietnam. If you recall, earlier I talked about facultative homosexuals. It's possible that a fellow prisoner infected Luc, during his POW days.

Luc also received several blood transfusions after a bad car accident, during my third year of medical school. It's possible that he may have received some blood tainted with HIV.

Hindsight is always twenty/twenty. I'm glad I didn't know then what I know now. I would have been a total basket case, worrying about Simone.

Remember to look out for the AIDS (STD) terrorists. Be mindful. Be careful. Protect yourself.

9

Julia and Victor

Marriage is for women the commonest mode of livelihood, and the total amount of undesired sex endured by women is probably greater in marriage than in prostitution.
—BERTRAND RUSSELL,
Marriage and Morals

Julia—November 29

Sex just isn't that important to me anymore.

And I'm not frigid! As a matter of fact, ninety percent of the time I climax within the first minute or two after penetration. Any activity after I have an orgasm is a waste of time. Because I'm not turned on anymore, I dry up. If he continues, it becomes very painful, and I end up with a damned yeast infection from the irritation. I've gone through so many tubes of Monistat this past year, I should've bought stock in Ortho Pharmaceuticals.

I do enjoy sex, but it's more of a stress reliever for me now than anything else. Vic believes we should see the heavens part, become one with the universe, and explode into "cosmic consciousness" while climaxing together. So far, I haven't seen anything other than the ceiling fan turning clockwise while I wait for him to finish. I've asked Vic a dozen times or more why it takes so long for him to cum, his response is always the same, "it feels so damn good just getting there."

I know his feelings get hurt because I cum so quickly, but he should be happy to have a woman who can have an orgasm as quickly as a man can. I learned a long time ago, from the men I dated before Vic, that if I wanted to get mine I'd better hurry up.

I wish Vic would stop his "Sir Lancelot" fantasy routine in the bedroom. I am not, and never will be, Queen Guinevere. When we got married seventeen years ago, I loved his romantic ceremonies. I even enjoyed the role-playing at first, but for the past five years or so, his romantic rituals have lost their zing.

I love Vic, but he needs to put things in perspective. Both of us are older now and there isn't time for his schoolboy antics. We're both at the peak of our careers. His architectural firm has just been awarded the contract to design and oversee the building of our city's new convention center. My new consulting contract with the hospital will keep me busy traveling back and forth to Washington, D.C., studying the president's national healthcare proposal. I've tried to make Vic realize that I need as much time as possible to network with the political in-crowd. I'm still aiming for a presidential cabinet position, and this contract gives me the perfect opportunity to rub elbows with the Commander in Chief. But Vic doesn't seem to understand that we can't make love every day of our lives.

I have several things to accomplish in the next couple of years; his marathon sex fests are not among them.

I don't have time for his foolish parlor sex games. I've tried wearing those outfits he brings home every week, but, let's face it, I'm not the petite little thing I was when we got married. Between power lunches and cocktails at happy hour, it's becoming increasingly difficult to keep the pounds off. Besides, I can't for the life of me figure out why he wants to see my sagging ass hanging below some skimpy lace-trimmed outfit. It's easy for Vic to stay in shape; he's a man. He doesn't have to worry about bloating, the hit-and-miss bleeding, or the headaches that keep me from exercising most of the time.

Until recently, I was able to tolerate Vic's sentimental ways. Now the hand-holding, his phone calls, kissing me in public, the greeting cards, and him constantly telling me "I love you" are taking their toll on me. I know my work can be stressful at times and maybe that's the reason I've had so many mood swings lately, but he's starting to get on my nerves. It seems like we're starting to change roles, he's becoming overly sensitive while I'm developing into a real hard-ass.

Some nights it's difficult to fall asleep because of Vic's candles and incense. Every night, regardless of the season, he lights two or three candles as he gets ready for bed. With his damned candles flickering and the smell of his burning lavender sticks, I can't get to sleep until he puts them out. I have to get up at four-thirty in the morning because of the two-hour commute to the office. I need to get to sleep early.

I have a hard time sleeping through the night because of the lingering smell of his incense. To add insult to injury, he closes the window each night complaining that it's "too chilly in here." Then he makes a wisecrack about my having a "private summer" or a damn "power surge."

I must admit he doesn't complain anymore when I reject his late-night advances. But when I think of it, he hasn't complained about my rejecting his early-morning attempts either. I guess he's gotten used to me having the headaches that have become my constant companions. I've explained to him how my libido takes a nosedive when my head is pounding.

Vic suggested I make an appointment to check on the headaches, because the frequency has increased over the past year. I have no intention of sitting in the doctor's waiting room all day—just because of some damn headaches. Vic knows I hate to take any type of medicine, especially the ones that dull the senses. You have to be in total control of your faculties when you're working on The Hill. If you don't pay close attention during a conversation with one of those politicians, their D.C. double-talk has you saying yes to the wrong thing at the wrong time. Hell, you might end up on the news . . . "An unidentified aide caught on video with Senator X . . . pantyhose around ankles . . . details at ten!"

I do need to see a dermatologist. These dry and itchy areas are getting worse. I know I should've used a heavier sunscreen last year. There was that special report on the radio at the beginning of summer that talked about the downside of too much sun. I should have heeded the warnings, but I really don't like being told what to do.

Next month we're taking a vacation for the first time in two years. Vic said he might reserve a club floor suite at the Ritz—with a Jacuzzi—the night before we leave, as a "prelude" to the days to come. I got a feeling he's trying a change of scenery in hopes that my libido will bubble back to the surface. Maybe I should buy a case of K-Y jelly and let him do me like the old days.

It wouldn't be so bad if we didn't have to "theme fuck." Like the time I was Cleopatra and he was Marc Antony, or when I played songs on the *biwa* [a Japanese lute] as Madame Butterfly, while riding his *goddamn* "jade stem!" Oh yea, if I could cut out his four-hour seduction rituals, sex would almost be normal. If only he knew how to get in, get off, and get out, our sex life would be just fine.

I need to get on the road before rush-hour traffic starts. Where did I put my keys? Damnit, maybe I *should* get some Ginkoba, if it would help me remember. Hell, the way I've been forgetting lately, I should get a backpack of liquid Ginkoba and run an IV drip into my arm.

I hope Vic doesn't pick up on my senior moments [momentary memory loss]; he'll get back on me about that damned HRT shit!

Victor—December 21

Lovingly, I removed the last orchid petal that clung to her wet body.

Slowly stepping out of the warm bath, she extended her left hand. Taking it, I softly kissed her wet fingertips and was momentarily blinded by the brilliance of her wedding ring. As she slid her arms into its bell-shaped sleeves, I draped the white terrycloth robe over

her petite shoulders. While tying the belt around her waist, she mentioned how warm the robe felt against her damp skin. Earlier I'd
asked housekeeping to place her robe in the dryer to heat and soften
its fluffy fibers; they brought it to me only moments before she
stepped out of the bath.

There is little I wouldn't do for my lovely lady.

Walking hand-in-hand to the suite's spacious bedroom, we were
greeted by the sound of Keiko's sensual "Light above the Trees"
flowing softly through the air. The huge four-poster bed went unno-
ticed by my lady. She was enchanted, or perhaps confused, by the
addition to the bedroom's décor. While I was bathing my beauty, the
hotel florist filled the room with crystal vases of various shapes and
sizes. They were on the floor. They formed a wall behind the head of
our bed. They adorned the nightstands, and covered the mantel
above the crackling fireplace. They were inside the paired mahogany
armoires, on the desk, and they lined the top shelf of the closet.
Each vase displayed a different bouquet of roses . . . white . . . yellow . . . peach . . . orange . . . and the deepest shade of red. I had
personally hand-picked each rose, the day before.

Resting on the down comforter, near the edge of the bed, was a
single cymbidium orchid. Its small outer whorls were an innocent
white, while the one large inner lip whorl was the soothing color of
lavender. The orchid has always been my symbol for nubile femininity—unique, beautiful, and elegantly inviting. As we reached the
edge of the bed, I took the orchid and nestled its stem into the hair
nearest her temple.

When I pulled the comforter and top sheet back, a rainbow of
fresh rose petals scattered over the white silk bedclothes and onto
the Oriental rug below.

Dropping to one knee, I carefully and very *slowly* untied the
braided cord of her terry robe. I relished the tanned strip of her
naked flesh that flashed before my eyes as the edges of her robe
parted.

Holding the terry cord, I leaned forward and kissed the exposed
skin below and above her navel; the central area, which physically
separates her heaven and her hell.

Above her waist was the peaceful paradise where her breast, arms, shoulders, mouth, tongue, earlobes, and sensual eyes were located. Her mature hips, round bottom, firm legs, manicured feet, and her very wet *yoni* fueled the fiery heat below my lady's waist.

I stood up, raised my hands, and gently ran my fingertips over her sensitive, swollen nipples. Soon my fingers found their way to her round shoulders. Lifting the robe ever so slightly off her shoulders, I extended my fingers and pushed the damp robe away from her body. Holding the robe above her shoulders for several heartbeats, I let it go. It fell and crumpled into a mountain of white terry around her gold-clad ankles.

As the terry cord slipped completely through my fingers toward the floor, I stepped back and took a long, full look at her womanly figure. From the red airbrushed nails of her toes, to the upswept hair that exposed her graceful neck, I marveled at God's work of art.

She is so beautiful, and she has willingly given herself to me—mind, body, and soul.

Moving closer, I watched as goose bumps slowly covered her. I wondered whether were they there because she was cold, or because she was anticipating what was to cum?

Taking one step backward, she lowered herself onto the bed's edge. Gracefully she slid back, then lifted her crossed legs up and onto the bed. My lovely lady raised her legs just high enough for me to see the welcoming smile of her wet *yoni*. I wonder . . . did Sharon Stone steal *that* move from my seductive siren?

Two thick strips of black hair covered the outer pair of her *yoni's* thick labia—lips that few have had the opportunity to smell, taste, or penetrate with their fingers, tongue, or their raised manhood. Still, none were worthy of anointing her nubile orchid.

My baby tried so hard to find someone to love her in that very special way. She tried so hard to be the woman of their dreams, in hopes that they would, in turn, become the man of her dreams. But, they always fell short. None of them could entice the caged woman buried deep within her to cum out. I got lucky. I listened, paid attention, and gave her what she desired and needed the most—unconditional love.

There's absolutely nothing I wouldn't do for my precious jewel.

Sliding her bottom toward the headboard, my playful nymph separated her legs and exposed more of her *yoni's* delicate parts. The outer whorls of her *yoni* glistened from the river of nectar oozing out of her golden canal—the same sweet nectar that has anointed my golden shaft so many times in the past, when I've gone in search of her golden cherry.

Leaning forward, my earth angel grasped a handful of silk, laid back, and then fluffed the sheet over herself. Gingerly, it came to rest on each elevation of her naked body. Her toes were the first to be caressed by the silken fabric. Next it covered her dimpled knees, thighs, and when it landed on her *mons veneris*, an intricate design appeared on its surface. It was a design created by the tuft of hair on her protruding mound. Venus would be proud to have her name associated with my goddess' tufted dumpling.

Continuing its journey, the sheet slid over her tummy, and tickled the fine hairs near her belly button. Floating still highter, the silk sheet embraced and emphasized the proud nipples that adorned my lover's breasts. The silken fabric's finally touched down on her pear-shaped diamond wedding ring; even covered, it glimmered.

Looking into her dark, exotic eyes, I realized that no painting, sculpture, or photograph could ever capture the beauty of her face.

She watched as I walked to the sitting room. I knew she was looking at me; I could feel it. I felt her eyes as they slapped my tight, tanned ass—a muscular mass of tissue that has the "promise of power" written all over it. It's the same sinewy mass that has driven my jade stem deep within her pink pagoda, over . . . and . . . over, so many times before.

I felt her eyes as they fondled my thick thighs and sculpted calves, by-products of my college speed-skating days. Next her eyes inspected my heels . . . and she wondered if I had inherited the curse of Achilles. What she failed to realize was that my weakness isn't in my heel; it has been, and always will be in the very fiber of my heart—she *is* my weakness.

Her eyes scanned the enormous span of my shoulders. Shoulders broad enough to support my cherry blossom's weary head or troubled heart when life gets too damned crazy.

She surveyed my back: strong enough for her to sit or ride like Lady Godiva. I felt her eyes groping my love handles, handrails that have come from too many chocolate soufflés, puddings, and pastries. I know she doesn't care about them; she accepts me just as I am. And I accept her, as she is, as I have and always will.

Soon, she'll know how *much* I worship her, how much I adore her. She'll know. She'll know by the slow and deliberate moves of my hands, fingers, mouth, tongue, and jade stem. She'll know by the way I take my time to penetrate, probe, and pluck her perpetual cherry from its hiding place tonight.

Curious, she watched as I dropped aphrodisiacs into the pools of melted wax. I used several drops of ylang-ylang, to relax, de-stress, and reduce any anxiety left over from the day . . . a few drops of sandalwood, to bring her into the here and now and to release our inhibitions so we can get into the way things "should be." To jump-start her animalistic nature, I used one drop each of narcissus, Madonna lily, and lilac. To completely open the love chambers within her heart of hearts, I added a mixture of rose and frankincense oil to the candle closest to the bed. Finally, I used the grandmother of all aphrodisiacs, the one Cleopatra applied whenever she wanted to have her way with Marc Antony—jasmine.

Unlike Marc Antony, tonight I will have *my* way with Madame Butterfly. As an insurance policy, I laced the pillowslips with an expensive sex pheromone I picked up in Chinatown.

My silk-screened beauty strained to see what was hiding in the shadows of my body. I turned, and gave her a full frontal view. Her breath became ragged with desire as she spied my heavy jade stem resting upon its bag of jewels. She stared long and hard, as if bewitched, while the flickering candlelight played hide and seek with my manhood.

It was strange, but it felt as if a collar had been attached to my stiffening jade stem and her eyes held the leash. Each time her eyes moved up my body; my jade stem jerkily followed.

Her groping eyes climbed upward, until she reached the windows of my soul. Instantly, she became . . . mesmerized . . . hypnotized . . . captured by my brown eyes. A flush covered her face, neck, and chest when she entered my soul's amber-stained windows. Inside, she heard my heart beating, rhythmically; she felt the scorching fires in my soul, heating my jade stem, preparing it for her hot, wet, hungry oven. She savored the pure ecstasy contained within the velvet-lined walls of my soul.

Last of all, she saw her immediate future, in moving pictures, on the cinematic screen in the theater of my soul. Vivid images, so erotically appealing, so consuming, so tantalizing that she unknowingly parted her legs and, in doing so, the silk sheet fell into Venus' valley and became wet with her love nectar.

Each step toward my Madame Butterfly strengthened my erection . . . lengthened it . . . raised it . . . but, she didn't seem to notice its metamorphosis. Her focus was still on my eyes, watching the vintage movies of our past escapades. Blue movies flashed quickly across the screen, exposing her feminine perversions of power . . . snippets of raw lust, bondage, and domination—secrets that she promised to keep about my occasional need to submit.

Sliding my tongue across my bottom lip, I licked the spillage of my Pavlovian anticipation of what was to cum. Wickedly smiling at my dog-like response, my cherry blossom parted her legs once again; however, this time, it was a conscious effort on her part. She deliberately widened her runway to make it easy for me to land. I couldn't wait to taxi, guided home by the shimmering pink beacon located behind the double-gated control tower.

Kneeling at the foot of her reclining throne, I snatched off the comforter and tossed it away. Hand over hand, I pulled the silk shroud away from her exotic body; revealing the delicate treasures I would soon savor. One by one they appeared . . . her supple neck . . . round shoulders . . . heaving breasts . . . deep navel . . . tufted pubic palace . . . trembling thighs . . . bent knees . . . cambered calves . . . and curled toes.

Like a serpent, I slithered toward the head of the bed. Stopping, I licked the insteps of her tiny feet. Wrapping my fingers around her right ankle, I gently turned her leg to expose the soft, sensitive underside of her knee. A dozen quick jabs from my tongue wet the flesh, then, slightly opening my mouth, I exhaled and released a stream of cool breath onto the moistened flesh. A garden of goose bumps blossomed, rewarding me. Her thighs quivered, then several low, vibrating moans of pleasure escaped from her throat. I smiled, and continued my pilgrimage.

Sliding my hand up her thigh started a chain reaction. She screamed, "Oh baby!" then locked her ankles behind my neck and quickly jerked my head to within a tongue's length of her moist temple. Just then, her temple gates flew open, and her South Seas' pearl greeted me with a salacious twitch.

She knew what was cumming. She knew it first, when I told her to join me at the Ritz. She knew it the moment she inserted the key in the elevator's VIP slot. She knew it the moment I unzipped her red dress. She knew it when I helped her into the bath laced with orchid petals. She knew. There was no question in her mind; she knew we were going to make love as never before.

My lady needed this time to rid her mind and body of stress. She needed the attention, pampering, and pleasure her man would give her tonight. I was ready, willing, and able to fulfill her every desire and grant her every wish. My baby knew she was going to receive the specialty of the house. She knew she was being prepared to receive the *hottest flames of love* that I could muster.

Moving closer, I inhaled the perfumed scent of the wispy black locks covering her domed temple. I marveled at the firmness of her thick gates, before sampling her river of plum nectar. Curling the tip of my tongue around her pink pearl, I pushed and pulled it, hoping that her inner gates would open and allow me to enter her sacred passageway.

Just as the tin man, the cowardly Lion, and the scarecrow entered the gates of the Emerald City demanding a heart, courage, and brains, I would enter the gates of her heavenly temple demanding to be her Alpha and Omega.

As I slowly inched my way toward her round face, my engorged jade stem left a glistening trail of crystal nectar on her thigh. Moving ever so lightly over her breast, I struggled to contain myself. I wanted to caress . . . lick . . . nibble . . . and bite it, but there was something I *had* to do before scaling her miniature Mount Fuji. I *had* to pay homage to her lips, and inhale her breath as she whispered, "I love you Victor."

We kissed, and suddenly, I was overcome with a yen so strong that my tongue quickly and without hesitation, penetrated her lips and journeyed deep within her hot mouth.

Eventually, my hands slipped down, then under her heart-shaped bottom. Instinctively her legs flew around my waist. Yelling at the top of her lungs *"Irete! Irete!"* She grabbed and *stuffed* my hardened jade stem between the wet lips of her hungry lotus blossom. Sinking her sunset nails into my ass, she screamed, *"motto fukaku irete!"* Then she recklessly thrust her hips up to *"make it go deeper and deeper!"*

I drove my clinched fist into the firm mattress, straightened my arms, and came into full view of her engorged nipples, flushed neck, clenched teeth, and eyes wide with excitement. At the same time, my knees drew up and then under her raised ass. Lunging forward, she reinserted my jade stem, and tightened her leg-lock around my waist. Digging my toes into the mattress, I thrust my pelvis up and delivered the "promise of power."

Later, after the in and outs . . . the rounds and downs . . . the sides and bottoms . . . the fire and sweat . . . the screams and yells . . . *that* moment finally came. It's that moment when heaven and hell fuse into one . . . that final moment when he's rock hard and you're sloppy wet . . . that brief moment of calm before the raging storm . . . that fleeting moment of the dark before the dawn . . . that moment when nothing else in your crazy-ass world matters . . . that moment when the two of us become one . . . that moment when we're breathing the same breath . . . thinking the same thoughts . . . when we're about to explode into waves of orgasmic ecstasy, and experience pleasure beyond belief . . . that moment when both of us cry out to each other . . . *"now? . . . now!? . . . now!! . . . yes!!! . . . oh hell yes, right n-n-now!"* As I flooded her rice patty with my fiery fertilizer, my concubine slapped my ass over and over as if to make sure every white drop was deposited inside of her swollen canal.

Screaming *"Iku! . . . Iku!"* my cherry blossom did just that, she came.

From sheer exhaustion, we collapsed into a lover's embrace. Minutes later, my lovely lady rolled me over and climbed onto my chest. She kissed me firmly on the lips, looked deeply into my eyes, smiled, and said, "I'm not sleeping on the wet spot tonight!" Laughing, she rolled off of me and onto her side, assumed the fetal position, and waited for me to spoon in behind her.

Breathing heavily, and desperately trying to catch my breath, I crawled in behind her. Crushing my graying chest hairs against her back and resting my leg over her hip, I gently embraced her torso. A faint scent of jasmine lingered on her body . . . enough to make me smile.

I ran one hand through her tangled hair, my other gently cradled the small, flattened breast closest to the bare mattress; we tore off the bottom sheet and mattress pad hours ago. Then we talked, snuggled, and cooed like a pair of lovebirds until the candles and incense burned out.

When I was sure she was asleep, I thanked my lucky stars for the evening and prayed that, one day, it *would* be her . . . that one day there wouldn't be a need to role-play . . . that my Julia would come back to me.

I got up, phoned the front desk for an eight o'clock wakeup call, showered, and wrote a note on the hotel's stationary:

Jade,

Thank you, cherry blossom, for the carnal pleasures you bestowed on me.

Remember, we can't get together until next month. I'm taking Julia on that cruise for three weeks. But not to worry sweetheart, I'll be back in time to celebrate the New Year with you on February 7.

I've memorized the love poems in Sei's *Pillow-Book* that turned you on so much. I watched the movie, and have been practicing my calligraphy. When I get back, I'll be ready to pen those words of love in sunrise red, and gold, on every part of your silky body.

Hey, I even made a new *Ryu* [fire dragon] *kokigami* [paper condom] for you to extinguish with your fountain of love. I can't wait!

Thinking of you, my lotus blossom,
Vic

I dressed, covered the "wet spot" with a towel, pulled the comforter over Jade, kissed her, and whispered "Good-night." I wasn't surprised that she didn't wake up or even move about when I kissed her fingertips. We've never been this wild before.

I thought that when I told Julia that I was taking Viagra, she might snap out of her denial and accept the hormone replacement therapy her gynecologist recommended. Still, I refuse to give up. Eventually something or somebody will break through, wake her, and bring Julia back to me—even if it turns out to be that senator she always talks about.

It's time to go. I have that ten-thirty groundbreaking ceremony tomorrow for the city convention center and I'm supposed to be there by six-thirty.

I picked up the orchid that had adorned her beautiful hair, placed it, the note, and two grand in cash on top of the Gideon Bible, and then headed for the door. Stepping into the hallway, I turned, took one last look at Jade, then closed the door on my fantasy come true.

Surprised?

Maybe you knew all along that Victor wasn't with Julia. Perhaps you thought Julia had changed her mind and allowed Victor to live out his "South Seas" sexual fantasy. What about Jade? Was she his lover? Was she a high-class call girl?

How do you follow an act like Victor's? What could I possibly say about his journal entry that would provide any insight into this *provocateur*? Could you handle a Victor or Victoria should one come along? How would you keep Victor a secret from your girlfriends who want to know about the person who painted that permanent smile of satisfaction on your face? You would keep him a secret, would you not?

Tyra gave me some sage advice during one session, when I asked if her girlfriends were jealous of her having a good man like Tyrone. She responded with, "Big momma told me, 'Gurl baby, don't *ever* tell them womens 'bout how good yo' man is. No sooner you leave yo' home fo' the sto', them thare heffas be all over yo' good man. And you kno' mens be weak 'bout them hip slangin' Jezebel's.' So you see, Doc, I keep my mouth shut just like big momma told me to do; I don't wanna haf'ta to break my foot off up in the ass of one of my gurlfriends! Know what I mean, Doc?" I certainly did. After the Luc incident, I never told anybody, man or woman, about how great a lover Simone was.

I'm sure that most of the women reading this book knew what Julia's problem was after the first or second paragraph of her journal entry. I've included this couple in the book partly for individuals who are ignorant of or who choose to ignore the natural phenomenon of menopause, more commonly known to the baby boomers as "the Pause." Another term that more accurately describes the change of life is perimenopause; this is the time of changes surrounding menopause.

I also chose this couple to show how a partner can be sensually, erotically, and sexually creative in their lovemaking. For those of you with a carnally challenged partner, have them read Victor's journal entry. Better yet, tell them it's a recipe for making you a happy camper and then have them act it out—word by word.

Just as the baby-boomer boys find it difficult to talk about their erection difficulties with their significant others, there are probably an equal number of baby-boomer girls with a similar problem. Many women have a hard time discussing their difficulties with their periods, or talking about the physical and emotional changes they go through during the process of perimenopause. Some women don't recognize the signs of the coming Pause. The reasons for being silent are numerous, but they boil down to what I believe is the same underlying reason in both the male and female—fear. The greatest fear is that of los-

ing our wo(man)hoods. "I won't be the wo(man) I used to be," for example, is a common thought among women and men going through the
'change.'

I would like to cover two important issues I noticed in Julia's journal
entry. The first is informational for men reading this book, and women
who may not be aware of the physical signs and symptoms associated
with menopause. The second is the emotional side of menopause, as it
relates to your significant other: You do want to share everything with
him, do you not?

It is sad to say, but during my time, most doctors dismissed peri-
menopausal changes by saying, "It's all in your head." And the most
common treatment for correcting the "it's all in your head" problem
was a complete hysterectomy. Heaven forbid, if you were a woman
under fifty seeking some relief, they wrote you off as being completely
nuts.

Julia was a walking menopause textbook, with the many classic
symptoms she manifested. The disclaimer she wrote in her second
paragraph— "And I'm not frigid!"—is equivalent to one from a man
with erection difficulties saying, "I'm not turned on right now." Both
statements are masks that cover the fear of being less of a wo(man).

Julia talked about her dryness after having an orgasm and the yeast
infections that occurred. In one of our sessions, Julia eluded to having
used a lubricant every time she had intercourse with Victor, because of
his ability to stretch making love past her minute or two wetness limitations. Most of the water-based lubricants tend to lose their effectiveness shortly after they are applied, and must be reapplied frequently.
The dryness, combined with the frictional irritation of Victor's tireless
penetrations, set up the ideal conditions for her yeast infections.

Julia's entries, "Sex just isn't that important to me anymore . . . for the
last five years or so, his romantic rituals have lost their zing . . . he hasn't
complained about my rejecting his early-morning attempts either," indicate her declining interest in sex. Menopause comes about because
of the decreasing levels of estrogen within a woman's body. Her reduced hormonal level is directly related to the drop in her libido. Julia's
desire to have sex—pardon the pun—had gone down the tubes.

Another change caused by Julia's decreased hormonal level was her increase in body weight. When she writes, "I'm not the petite little thing I was when we got married . . . becoming increasingly difficult to keep the pounds off . . . sagging ass hanging", Julia attributes the weight gain to lack of exercise and too many "power lunches." Her lack of exercise is certainly a contributing factor, but the truth is, many women experience a weight gain during menopause.

In theory, the key to maintaining or losing weight is quite simple: eat less and exercise more. There are, however, several caveats: You must take into account the emotional, genetic, hormonal, and societal factors that also govern your body weight. If you should come up with a foolproof method of handling those factors, the world will beat a path to your doorstep—not to mention the zillions of dollars you'll make in the process.

When Julia wrote, "Until recently, I was able to tolerate Vic's sentimental ways . . . work can be stressful at times . . . maybe that's the reason I've had so many mood swings lately," she was referring to the pendulum-like mood swings associated with perimenopause.

The sleep disturbances, night sweats, migraine headaches, memory loss, dry and itchy skin, and increased anxiety that Julia experienced are also a result of the hormonal changes associated with perimenopause.

While many women over thirty-five will experience some, if not all, of these symptoms from time to time, they should consider seeking a professional diagnosis if they're bothered with several symptoms regularly.

Throughout the book, I have emphasized one theme over and over—communication. Whether you're faced with a conflict like the one Dexter and Epiphany had to deal with, or the problem that Simone and I faced, you must open your mouth and speak from your heart. It is better to bring the conflict out in the open than to keep it behind the closed doors of your heart.

Realistically, some things should never be revealed. But for the things that won't devastate your partner, especially in the case of menopause or erection difficulty, please talk to each other. Don't wait until you are at each other's throats; then, it may too late. You'll become the topic of discussion within your circle of friends: "Can you believe they're getting a divorce after thirty-five years of being married? I bet s(he) cheated!" and they will be right. Julia cheated in that she denied what was happening to her, and as a result, refused to seek professional help regarding the menopausal changes she was experiencing.

There is a positive side to menopause. For instance, there's no need for birth control, so the two of you can enjoy spontaneous lovemaking without the fear of getting pregnant. You aren't troubled with bothersome periods, bouts of PMS, cramps, or having to plan your vacation around when your period is due.

Menopause is a new era in your life; you can make of it what you like. You can choose to make this new era into the Dark Ages, a Renaissance, or a *belle époque*—a beautiful era. It's all up to you.

Many good books address the physical, emotional, and relationship issues that occur during menopause and when erections are less than firm. Browse your local bookstore's shelves and buy several of these books. Don't let ignorance destroy you or your intimate relationship.

With a complete and thorough physical exam, including specific laboratory tests to check Victor's hormone levels, we were able to rule out physical causes for his erection difficulties. After several months of unsuccessful therapy, I referred Victor to a licensed sex therapist. That's how Victor met Midori, the lady he called Jade. She was a sexual surrogate who worked in conjunction with the sex therapist.

Shortly after Victor started his therapy sessions with Midori, Viagra was approved and released by the FDA for treating sexual dysfunction. I prescribed the 50 mg tablets for Victor and asked him to write about its effects on him. I was especially curious to hear from him, because he was one of the first patients for whom I had prescribed this pill for erection difficulties. During his next session, I asked Victor about the medication's effectiveness, he smiled and said, "I bought ten thousand shares of Pfizer stock."

Because of the rave reviews Victor gave that little blue pill, I was surprised when I read his last entry and discovered he was still seeing Midori. I knew he had stopped seeing the sex therapist after his "jade stem" responded so well to the Viagra. At the time, I wasn't sure if Midori continued the sessions with Victor because she wanted him to overcome his psychological problem so he could stop taking Viagra, or if she continued with the sessions because she got caught up in his fantasy world.

I suspect Midori became enamored with Victor's hedonistic approach to lovemaking and allowed the sessions to go beyond the professional therapist-patient relationship. That Victor was handsome, kind, and extremely charismatic—qualities that are difficult to resist—surely didn't help matters.

What do you think about Midori? Was it difficult for Midori to maintain her professional ethics once Victor lured her into his web of seduction? Did he, as Tyrone would put it, "turn the sista out"?

His relationship with Midori was one of the reasons Victor is back in therapy with me. Before he started the sex therapy, I met with him and Julia to discuss this alternative and *controversial* treatment approach. I told Victor about couples who created a new conflict in their relationship because the partner didn't inform, understand, or approve of the surrogate-assisted sex therapy.

During our meeting, I explained the fine but definite line between a sexual surrogate and a prostitute. A surrogate performs a sexual therapy regime prescribed by a licensed sex therapist. The goal is to overcome the emotional blocks that prevent a person from enjoying a healthy sex life. A prostitute, on the other hand, is paid to render a service—providing pleasure by stimulating the "Johns or Janes" to orgasm. This is not to say that a prostitute isn't capable of removing an emotional block to a healthier sex life for someone. I'm simply saying the odds of a prostitute hitting the emotional block on the head and licking the problem—no puns intended—would be very slim.

Let me digress for a moment. I wonder how many of you thought that Jade was a high-class call girl. I bet most of you thought she was something other than a professionally trained sexual surrogate, did you not? The two thousand dollars Victor left for Midori was, as he put it, "some spending change for the holidays." I told him I could use a few extra dollars for the holidays as well, but only if I didn't have to play his parlor games.

I mentioned that the surrogate issue was one of the reasons Victor resumed his therapy sessions with me. I thought Julia was having a problem with him seeing Midori, but that wasn't the case. Actually, I think Julia welcomed the surrogate and looked upon her as a reprieve from having to participate in Victor's sexual fantasies.

Victor was having a problem; in fact, he had several of them. He felt guilty because he was enjoying the time he spent with Midori much more than the time he spent with Julia. He continued to see Midori because she appreciated and enjoyed the way he expressed himself sensually, erotically.

Another problem he had was common among those patients who are prone to infatuation. Victor was appreciative of all that Midori had done for him—allowing him to live out his fantasies. He also knew she enjoyed being a part of them. He was so taken with her that he started to transpose his emotions for Julia onto Midori. Remember how Christian transposed his feelings for Ellen onto Dominique?

Certain patients overlook the fact that they're paying a professional to help them with a problem, and begin to view it as personal. They exhibit this behavior because the therapist has helped them overcome a crisis, and they "fall" for their hero(ine). The same is also true of the therapist who believes that (s)he has "saved" the patient, as opposed to assisting them out of their stuck state. They'll form a romantic attachment to the patient even though they know it is unethical and amounts to taking advantage of the situation.

Has a friend ever pulled you out of an emotional or financial bind? How did you feel toward that person afterward? Did you find yourself wanting to repay them, or feeling that you owe them something for saving you? Did you find yourself placing that person on a pedestal? Imagine how Victor felt, especially with how he lives part of his life in a fantasy world.

Then there is also the normal attraction people have for one another. For instance, Tyra was extremely attractive, intelligent, and quite a pleasant woman to be around. If you take into account that something about assertive women makes my heart race, and if I had a weak constitution, I could've tossed my ethics out the window and let nature take its course.

As a final note, I'm sure millions of women would lovingly welcome a gentle, attentive, passionate, thoughtful, carnal-minded, compassionate, and romantic man like Victor. "Jade" couldn't have been the only one. There's probably an earth full of: Topazes, Rubies, Opals, Ambers, Sapphires, and other women who would love to have Victor in their lives.

If you already have a Victor in your life, God bless you, and remember big momma's advice—"keep yo mouth shut!" If you don't have a Victor at home, wouldn't you welcome a man like him with open . . . arms? I bet you some woman right now is saying, "Hell, if I found a man like Victor, I'd give *him* two grand for a night like that!"

Incidentally, Victor was in the habit of naming his penis. For each fantasy he would name it to fit the particular "sex theme" that was to be acted out. He coined it "jade stem" because; the *Kama Sutra* uses the word stem to describe the type of penis Victor had; the Japanese word, *midori*, translates as *green*; green jade is a gemstone that comes from eastern Asian; and Midori was of Japanese decent. Hence, "Jade's Stem."

How are menopause, impotency, and the surrogate issue relevant to my life? To begin with, Victor had an erection difficulty, something, as you know, I've experienced on more than one occasion.

During another period in my life I experienced erection difficulties that I didn't mention in Tyrone and Tyra. After Amileé was born, I couldn't get it up. It had been a rough pregnancy for Simone because she was a high-risk patient. She received several blood transfusions because of her condition, and she was prone to severe infections. Simone was *still* dealing with the emotional trauma of being abused, and she was suffering with "normal" postpartum depression. The last thing I thought Simone needed to deal with was my limp "redwood."

Fortunately for me, but unfortunately for her, Amileé was a preemie and sickly during her first year. She developed a new bout of colic at six months and spent most nights crying her little heart out. I insisted on taking care of Amileé during the nights, so that I could sleep in the nursery and avoid Simone's amorous advances. I told Simone that she needed her rest so that she could take care of our little bundle of joy during the day. That was the truth. When she argued that it wasn't fair for me to stay up because I had to work, I'd give her the ultimate doctor guilt trip, "Sweetheart, because Amileé is so frail, it would be better for 'doctor Daddy' to take care of her just in case something should happen." It worked every time.

Darren's mother, queen of the ultimate guilt trips, would've been proud of me—but I wasn't.

At some point in time, I knew Simone would ask me why I was avoiding her advances. I couldn't lie and risk losing her again, but I knew I couldn't tell her about the flashbacks and horrible pictures of her and Luc that were being triggered for some reason; she was much too fragile. I needed a miracle.

Do you know the old saying, "God may not always come when you want him to, but he's always on time"? Simone developed some complications that prevented her from having intercourse the first six months after she delivered Amileé. As a result, we were limited to cunnilingus as the only means of satisfying my love's hearty appetite.

By the way, oral sex is the recommended solution for older couples who would still like to be sexually active, for women who suffer from post-menopausal vaginal dryness, and when the man's penis isn't firm enough for penetration.

Oral stimulation applies more pressure to the penis, which in combination with vigorous hand stimulation enables an older male suffering from erection difficulties to reach orgasm. Because vaginal dryness is an issue during perimenopause and a definite problem after menopause has occurred, oral stimulation provides an ideal solution. Because the clitoris is external to the vagina, self-lubrication is no longer a concern; her partner's saliva acts as a lubricant.

Fortunately, my erection difficulty went away not too long after Simone could resume intercourse. Actually, it disappeared serendipitously as a result of my being exhausted from six months of late-night hours, taking care of my Amileé. When she got over her colicky spell, I didn't have a choice—I had to sleep in the same room with Simone. The first night I slept with Simone, the fear of not being able to "perform" popped-up in my head, however, the thought was immediately overridden by my physical state of exhaustion. I was *so* spent; I said to myself "To hell with it. I don't care if I can't get it up. I just wanna sleep." Later that night, Simone rubbed her butt against my limp redwood, it slowly came to attention, entered Simone's gateway to pleasure, and repeatedly saluted her into the wee hours of the morning. It happened because, in giving up, I *relaxed*, and allowed nature to take its course.

The change of life for both men and women is one conflict every couple will eventually experience, if they stay together long enough. The inability to maintain a firm erection is going to happen to every man one day, just as menopause will happen to every woman who reaches that stage in her life. Unfortunately, my Simone didn't live long enough for me to tackle, "the ultimate PMS challenge."

As with any challenge, you can make your life a living hell or a wonderful heaven; it all depends on your point of view and how you approach the situation.

The surrogate issue affected me more than any other issue has in my life. It has been emotionally draining because its ill effects have been constant companions throughout my life. Two incidents of this surrogacy issue made major life changes within and around me. The first incident changed the course of my life, while the second one tested my love to the *n*th degree. Both situations involved family.

When I spoke in terms of my surrogate issues, I wasn't referring to a substitute sexual partner. I was speaking in terms of a surrogate parent, as when someone adopts a child. I was Amileé's surrogate father; her biological father was, Luc.

When I realized Amileé was not my child, I wanted to divorce Simone. My father intervened; he saved my marriage, and kept me from losing my best friend. He said, "J-P, the love you and Simone share is rare, you'll never find another like her. Can you live the rest of your life, knowing that you walked away from your one and only chance to experience perfect love? If you divorce her, you'll be miserable for the rest of your life."

I knew he was right. Simone was my soul mate, my kindred spirit, my female counterpart, and the only woman for me. I couldn't let anything keep us apart—not even my foolish male pride.

Amileé was a part of Simone, and because I loved *every* part of her with all my heart and soul, I couldn't do anything but; accept Amileé, love her, and raise her just as if she were my own flesh and blood.

Rather than complicating Amileé's life, I chose not to father any children. I didn't want a child of mine to be born, and then raised with Amileé. I would've treated my child with more favor, which would have been wrong, and that was *not* going to happen. Amileé already had a hard enough road to travel. She didn't need anything else to complicate her journey.

The other reason I didn't want Simone to have my child was because of her medical condition; she almost died giving birth to Amileé. Simone was a high-risk ob-gyn patient, because of her sickle cell disorder. The decision not to put Simone through childbirth again was purely selfish on my part. The fear of losing Simone was much greater than my desire to father a child; I was frightened to death of losing the love of my life. To ensure she would never become pregnant, I had a vasectomy.

There was no doubt about Amileé being Luc's child; Amileé was a perfect blend of Simone and my brother. Simone had island bronze skin, while Luc's was creamy white; Amileé's skin was the color of milk tea. Simone's brown hair was thick and crinkly, while Luc's was blond and straight; Amileé's hair was ash blond and wavy. Simone had gray-green eyes, while Luc's were blue; Amileé's eyes were gray-blue.

The other surrogate issue occurred much earlier in my life. When I was five, my parents took me on holiday to Germany. We were traveling on the autobahn when a drunk driver crossed the median and crashed head-on into our car. I walked away from the accident without a scratch. My parents, however, were not as fortunate. The impact killed both of them.

The Lefervres were kind enough to take me into their home, because of the close relationship they had with my parents. My father and Dr. Lefervre were classmates at medical school, and they were the best of friends. They eventually adopted me as their second son. This surrogate issue completely changed the course of my life.

If I had been Luc's blood brother, it would've been more difficult to tell which of us was Amileé's father. But when you're black as me, and have hair the texture of nappy wool, I don't care how far you go back in my ancestry; there aren't any genes for wavy blond hair, gray-blue eyes, or light-colored skin in my African roots. About the only thing Amileé could've inherited from me was her big butt. Thank God that Simone's Jamaican genes for a big butt were stronger than Luc's genes for a flat ass.

Simone and I knew Luc was Amileé's father. We knew it the first time we saw her. Foolishly, we kept it a secret from her. When she was going though her inquisitive years, I fed Amileé the "gene pool" theory. I told her that black women were raped and bred like cattle during slavery times; and, because of those horrible acts, we have a multitude of different races within our gene pool. I told Amileé that you never knew what color skin, eyes, or hair type your child would inherit until the child was born. That was the only lie I ever told my daughter.

There was no other way for me to explain why she looked so different from the man she called her *Papa*. Amileé accepted the gene pool explanation until she was in her late teens; then she stopped asking. I suspect she figured it out on her own and continued to play along with the rest of us in keeping our family's deep dark, or maybe I should say deep white, secret.

Amileé is the reason Simone agreed to see Luc when he was dying. She didn't want to deprive Amileé of saying good-bye to her father before he died. I'm sure she thought it was the right thing to do and, knowing Simone, she would never have forgiven herself if she denied Amileé that right, especially once Amileé figured out that Luc was her biological father. As much as I hate to admit it, Simone's soul probably wouldn't allow her to deny Luc the opportunity to see his daughter before dying.

Amileé and I talked about Luc being her real father, after Simone made her transition. She said, "Papa, I know you're not my biological father, but I have always known you as being my *real* father . . .

the father who stood by me and Mom when it was your right to walk away from us and never look back . . . who wiped my tears away . . . who would drive to the other side of town just to get my favorite ice cream . . . who understood my wild and reckless college years, even when Mother had given up on me." My chest swelled with pride as I listened to *my* daughter's words.

Amileé continued by saying, "You were the father who told me, 'You will always be my little girl' and made me feel special when I cycled into womanhood . . . who taught me to live, function, and be proud of my dual ancestry." I marveled at the way she had carefully chosen her words.

"I know you altered yourself so you wouldn't have any children of your own; Mother told me all about it. She knew about your vasectomy, yet she played along with your charade, the same way you played along with ours. You are more than a father to me, Papa. You are a Saint. You stayed when you didn't have to, and you did it with lots of love in your heart for Mother and me. You were our blessing from God. Papa, I love you."

My little girl had pushed every one of my emotional buttons and, in the process, reduced me to a quivering bowl of mush. I hugged Amileé and, for a brief moment, I forgave Luc.

For the rest of that day, the only thing running through my head was a song Maurice Chevalier sang in *Gigi*, "Thank Heaven for Little Girls."

Maybe I was a fool for staying. But if staying with the woman I loved with all my heart and soul, and being around the sweetest daughter a man could ever hope for, was foolish, then I'm the biggest fool in the history of mankind.

So many times since Simone made her transition, I wished I had offered her my forgiveness for Amileé not being my child. But denying her the right to hear those words, or for her to tell *me*, was my foolish way of punishing her for sleeping with Luc. That's why she always begged me to forgive her, to let her tell me about Amileé, especially whenever she thought the end was near. I would never let her finish her sentence. I wanted her to suffer throughout her lifetime, as *I* had; but that was wrong. When I finally realized it was wrong for me to treat her that way, we were in the ER.

The ambulance doors opened, and they lowered Simone's gurney onto the pavement. It was just a short distance to the ER from the ambulance, but, because Simone was in so much pain, it seemed to me to be *miles*. She tried to speak, "Jean-Paul . . . I love . . . " but like so many times before, I stopped her. "Shhh! Mone, save your breath, we'll talk later." However, this time was different.

She ripped the oxygen mask from her face, lifted her head towards me, and said, "Jean-Paul . . . I love you . . . and only you . . ." Suddenly her eyes widened and her voice broke. She began mouthing her words to me while straining to keep her head up. Suddenly her body jerked and snapped her head hard, back onto the gurney.

Struggling, she raised her hand and caressed my cheek, much as she did on the day I asked her to marry me. Taking a quick and shallow breath, she mustered a smile and whispered, "Please forgive me Jean Paul . . . I love you . . . and only you . . . I'm sor . . . "

Her body convulsed in pain. Her eyes widened as her face contorted from the pain. In one violent and abrupt movement, Simone's entire body stiffened. Then it went limp, and the hand that was caressing my cheek, fell down onto the cold gurney. She took one last look at me before her eyelids slowly covered the beautiful gray-green windows of her soul. There was one long and quiet exhalation, followed by silence. "Simone? Simone? Simone! No! Oh my God, no." I faced my greatest fear; Simone was gone, forever.

Like so many times in the past, she didn't get a chance to finish her sentence. But unlike the past, I wasn't the one who stopped her. That day, Death had not taken a holiday; it was he who stopped my Simone this time. Simone never got a chance to make peace with me . . . and I . . . never told her, "I forgive you, Simone."

The pain I felt about Amileé not being my blood child ended when I stopped wanting to hurt Simone for running to my brother's arms, his bed, and possibly his heart. The reality of not telling Simone, "I forgive you" is a cross I carry to this day. This has been the reason I've asked and *begged* you to open up—talk to your loved one. If you don't, you may end up like me—feeling empty, incomplete, and guilty for the rest of your miserable life—never able to say you're sorry, or worse, never able to tell that special someone, "I love you."

Do it while you can. Do it while they're still alive. Do it now. Damnit, just do it!

I'd like to share one last journal entry with you. This is a small portion of a very long and detailed entry. Despite its abbreviated form, I'm sure you'll gain a little more insight into Victor's elaborate seductions, his attention to detail, and the effort he puts into making his loved ones feel special.

Midori—December 27

I heard the door close. I heard the deadbolt sliding into place. I even heard the squeaky sound of the security latch as it swung to. Those sounds were my last contact with reality after I entered fantasyland.

Walking toward the tall, ornate bathroom door, I noticed a faint light reflected from its lacquered surface, while a seductive saxophone whispered to me softly from the adjoining room. When I entered the bathroom, I couldn't believe my eyes. My words will never do justice to what I saw.

Surrounding the antique, rolled-rim bathtub were dozens of candles in various shapes, sizes, and colors. Each flame flickered and swayed rhythmically to the soothing sounds of the music flowing in from another room . . . the room he said was, "a surprise, it's a surprise blossom." When I asked what kind of surprise he replied, "Just let your imagination run *wild.*"

Each candle had been strategically placed to make my eyes dance from one delightful flicker to another. He had transformed the bathroom into a shrine. A sacred place whose sole purpose was to make me feel good. I felt so special.

A light haze of Russian amber incense blanketed the darkened room. How did he know it was my favorite incense? Then again, how has he come to know about everything else I like? The sweet smell of that amber resin sedated my senses. I had no choice but to *relax* and *respond*. I inhaled the spicy scent once more and released the stresses of the day. Victor's only goal is to please me, and he's damned good at it. I only hope that I am as good to him as he is to me.

The bathtub glistened with the rainbow bubbles dancing over the water's surface. Several of the little bubbles burst, seemingly just for my entertainment. Has he trained the bubbles to give me pleasure as well? Is there anything this man can't do?

A shroud of pink-and-white orchid petals floated lazily on the bathwater between the breaks of the mountainous bubbles. A large, lavender-and-white cymbidium orchid bobbed with each drip of the golden faucet. I think it was anxiously awaiting the arrival of my toes; so they could play a game of hide and seek.

A large white candle drew my eyes to the silver-and-crystal ice bucket. Towering above the rim of this sparkling container was a bottle of 1953 *Dom Perignon*. Slowly, a lone drop ran down the bottle's neck and onto the outer surface of the bucket. Gaining in size and speed as it rolled effortlessly toward the floor, the drop stopped momentarily, at the bottom of the silver bucket. Swelling, the way my nipples puff up whenever Victor cups my face in his large hands and kisses me, the drop detached from its silver perch and dived onto a square, rice paper note card. Was this drop of water under his control too? I wouldn't be surprised if he did control it. He definitely controls my emotions, and I love it.

In the center of this sunset red paper square was one beautifully drawn character, representing the word "imagining." What must I imagine? Will my imagination be good enough to prepare me for the pleasures he has in store for me this time? A gold *mizuhiki* string attached the paper note to a stalk of white-and-lavender orchids.

I placed the note and orchid stalk back on the black bathing stool. Moments later, I felt Victor's warm hand upon my back. With one s-l-o-w downward movement, he unzipped my red silk dress. Without a thought, I my dropped shoulders, lowered my arms, and watched as the dress cascaded down my body and onto the floor—

the way all the other dresses and gowns have done over the past twelve months. Seconds later, I shrugged out of my red shelf bra.

Except for a pair of thigh-highs, I was completely naked. I had stopped wearing panties months ago; Victor doesn't like panty lines. He says they disrupt the beautiful lines of my backside. He said my panties were silk barriers—they got in his way.

He wanted "instant access" whenever the opportunity presented itself for him to pleasure me—like the day when he draped me over the hood of his red Diablo, in the airport parking structure. I had to hold onto the windshield to keep from sliding off as he ripped my panties in half.

Now Victor's gentle hands began rolling the seamed, red thigh-high down my left leg. He placed his soft hands up high, almost touching the moist outer *kuchibirū* of my "pink pagoda."

Meticulously, *slowly*, and ritualistically his hands slid down my thigh until a perfect roll formed around the laced top of my stocking. I quivered from sheer ecstasy for what seemed like hours before he gently lifted my heel, rolled the stocking over my instep, and off my red-painted "little piggies."

He placed the rolled-up stockings, my bra, and dress on the Ming chair next to the tub. I turned to kiss him, but he gently redirected my head toward the foot of the gold-rimmed tub. It must've been magic, it had to be. Was he a master magician in addition to everything else?

Maybe I just didn't see it before, but to my surprise, my eyes spied a silver charger covered with a blanket of gingko leaves. Spread out on the fan-shaped leaves was an assortment of fresh fruit . . . ripe strawberries, peeled red seedless grapes, bite-sized balls of melons, long thick bananas, sliced kiwi, a wonderful dish of every fruit I love to eat.

Godiva chocolate truffles, cherry-filled cordials, and of course, more orchids, decorated the center of my miniature Garden of Eden. He did all of this for me, and me alone. God, I'm so fortunate to have Victor in my life. Unlike my pathetic boyfriend, Will, Victor knows exactly how to please a woman. He makes me feel good to be me.

Helped by a strong-but-gentle hand on my elbow, I stepped into the tub's perfumed water. With both feet were firmly set, I placed a hand on Victor's shoulder and lowered myself into steamy water. I laid back, closed my eyes, and made a wish. I wished I were Victor's wife.

One lone bubble appeared from nowhere, and landed on my nipple closest to Victor. I looked at him . . . he glanced at the bubble . . . looked at me . . . I nodded . . . he smiled . . . then he popped that mannish little bubble with the tip of his gifted tongue.

Victor gave Midori a multitude of warm fuzzies that Will, her boyfriend of two years, was incapable of providing. Actually, Will didn't care much about warm fuzzies, and wasn't the least bit interested in any of that "mushy" chick-flick stuff.

Midori, became my patient shortly after her boyfriend literally kicked her out of the house. Will rejected Midori when he learned that the child she was carrying wasn't his.

I'd love to go into the details of her journal, the other reasons she became a patient, and who had fathered her child. However, that's another story for another time, or maybe another book. You *would* like to be the proverbial fly on the (heart) wall once again, would you not?

Epilogue

I received some disturbing news about one of the couples. Blair finally lost control and committed the ultimate crime . . . murder. According to the court report, a neighbor allegedly saw Tim, the paper carrier, delivering the morning paper as he routinely did to Blair's house. It seems that Blair went berserk when he overheard Marcy talking to Tim. The neighbor said that Blair screamed like a madman as he pulled Marcy by her hair back into the house.

Foolishly, Tim ran inside to help. The neighbor who witnessed the incident heard one gunshot, followed by a long, silent pause. Then she heard a second shot. Moments later, she saw Tim backing out of the house.

During the trial, the neighbor told the court, "Tim stumbled down the steps and fell on his side. His body started twitching and when he rolled over, it was horrible! His T-shirt was soaked with blood. When he tried to get up, Blair stood right over him and put four more shots into his body!"

The neighbor continued, "As if that wasn't enough, Blair started to go back to the house, but then hesitated for a moment, turned back around and shot that boy in his privates. If I hadn't seen it with my own eyes, I wouldn't have believed it. Why, I never would have thought that Blair would do such a horrible thing! He was always such a nice man."

Pay attention to what people say, and how they say it. You'll discover all that glitters isn't gold. Remember . . . most batterers are extremely charming.

Blair is presently serving two consecutive life sentences, with no chance for parole. Marcy works as a counselor in a shelter for the abused, and is quite content living with her new best friend, Fluffy Too.

Dexter moved his family to the States and landed a teaching position in the English department at a small New England college. He left that job a few years after their second child was born and began teaching God's word. He continues to do so as Bishop, Rev. Dexter in an Episcopalian Church. Maybe his grandmother was right after all; he was born to be a messenger of God. He and Epiphany have recently become great-grandparents.

Tyrone expanded his operations to include several small plants in Michigan. Tyra is the producer and host of the national cable show, *Affordable Styles*. Whenever he is questioned about producing some heirs to his dynasty, Tyrone replies with, "I need just a little mo' practice, to make a baby as pretty as Tyra," then he breaks into his knee-slapping laughter routine.

I saw Christian at the last board meeting of Simone's foundation. He's still struggling with the aftermath of his decision concerning Ellen. Unfortunately, he's suffering from that useless human emotion I call 'bad' guilt. However, I believe he will be back to his old self in no time. I know he will, because he has the support of, Dominique, his loving and very pregnant wife.

As of this writing, the price of Harriet's cognac has soared to $495. Joel still dries her tears whenever she watches *An Affair to Remember.*

Claudia, believe it or not, has been trying to get back with Darren, since she found out about his wife's fatal boating accident.

I'm working with the journal entries of several new couples, and considering how similar conflicts have affected my life. I'm also working with my lifelong and most-loving patient—Amileé. She's dealing with the outcomes of her teenage daughter's experimentation with drugs and sex.

No matter how hard you try to instill solid values in your children, or how great a parent you may have been, sometimes things don't work out the way you planned. My fifteen-year-old granddaughter, Gisele, is going to make me a great-grandpapa within the next three months.

Somali, the oldest of my four granddaughters, is studying to become, of all things, a psychiatrist.

I hope I have accomplished my purpose for writing this, your "crystal ball" book. If your soul found peace while you were reading . . . if your heart was quieted by a halcyon thought . . . if you are now able to foresee a brighter future . . . if you had an enlightening "ah-ha" in which something made perfect sense . . . if you are able to stand a little taller . . . if you can prevent relationship Armageddon because of something you've read in this book . . . if you can see the real emotion under your partner's mask of anger . . . if you've regained control in your life . . . if you have forgiven yourself for blaming the person in the mirror when it wasn't their fault . . . or if you think you can or are willing to give love one more try . . . then this doctor has accomplished his purpose for writing this book—to relieve at least one reader's pain and suffering.

Relationships are complicated and full of challenges. But, just as avoiding or removing a rose's thorns makes it a pleasure to behold, avoiding or removing the communication blocks that loom in your relationship will allow you to enjoy a wonderful life with your partner. Remember, when you come to a crossroads in your relationship:

> pay attention,
> talk openly and honestly,
> and trust the small-but-powerful,
> voice coming from your heart of hearts.

You will do those things for your old friend, the incurably romantic doctor, will you not?

In closing, this is my prayer for you . . .

May someone love you so much that everything
seems to remind them of you.